DEATH AT DEAD MAN'S STAKE

DEATH AT DEAD MAN'S STAKE

Nick Oldham

SEVERN
HOUSE

First world edition published in Great Britain and the USA in 2024
by Severn House, an imprint of Canongate Books Ltd,
14 High Street, Edinburgh EH1 1TE.

severnhouse.com

British Library Cataloguing-in-Publication Data
A CIP catalogue record for this title is available from the British Library.

ISBN-13: 978-1-4483-1441-6 (cased)
ISBN-13: 978-1-4483-1484-3 (e-book)

All Severn House titles are printed on acid-free paper.

Typeset by Palimpsest Book Production Ltd., Falkirk,
Stirlingshire, Scotland.
Printed and bound in Great Britain by TJ Books,
Padstow, Cornwall.

MIX
Paper | Supporting
responsible forestry
FSC
www.fsc.org   FSC® C013056

Praise for Nick Oldham

"A brutal, gut-wrenching read with a roller-coaster ride
of a plot"
Booklist on *Death Ride*

"Riveting . . . A nail-biting level of suspense"
Publishers Weekly on *Death Ride*

"Oldham continues to push the envelope"
Kirkus Reviews on *Death Ride*

"Pulse-pounding action, nail-biting suspense . . . perfect
for Ian Rankin fans"
Booklist on *Scarred*

"This edge-of-the seat narrative, with constantly ratcheting
tension, features a twist-a-minute plot and a thoroughly
unexpected shock ending"
Booklist on *Transfusion*

"Understated exposition and violent set pieces, all
professionally handled throughout"
Kirkus Reviews on *Transfusion*

About the author

Nick Oldham is the author of the acclaimed Henry Christie series and the Steve Flynn thrillers. He is a retired police inspector, who served in the force from the age of nineteen. *Dead Man's Stake* is the first book in the Jessica Raker series.

@NickOldhamBooks

*This one is dedicated to the memory of
my father-in-law, Alan Mercer.*

ONE

B art Morrison knew in all probability that he didn't have much time left on earth, but he didn't expect to die quite so soon. At the age of eighty-two he'd survived prostate cancer, lived with Parkinson's Disease for over four years, and had just been diagnosed with aggressive liver cancer, so the odds of making it to an even riper old age were stacked heavily against him.

He knew this and accepted it with the ill-grace of the old curmudgeon that he was.

But he also knew that for the moment his mind was as sharp as it ever had been even if the rest of him was grinding to an unpleasant halt, and within the limits of his declining physical abilities he still intended to make the most of what remained of his earthly existence.

Which meant the occasional escape, just for the sheer fun of it and to annoy others, and to get away from the daily drudgery his life had become. Escape obviously required a plan of sorts and cunning, which he had aplenty, and also had to be a challenge to both mind and body.

On the morning of his latest escape, his third one in the past two months, he bided his time for the moments when the people, being the cynical old man he was, he called his guards, or occasionally the Waffen SS to their faces, were otherwise engaged or distracted.

He began to prepare himself even before breakfast in his cell – although to call a very comfortable, self-contained apartment with an ensuite bathroom, a separate kitchen and a nice living room with a balcony overlooking a pretty quadrangle festooned with flowers and hanging baskets (which Bart called the exercise yard), plus a nice big bedroom, a cell was stretching a point.

Bartholomew Roger Morrison was a resident at the Pendle View Care Home situated on the outer edge of the ancient market town of Clitheroe in the Ribble Valley and, as its name suggested, the home had an excellent view of the that big, dark, brooding, mysterious hill, although Bart's room was one that faced inwards which annoyed him intensely, especially considering the amount of money he – as he described it – was robbed of to live here, even if that inner square his apartment overlooked was well tended and pretty.

That Monday morning he was up at seven a.m., shaving and showering, but was back in bed by seven fifteen a.m. having pulled his pyjamas and dressing gown back on over his clothes, buttoned up to the neck.

Alice, one of his regular carers (one of his 'guards'), came in to his apartment at seven thirty a.m. with his breakfast on a bed tray. She chirped noisily, happy as usual, going through the motions without actually paying him much attention it seemed, and left the meal on the tray across his knees, then went on to serve Julia, the lady next door.

The fact that the cheery, humming Alice didn't even seem to register Bart's exaggerated scowl only served to irritate him more. However, although Bart obviously did not know this, when Alice stepped back out into the corridor her facade of good nature dropped and her own face changed into a scowl of contempt as she pushed her trolley along to Julia's door. Julia was a nice old person, unlike Bart. Who was a git.

Bart dismissed Alice from his mind, wolfed down his scrambled eggs on toast, then clambered out of bed and slid off his dressing gown and pyjamas from over his clothes to reveal his get-up for the day: tweed jacket, moleskin trousers, brown brogues, topped with his flat cap, which he'd hidden under his pillows, and his silver-tipped walking stick.

Then, with a dithering, arthritic hand he opened his door, checked both ways along the corridor – all clear: Alice's trolley was still parked outside Julia's door, a sight which provoked another scowl from Bart who was incandescently envious of that relationship. Alice had never, ever, had a laugh and joke with him, oh no, but with goody two shoes Julia it was a different story.

He pulled himself together with a grunt, turned in the opposite direction and scuttled away at what he thought was quite a quick pace.

It wasn't as though residents were under lock and key, although some of the more far-gone dementia sufferers were closely monitored, but everyone was observed by the watchful eye of the general manager with the addition of a few security cameras dotted strategically around the place, which were more to deter unwelcome intruders than anything. And Bart knew the position of each one anyway.

Monday, as ever, was a pretty good day for an escapade because there were quite a few comings and goings which Bart used to his advantage.

Fresh produce for the kitchen always arrived that day in a large, refrigerated van; the bin men called, reversing their whopping big wagon all the way up the drive; plus several other residents went on trips, taken out in a minibus to hospital appointments such as for chemotherapy at the local hospital; others taken for hairdressing appointments and some were dropped off in town to do some shopping, to be picked up later.

But whatever the cause, all this activity distracted the staff of the home and gave the freedom-loving Bart the opportunity to sneak out.

But actually, Bart Morrison was a creature of habit. He revelled in the thought of adventure and royally annoying others, but in reality he always made his way to the same location on his unannounced jaunts, not least because he didn't want to get lost (that had happened a couple of times and it had scared him) or jeopardize his lift home.

He would walk out for about an hour, shuffling along his usual route until he reached the fast treacherous road that was the A59 which went to Skipton in one direction, Preston in the other.

But he did enjoy his moments dicing with death as he negotiated the crossing of this road that Monday morning. He shaded his eyes to check traffic on a horrifically fast highway on which numerous people had been killed over the years. The beauty for Bart was that he was fully aware of this, knew his limitations both speed and vision-wise and there was also a central reservation in the middle of the road at the point where he crossed which provided a safe refuge more or less and which he aimed for. He'd had one or two near misses but nothing too dramatic and he had no intention of making this Monday the day on which he would meet his maker by being flattened by a car or lorry.

Timing the first half of the road-dash to perfection, he reached the central reservation and paused for breath.

No drama so far.

He waited until a couple of HGVs had thundered past, the shockwaves of their slipstreams almost uprooting him like a tree in a hurricane, then he made it across the second half of the road safely, continuing his hiking adventure up towards the pretty little village of Pendleton on the lower slope of Pendle Hill. Then he turned towards Audley Reservoir, cut off the road up the footpath and found his usual bench by the waterside and sat down, now breathing heavily. He wanted to watch some bird life for a while and see if any anglers were fishing that morning at that time. None were. In fact, very little seemed to be happening, though the bird life was quite busy and he enjoyed watching various species flitting around the water, amazed as ever by the patience of a heron on the water's edge. Still as a statue, focused, before that long and deadly beak jabbed forwards into the water and then came out with its wriggling catch.

Bart almost applauded with delight.

And then his mobile phone rang. It was one of those designed for the 'older person' (translated in Bart's mind to 'dodderer') bought from the pages of a Sunday newspaper's magazine. It had extra-large buttons on the keypad, a loud ring tone and a vibration that felt like a pneumatic drill in his pocket. He muttered as he fished it out and peered at the large letters on the screen which told him 'ALCATRAZ' was calling him, in other words the Pendle View Care Home. Reluctantly he thumbed the answer-call button.

'Hello, Bart,' came the patient voice of the home's general manager, Mrs Elsie Dean. Bart recognized her plummy, friendly tones right away.

That still did not prevent him from answering, 'Mrs Dean,' with as much venom and impatience he could inject into those two words.

'I take it you are OK, Bart?'

'I am.' His voice was stern, even though he secretly quite liked Mrs Dean, probably more than most other members of staff – his guards – who he generally detested.

'We've noticed you've gone on walkabout, sneaked out while we were busy,' Elsie Dean said, but not with animosity. 'This really must stop happening.'

'Aye,' Bart said laconically.

'Do you need a lift back, my love?' Elsie Dean asked. 'Or are you on your way?'

Bart considered how he was feeling. 'I'll start strolling back,' he said finally, realizing the day's adventure was over.

'I'll come up in the car if you want?'

'I'll call you if I need you,' Bart said abruptly, ended the call with a jab of his thumb and slid the phone back into his pocket.

He stood up from the bench, feeling his hips and knees grating and hearing the click of his joints. There was just one more thing to do before starting the journey back and that was to complete his customary walk around the perimeter of the small body of water. He steadied himself, inhaled a breath into his aging but serviceable lungs. He liked to stroll around, in particular over the dam at the far side from which there was a great view right across Clitheroe, one to be savoured even by an old, cantankerous codger.

But before he could put one step in front of the other, a voice called him from behind. 'Bart, Bart, I've come to take you back.'

Bart turned with a quizzical expression on his face. 'How come you're here?'

'Mrs Dean sent me.'

Less than a minute later, Bart was drowning.

TWO

Following an urgent-sounding knock, the sergeants' office door was flung open.

A young police community support officer stood on the threshold – female, early twenties, breathing heavily. She blurted, 'Sarge – job on! Up at Dead Man's Stake . . . old Bill Ramsden's got a fireman held hostage . . . and he's got a shotgun.'

Sergeant Jessica Raker blinked, open-mouthed, and very, very much unlike her, hesitated.

'We need to get going now, Sarge,' the PCSO said. 'That is if you're turning out to it. If not, I'm on my way. It sounds like a crazy job.'

'Yes, yes, of course I'm coming,' Jess said.

'You got your stab vest? You probably won't need it, but you never know old Bill . . . he's an absolute nutter. I know it won't stop a shotgun blast.'

'Yeah, yeah, somewhere in this lot.' Jess indicated the pile of new uniform and equipment she had just heaved unceremoniously into an untidy heap in one corner of the office. In amongst it was her stab vest.

The PCSO – whose name Jess didn't even know – stood there

expectantly on the balls of her feet, her body language urging Jess to get a shift on.

However, Sergeant Jessica Raker had only just arrived at the police station ten minutes earlier and had only just lugged her belongings in from her car parked in the backyard of the nick. Now all her uniform, including everything – her extendable baton, rigid handcuffs, stab vest and all the other odds and sods that go to make up a modern cop's uniform – was in that pile. Her plan had been to take her time, hang stuff neatly in her locker and literally get her feet under the – she noticed – very old desk on her first day in the job. She planned on getting a brew and only then venturing out to explore her new world of policing.

It shouldn't have surprised her that all these nicely laid-out plans of taking her time, getting that first mug of police station tea, logging on to her computer for the first time and doing the rounds, introducing herself to whoever else might be on duty, would never come to fruition because in all her eighteen years of service she'd never once known a tour of duty which went completely to plan. Such was the nature of being a cop, even here in Clitheroe in the heart of the Ribble Valley in Lancashire, the place where Jess was born and bred, but also a place her husband described sweetly as 'the backside of beyond'.

Jess quickly began to scramble through the pile to find the vest which she threw over her head and fastened.

She then nodded at the PCSO whose body language was still screaming, 'Hurry up, Sarge.'

'Radio!' Jess said suddenly. 'I haven't got a radio!'

The PCSO held out a personal radio (PR) in a harness. 'Thought you might need one. This is a spare. I presume your own will be somewhere amongst all that clutter? Can we get going? Ramsden's volatile enough without a drink in him.'

'He's drunk?' Jess asked. 'At this time of day?'

'Apparently.'

'And he's got a shotgun?' Jess said just to confirm what she'd heard.

'Yep. Shouldn't have but has, even though last time this happened he got his certificate revoked.'

'It's happened before?'

'Several times . . . Ramsden has a very big problem with trespassers . . . and everyone, if I'm honest. And drink, obviously.'

The pair were having this conversation as the PCSO led Jess through the corridors of the old police station, out past the public enquiry desk and on to King Street where a police car was parked on the double yellows. The PCSO scuttled around to the driver's side whilst Jess dropped into the front passenger seat. Almost before her bottom hit the seat the car was accelerating away from the kerb. She grabbed her seat belt and tugged it across her body, glancing at the PCSO who, whilst driving, changing gear and putting her foot down was also fitting her seat belt.

'Are PCSOs allowed to drive in this neck of the woods?' Jess asked as she was chucked sideways at the next junction.

'No bugger else to do it,' the young woman said, gripping the steering wheel tight and leaning into it. 'We get a one-day course, dead basic. We pass if we don't mow anyone down, but we're not supposed to blue-light it or chase anyone.' She grimaced. 'So I don't blue-light it but I go as fast as I can when I have to and only chase people from a distance . . . if you get my drift, Sarge?'

Jess grinned, then introduced herself. 'Sergeant Jess Raker, by the way.'

'I know. I'm PCSO Samira Patel, a twenty-two-year-old wannabe cop, an ambition that might be pie in the sky, but which I hope to achieve before my dad tries to marry me off. Anyhow, welcome to the Ribble Valley, Sarge.'

'Thank you. I was hoping not to have a baptism of fire.'

Samira chuckled. 'You've set tongues wagging, by the way.'

'How come?'

'Cos no one knows anything about you.'

'And long may that remain, Samira.'

'You can call me Sam, if you want. Everyone else does.'

'What do you prefer?'

'Samira.'

'Samira it is, then,' Jess said, hoping they had got past the uncomfortable origin speculation stage, though she said, 'I was hoping to get a rest from this sort of thing.'

'It can come thick and fast here, believe me,' Samira warned her, 'don't think it can't.'

'Fair enough . . . to business . . . how many patrols are enroute, Samira?'

She guffawed.

'Just us, then?' Jess guessed.

'Our other mobiles are tied up with warrants and an inquest . . . the closest armed response is half an hour behind us in Blackburn.'

'Bugger.'

'Indeed,' agreed Samira. 'And we have a bit of a journey ahead. Dead Man's Stake is out in the sticks and it'll take us the best part of twenty minutes to get there, even with a tail wind.'

'In that case . . .' Jess reached out and flipped the dashboard switch for the blue light. 'Pedal to the metal,' she instructed the PCSO, then looked for the switch for the two-tone horns but could not see it. 'No sirens?'

'Not on bog-standard patrol cars like this.'

'OK.' Jess leaned back, braced her feet against the slope of the passenger footwell, now quite pleased that her first day in a new job in a new police force might well be a baptism of fire, the sort of thing that would be good for her reputation . . . if it all went well, that was, and this drunken old man Ramsden didn't start blasting away with his shotgun.

She held on tight, already quietly impressed by the PCSO and her enthusiasm.

THREE

Twelve months earlier, almost to the day, Jess Raker had been doing something similar two hundred and fifty miles to the south of Lancashire in London, something which would be the catalyst for her move back north.

It had been one of those very trying mornings at home in the terraced house on the edge of Greenwich she owned and shared with her husband Josh and their two children, daughter Lily, fifteen, and son Jason, twelve.

Josh, a marketing director for a multinational company across the River Thames in the City, had left for work at six a.m. for the relatively short Tube journey under the river to the very shiny skyscraper office block, amongst many other similar megastructures, in which he worked. He was always at his desk by six thirty a.m. and often did not make it back home until, usually exhausted, twelve or fourteen hours later, drained by his high-powered role.

Which always meant that somehow, Jess – who was a police firearms sergeant – had to get the kids ready and chivvy them out for school by eight thirty a.m. and then get herself down to New Cross Police Station where she was based. Fortunately she could usually manage to sort the kids, though more regularly than she liked she had to rely on help from her widowed mother who was usually on-tap to assist.

But that particular morning, Jess was pretty much in control. It was an admin day so there was just a slight leeway with her start time.

Lily was fairly self-reliant and could be trusted to be ready to step out of the door to make her way to the school bus stop. Mostly she had her head angled down to her mobile phone, ate her cereal without ever looking up, then bade goodbye without looking up again. Jess always had to stop her before she ventured out to make her look her in the eye so she could tell her she loved her.

Without exception, Lily rolled her eyes and said, 'Whatev,' but there was always just that crack of a smile for her mum before she left. Their little ritual.

Jason . . . completely different matter.

He was into Xbox games in his room and prising him away from the console each morning was always a challenge for Jess, usually resulting in a sulk and the dragging of his feet around the house, just like most lads on the cusp of teenhood. He didn't mind school actually, loved the sports side of it, but considered most other subjects to be pointless.

Jess managed to get him to the school gates and even though she was running a tad late that morning, she still watched him trudge all the way to the school entrance and her heart almost shattered when he looked back over his shoulder, smiled and waved at her. She blew him a kiss, then he was gone. 'Soft arse,' she thought, though she wasn't sure if she meant herself or Jason. Maybe both.

Then she dashed back to her car, a battered old silver Citroen Picasso diesel, 130,000 miles on the clock and still going strong, and drove into work.

It didn't matter she was a few minutes late as she walked swiftly into her office in the Firearms Department. Admin meant a relatively relaxed day and none of her bosses begrudged her a late start after all the extra time she put in, often without recompense. Plus, unless something serious happened out there on the streets of London, she also expected to have what cops called an early dart at the other end of the day so she could surprise both kids and pick them up from school, which was a rare treat but would mean a quick call to her mother, who lived nearby, to stand her down from that duty today.

The problem with London though was that there was rarely a day when nothing serious happened which didn't involve a firearms team.

And that day, twelve months ago, was no exception.

FOUR

S amira was both grimacing and grinning at the wheel of the police car at the same time and was clearly loving the order to put her foot down, blue lights flashing, using the heel of her hand on the horn as a substitute for a two-tone, accompanied by angrily flashing the headlights. She and Jess swerved impressively through traffic which thinned out considerably as they left Clitheroe and hurtled into the countryside.

Within moments they were zipping fast through narrow lanes heading through villages and hamlets Jess remembered from her youth; pretty places which often didn't look as though they'd been touched by the progress of time. After London, which was undoubtedly a breathtaking city, these rural places were in their own way equally stunning but in a much more subtle way with evocative place names hinting at their history.

But there wasn't time to sightsee.

Hedgerows, stone buildings, old halls and churches whizzed by at an alarming rate.

In the meantime, Jess got to grips with the radio, introducing herself quickly to the comms operator based at police headquarters near Preston, announcing she was enroute with PCSO Patel and asking for more officers to be deployed, possibly with the helicopter as well due to the remote nature of the location of this incident. She also asked if there was any update from the fire service.

There was no joy from Comms. No other patrols were available:

the ARV, as Samira had already said, was blue-lighting it from Blackburn – miles away – and the helicopter was grounded due to a technical fault. And there was no update from the fire service, which was worrying.

Samira commented, 'Bit of a bugger. Hopefully Ramsden will have succumbed to excess alcohol by the time we get there and won't have done any damage to anyone.'

'Mm,' Jess said doubtfully. 'Have you got a taser?'

'In the boot. I'm not allowed to use it, though.'

'Might come in useful. Is it charged up?'

Samira nodded as she gritted her teeth and negotiated the tightly winding road past the Inn at Whitewell. They were then on the road to Dunsop Bridge, crossing over the fast-flowing River Hodder before reaching the village and then speeding up the road towards the Trough of Bowland. They clattered over a cattle grid – something that Jess hadn't experienced for years – and it seemed to rattle the cop car right to its chassis and did the same to Jess, though it was her bones that rattled.

After about quarter of a mile of dips and sheep avoidance – they roamed unfettered across this land – they plunged down a steep hill at the foot of which Samira stepped on the brakes and turned through a five-barred gate on to a tight farm track leading up to the moors. She slowed right down here on the deeply rutted surface taking extra care so as not to rip out the bottom of the car.

'Job for a Land Rover, this,' Samira said as the offside front wheel dropped into a muddy hole and the steering wheel was almost torn from her grip.

'Do we have one?'

'Yep, but Dave's got it.'

'Dave?'

'PC Dave Simpson . . . locked a guy up on warrant this morning and took him over to Blackburn nick.'

'Blackburn?' Jess threw a steadying hand on to the dashboard to stop herself jerking wildly forwards.

'Divisional HQ.'

'Twenty miles away!' Jess exclaimed.

'And counting.'

Jess blew out her cheeks and thought, Hell! Most of the DHQs in the Met are only a few miles from anywhere at most. She was beginning to appreciate how vast an area she was now responsible for.

Samira continued, 'Which is why everyone thinks twice about making arrests because it takes you out of the game for so long. Even just dropping a prisoner off and coming straight back is an hour minimum, even with a tail wind.'

Jess shook her head in disbelief.

'Not far now,' Samira said as the front wheels of the car thudded into another deep rut on the track.

FIVE

Traffic from Jason's school to the police station in New Cross in south London was excruciatingly slow that morning twelve months before.

To be honest the extra time stuck in traffic gave her a few precious moments to wind down after the rush of sorting the kids . . . and to ponder about the state of her marriage to Josh, how distant he'd become recently and whether that was any of her fault. Jess knew he was working gruelling hours but the pay-off was an immense salary in comparison to her decent enough police wage, plus the possibility of a nice, comfortable future.

But at what price? she asked herself. Two people staying together for the sake of the kids yet at the same time drifting apart, not being that single entity she believed a married couple should be. Or was she just being silly? She knew Josh was currently working with huge, influential, massively wealthy international clients and was completely embroiled in that, understandably perhaps. But he'd assured her that once everything was up and running with them, he would be able to ease off. So she had taken his word on that: things would get better.

By the time she'd mulled all this through (and reached no conclusions) she was parking at the nick but with one lingering question in her mind: do I still actually love Josh?

The answer to that would have to wait, so she filed it away for further research later and turned her attention to today and what lay ahead.

Yes, mostly admin with a couple of operational meetings with CID and the National Crime Agency who were planning some big armed raids later in the week which required her and her boss's input. It wouldn't all be desk work.

That was the day she had in her mind, but as she turned into her office, calling out greetings to her colleagues, it went in a completely different direction.

SIX

With a nasty scraping sound, the police car bottomed out once again on the track leading up to Bill Ramsden's farmhouse near Dead Man's Stake.

'Essentially it's a shithole, pardon my French,' Samira said. 'Used to be a thriving farm by all accounts but his excessive boozing, a bad divorce or two and terrible management by Bill took the place to wrack and ruin,' the PCSO went on. 'Now it's a crumbling mess. No animals other than a few scraggy hens, I believe. He did breed donkeys and ponies but the RSPCA shut that down and took him to court for animal neglect, which included failing to bury carcases. Now he's banned for life from owning all livestock, I think . . . not sure about the hens but they could be running wild. Anyway, that and other similar convictions turned him against authority. I dunno.' She shrugged. 'I'm no psycho-therapist, or whatever.'

The car bottomed out again as Samira negotiated a tight kink in the track where they came across a stationary fire engine, slumped at an angle in a rut, facing up the track completely blocking any further progress.

A burly, sweaty firefighter jogged towards the police car but stopped in his tracks as Jess and Samira got out.

The man seemed flummoxed and disappointed. 'I was going to say, thank God you're here,' he gasped. 'But is this the best the police can offer?'

Jess walked up to him, tripping a little on a muddy ridge, already fuming. 'What are you trying to say?'

'Well . . .' His eyes flicked back and forth between the two officers. Samira was standing behind Jess.

'Two women?' Jess guessed. 'Not good enough?'

'Where's the firearms team, for example? This guy's got a shotgun and he's holding my mate hostage. He needs fucking wasting!'

'And you need to keep calm,' Jess told him firmly. 'What's actually happened here?'

As she asked this question another firefighter trotted up behind the first. He was younger and pretty good looking, Jess noted – but only in passing.

'I'm the crew manager – Joe Borwick.' He was carrying his yellow helmet with the two black bands under his arm. He looked sweaty, too. But good sweaty.

The first guy looked annoyed but stepped aside.

'What's gone on?' Jess asked him.

'We got a call out here to Dead Man's Stake Farm to what was reported as a rubbish fire and we turned out with just the one tender and found a whole mound of old tyres, old oil cans et cetera, blazing just outside the farm gates.'

'Who reported it?'

'A guy out walking on Wolf Fell.' Borwick gestured to the steep moor side on the opposite side of the valley. 'Anyway, we drove up here, which as you can see is pretty hairy and narrow for a fire tender. We dealt with the fire, which is still smouldering, but there was no way we could reverse all the way back down . . . well, we could, but y'know?'

'I get it,' Jess said. It would take some doing going backwards.

'Anyway, the fire was just this side of the farm gates which were locked but we could see the farmyard has plenty of room to swing the machine around, plus we wanted to speak to the farmer to see what he knew about the fire in the first place, because it seems obvious, to me anyway, that he's the one who started it. So we needed words. I asked one of my crew to jump over the gate and go knock on the front door. The rest of us watched from the gate; next thing, door opens, guy comes out with a shotgun and drags my officer in with it pointed at his head.'

As Borwick explained all this, they had walked up to the gate and leaned on it, looking at the very dilapidated farmhouse across a wide, cobbled and concreted yard. A sign on the gate read: Dead Man's Stake Farm. The farmhouse itself was a good seventy-five yards away, constructed of dark stone with some boarded-up windows and a very sturdy-looking iron-framed front door. On either side of the yard, which was as large as Borwick had described, were farm buildings in a terrible state of disrepair, with damaged or missing roofs and doors. The whole place looked as though it had been neglected for many years.

'So he's in the house?' Jess clarified.

'Yep. I went over and he opened the door using my guy as a shield in front of him, with the shotgun jammed up under his chin. I tried to reason with him but in the end he pointed the shotgun at me and fired. I threw myself to one side as soon as I saw it moving, then scuttled back here like a friggin' crab.' Borwick exhaled a stuttering breath. 'He dragged Col back in with him. Colin's my guy, by the way.'

'What did you say to the famer?'

'I just asked him to let Colin go and we'd just back off, then step aside for you guys . . . and gals,' he added for the sake of political correctness. 'Though I didn't say the last bit about you lot coming.'

Jess took a deep breath, glanced at a very worried-looking PCSO, but before she could say anything and sort her mind out – and rid her thoughts of another nasty firearms incident – the front door of the farmhouse opened and a man, who Jess would later learn was Bill Ramsden, ran out a few paces brandishing a machine pistol, not a shotgun, and opened fire, strafing the cops and the firefighters lounging by the gate, laughing manically as he did.

Jess saw it, processed it, and before he actually opened fire she screamed a warning and launched herself into the hunk that was Borwick, barged him to the ground. She landed on top of him, paused for a millisecond as their eyes locked inches apart, but then she scrambled up on to her knees, checking that everyone else had reacted and dived for cover.

They had.

'Hell of a first day,' Jess muttered breathlessly as she took a quick peek around the gate post to see Ramsden backing into the farmhouse and slamming the door, behind which he was still holding Colin, the firefighter, hostage.

SEVEN

As Jess spun into her small office at New Cross nick, almost a year before, her boss – the firearms team inspector – was waiting for her, geed-up, raring to go, already in his firearms kit, ballistic vest, overalls, boots and a holster in which nestled a Glock pistol.

'And you, Mrs Raker, thought you were going to spend the day fannying around at your desk.' He smirked triumphantly.

'Apparently not?' she guessed.

'No, you are not . . . gear on, briefing at nine fifteen, which gives you' – he checked his watch, which Jess knew was a Rolex – 'seven minutes. NCA have an urgent, if vague, job for us. Chop, chop.'

Jess shrugged and sighed, unsurprised. 'I'll be there.'

And she was.

And thirty minutes after the briefing she was in the passenger seat of an unmarked firearms response vehicle heading towards Greenwich where intelligence had it from the National Crime Agency that an armed raid was going to take place at either a jeweller or a bank.

It was as ambiguous as that.

'It is good intel,' the guy from the NCA insisted at the briefing. 'Good source, one of our best.'

The firearms team all had to stifle their guffaws and keep straight faces.

'Though the actual target isn't known?' Jess tried to clarify.

The detective acknowledged that with a half-nod and began to hand out a list of jewellers and banks in the Greenwich area, any of which could become the target for a ruthless armed gang specializing in this quite old-fashioned type of crime, but which still terrified victims and witnesses. The plus side of it was that the gang were a well-known South London outfit operating out of Peckham and mugshots of the main gang leaders had been distributed amongst the firearms team. Jess recognized a few of them as she had been on a house raid a few months before where some of them had been holed up and wanted for serious offences. That job had gone smoothly.

But she got a vibe from the NCA briefing team that today, if the police engaged the gang, things might not go so easily, especially when the NCA guy said their source had overheard that if the police did show up, the gang was up for a shoot-out and car chase and the death of a cop wouldn't worry them unduly. It didn't help Jess and her team when the NCA guy also admitted that the gang leaders had managed, either by luck or deliberately, to shake off a six-cop surveillance team that had been tracking them for a week. An omen that did not bode well.

When the main briefing was over, Jess stepped up to the podium to address her team, as she had done on many occasions. The team consisted of three double-crewed cars, two of which were liveried and one, hers, which wasn't.

She spoke succinctly after waiting for the NCA detective to leave.

'I know the NCA want to nail this crew and rightly so, but as they've already admitted losing track of some of the targets, that don't impress me much,' she said. 'It probably means the gang means business, so what I say to you is this: prevention is better than cure. Your safety is paramount. You guys in the marked vehicles, keep a high profile, OK? This just seems a half-baked operation on a nod and a wink, and I don't want it going t-up and anyone getting hurt, OK?'

They all nodded agreement as, despite often being labelled as gun-toting and trigger-happy, the best result for them was always no shots fired. Always.

The team turned out and half an hour later Jess settled herself in the passenger seat of the ARV as the driver made his way slowly along the snarled-up main street of Greenwich towards the *Cutty Sark*. She skim-read the briefing pack and operational order again, both of which were a bit too vague for her liking and she sifted through the photos and pen pictures of the gang leaders, unable to quell a certain amount of disquiet, a continuation of the trepidation she'd felt at the briefing itself.

It all seemed a bit too . . . 'meh' for her. She shivered.

'You OK, Sarge?' the driver asked, glancing at her. He was a very experienced firearms officer called Mark Rigg, a PC with almost twenty years under his belt and just over ten on the team. He had drawn his weapon many times and been forced to discharge it only once.

'This is one of those days when the place should be flooded in uniforms. It's all too . . . unspecific for my liking, Mark. I'd rather just put the villains off.'

'Agreed,' he said.

She shuffled the paperwork back into a file and tossed it on to the back seat.

Which was the moment when the call came over the radio: a silent alarm had been activated at a high-class jeweller's shop on Greenwich High Street, a shop that backed on to the famous market.

Jess and Rigg were perhaps thirty seconds away from the premises.

'Maybe we are in business,' Jess said grimly and grabbed her seatbelt.

EIGHT

J ess peered worriedly around the gatepost towards Dead Man's Stake Farm. The front door was closed and definitely locked: the sound of bolts being slammed into place had been distinctly heard. She had been on the radio to Comms to gee up the backup, but with the best will in the world, cops toting guns were still fifteen minutes distant at best. She saw a shadow cross the front window – Ramsden with his shotgun.

'Bad, bad, bad,' she said.

'What are we going to do, Sarge?' Samira asked as Jess dipped behind the protection of the gatepost and tried to get her breathing under control and reduce her heartbeat a few notches.

But even though her inner body was pounding, her exterior remained as calm as a mill pond. She hoped.

'We need to engage him in some sort of dialogue,' she replied, knowing this was one of the many corny lines straight out of the hostage negotiators' manual. 'If only for quarter of an hour.'

She glanced at Joe Borwick who, like all the rest, was looking at her expectantly, the senior police officer on the scene, the one from whom miracles were expected. Borwick said, 'That's one of my men in there.'

Jess nodded. 'I get it.'

She blinked a couple of times to get her thoughts in gear, licked her lips and said to Samira, 'Get the taser out of the boot, will you?'

It was Samira's turn to blink. 'You're going to tase him?' she asked incredulously.

'Yes, from fifty yards . . . duh! Just get it, OK?' Jess reiterated.

Samira got the message and scuttled back down the track to the car.

Jess stood up and swivelled out from behind the gatepost, cupped both hands around her mouth to form a loudspeaker. She cleared her throat, which had suddenly dried up, then shouted, 'Bill! Bill Ramsden! I'm Sergeant Raker from Clitheroe police station . . . we need to talk. We need to talk without you holding and pointing a gun. Can we do that? Can we work a way out of this situation?'

Behind her Samira appeared with the taser. Jess gave her a hand signal to keep out of sight because she didn't want Ramsden spotting any kind of weapon which might inflame him to respond in an even more dangerous manner.

She cupped her hands again. 'Bill. Come on, let's talk.'

Jess tensed up when she heard the bolts being drawn back and saw the door handle begin to move. Ramsden was coming to the door again and Jess felt a huge sense of relief when, as he stepped into view, he was holding the neck of a half empty bottle of whisky in his right hand and the MP5 carbine was in his left, dangling loosely down his side.

He brought the neck of the bottle up to his lips and necked a few slurps, wiped his mouth with the back of his hand, cackled again and brought up the gun and pulled the trigger. Because he was holding it in only one hand, the recoil made the weapon leap as each bullet exited the barrel and he had no control of its aim and the slugs went everywhere, but mostly upwards into the sky and harmlessly away with no real danger to Jess and the others who still cowered behind the wall and the gateposts.

Ramsden disappeared back inside the farmhouse, the bolts once more being slammed into place. Jess could hear muted shouts from inside the building and realized that if things were bad to begin with, they may well have just taken a turn for the worse.

Her face twitched, her nostrils flared, but she stopped doing those things when she realized that everyone was looking at her and must be thinking how very weird she appeared, twitching like mad. Then she turned to Samira. 'Taser.'

The PCSO handed it over and Jess quickly checked the charge: fully loaded.

'What are you thinking, Sarge?'

'I'm thinking of using this.' Jess weighed it in her hand. She'd used one on a number of occasions while in the Met and was very highly trained, knew their strengths and weaknesses, but knew that mostly they were effective, though on occasions they failed to stop some people, mainly those high on drugs, out of their minds and intent on violence.

'Right,' she decided. 'There's at least another ten minutes before the cavalry arrive and I see this as a crucial time here and now. Ramsden doesn't want to talk or negotiate and that firefighter's life is in extreme danger, so to do nothing is not an option in my opinion,' she explained to Samira, who understood but was also puzzled.

'What are you going to do?'

'Have you got a loud voice?'

'Er, yeah. At least my boyfriend says I have.'

'In that case, count to sixty and then do what I did, make a loud-speaker for your mouth, stick your head around the gatepost and shout for Ramsden to come out and put his guns down. If the door opens, take cover immediately and radio me the word "Go!" Yeah?'

Samira nodded uncertainly.

'Do you understand?' Jess asked more firmly.

'Yeah, yeah . . . what are you going to do?'

'See if there's a back way in.'

NINE

Like many shops in Greenwich, Royale's Jewellers was inde-pendently owned, adding to the rich variety of small businesses in that area. The double-fronted shop specialized in high-class watches and beautiful diamond-encrusted jewellery, much of which sold for thousands of pounds, items that most people could only dream of owning unless they were wealthy. Or villains.

Jess and her husband Josh had strolled past the ornate plate-glass fronted shop on many occasions as Greenwich was one of their favourite haunts for a walk and a meal. Jess had once pulled Josh to a halt and had looked at him, then at a display of highly expensive rings, then back at him and lifted up her hand and twinkled her fingers, then ran a fingertip delicately across her throat to indicate that a necklace wouldn't go amiss either, until both of them ended up chuckling at the idea.

Neither was going to happen, but Jess didn't mind. She was more than happy with the rings on her fingers, the engagement and wedding rings and the eternity ring which had all been relatively inexpensive items, bought for her by Josh years earlier. They meant everything to her.

So, Jess the cop knew exactly where the shop was when the alarm sounded.

'Hundred yards on the right,' she snapped at Rigg, who nodded and eased across the road through a break in the traffic, mounted the footpath and stopped, leaving them perhaps a twenty-yard sprint to the shop which from the outside looked normal, business as usual.

Until Jess noticed the van on the kerbside. Transit. Sliding door slightly open.

She glanced at Rigg.

'Seen it,' he said through gritted teeth.

'Anything more from the shop?' Jess asked Comms.

'Nothing – just the silent alarm,' she was informed, 'which will go audible soon.'

'Roger that . . . just arrived on the scene, nothing apparently amiss but there's a suspicious van parked outside.' She relayed the registration number for a PNC check as she got out of the car, drew her handgun, and approached the van along the footpath. On the other side of the van, in the road, Rigg was mirroring her, creeping swiftly towards the vehicle with his MP5 machine pistol ready to fire.

Both officers had turned on their bodycams, recording the incident and their approach.

About fifteen yards short of the van, the whole thing kicked off.

TEN

'A *back way*? You're going in the back way?' Samira asked incredulously.

'If there's a door open,' Jess confirmed.

'Wow!'

'You just do what I ask,' Jess told her firmly again. 'Just don't get shot. If the door opens and he comes out with a gun, get under cover. No heroics.'

'Don't worry, I will.'

'Right . . .' Jess glanced at Joe Borwick, the crew manager who seemed stunned by her intentions. Her quick shake of the head made him zip up any observations he might have whilst also ensuring she didn't allow herself to veer from her chosen path which she knew was perhaps slightly crazy. But that was how she went: she was here to protect life, no compromise.

She checked the taser charge once more. She had once been let down by one during a big public order operation in the Met which had ended up with her getting a broken cheekbone and the bad guy a concussion, and she knew she wouldn't have chance to check it again before discharging it today if that opportunity presented itself.

She timed in Samira to begin the countdown then ducked down below the line of the wall and, counting silently herself, began to move in a fast, crab-like crouch, keeping out of sight of the farm-house, scurrying her way around the perimeter of the premises, making use of an old tractor and trailer for cover as she made her way to the rear of the farmhouse.

She could not help but notice the abject disrepair of all the build-ings and equipment and the terrible stench that seemed to pulsate particularly out of one of the outbuildings, which she guessed was or had been a cowshed at some point, although there was no sign of any actual livestock on the farm. In passing, though she knew Samira had touched on it, she wondered what the full history of the place was, why it had really come to its current state which was dire in the extreme.

Finally she made the short dash from an outbuilding to the gable end of the farmhouse and backed herself up against the stone wall with the taser held up between both her hands just under her chin like a Glock, but without a finger on the trigger.

From there she could see along the side of the house, across the farmyard to the bobbing figures on the other side of the gate.

She reached sixty in her head and gave an exaggerated nod which she hoped Samira would see and when she saw the PCSO reveal herself slowly at the gate, Jess knew the message had been received, particularly when Samira cupped her hands around her mouth and bellowed, 'Bill Ramsden, Bill Ramsden, you come to the door unarmed and talk to me now!'

Jess twitched a smile: Samira certainly could project her voice. Then she ran to the back corner of the farmhouse, paused and placed the tip of her right forefinger on the trigger of the taser.

She peeked quickly around the corner to look along the back wall of the property, seeing a back door about four yards away, with boarded-up windows either side of it.

She could still hear Samira shouting but could not discern if Ramsden had responded.

She ducked and crouch-walked along the wall, keeping low, then rose slowly to her full height by the back door. Her chest constricted as a fresh but welcome gush of adrenaline spurted into her system.

The door was solid, constructed of very thick wooden panels which could easily have been a century old. Carefully she reached out with her left hand and laid it on the door and tested to see if it was open or not. She had been in situations in London, all revved up to bash doors down only to discover that a quick check would sometimes find the door would actually open with a gentle push, often a huge disappointment to the rapid-entry team who were raring to deploy their door-opening equipment.

A shimmer ran all the way through her as she put the weight of her hand on Ramsden's door and pushed. It opened. Not willingly, but at least silently.

She clamped her teeth together. Tight.

She pushed the door a little further, fraction by fraction until the gap was just wide enough for her slim frame to slide through.

She kept moving silently, the taser in her right hand, supported by her left, elbows locked forming an isosceles triangle with her chest.

She entered the kitchen.

Her mind was sharp, taking in and analysing everything as her keen eyes scanned the disgusting room, which reeked of rotting food waste, and saw an array of small farming implements laid out on a workbench, such as a sickle, a pair of hedge shears and an axe fixed into the jaws of a vice . . . but that wasn't important. She stepped across the large, uneven but shiny stone slabs that formed the kitchen floor to the inner door which was slightly ajar and on the other side of which was the large living and dining area at the front of the farmhouse. She paused here and listened. Her breath shallow and controlled as she concentrated and imagined her next move.

Now she could hear Ramsden's voice. He was mumbling and Jess could visualize him as he stalked around the living room, muttering drunkenly to himself. She could hear horrible swear words as he ranted against authority to the firefighter he was holding hostage.

Then there was a pause during which Jess heard Samira still shouting for Ramsden to come to the door.

'And what do you think?' Ramsden demanded.

Jess was sure the question was directed at the trapped firefighter.

There was a slurred, incomprehensible response from the captive making Jess wonder if he'd been badly assaulted by Ramsden, maybe bashed about, struck by the butts of Ramsden's guns.

'You should never think you can come on to my property,' Ramsden growled.

Jess heard a dull thud and the firefighter emitted a groan of pain.

'And because you did . . .' Ramsden went on, then paused and Jess heard the glug of liquid making Jess assume he was drinking from the bottle. This was followed by an 'Ahh' sound from him as the mouthfuls of whatever it was sank down his throat. 'And because you did,' he then continued, 'I'm going to kill you.'

The blood inside Jess turned to sheer ice.

And then she heard a sound which chilled her even more. A sound she knew all too well from her time as a firearms officer. A sound she herself had been responsible for making often: that of a shotgun being racked, when a fresh cartridge is loaded into the breech.

Unmistakeable.

Shit!

She glanced at the taser, prayed it would not let her down.

'Gonna blow your head off and stuff the consequences,' Ramsden declared, still slurring his words.

Jess moved.

With athletic ability she pivoted through the kitchen door.

Ramsden had his back angled to her, thankfully. That gave her precious moments of advantage. But he was standing over the prostrate figure of the firefighter with the shotgun pointed down at him.

Jess took it all in immediately, weighing up every single option, angle, possibility and probability. She saw the blood spreading from a wound at the back of the fireman's head, the unfortunate officer looking terrified at the double barrels of the shotgun inches from his face.

She knew for certain there was no time for any warning, none of that 'Police! Put your weapon down' malarky.

The firefighter was in immediate danger and Jess had no choice in the matter.

But then, maybe Ramsden felt a change in the air, sensed movement behind him perhaps, or saw a shadow or something move out of the corner of his eye and for a nanosecond his whole body seemed to freeze and in that moment Jess knew her presence had been detected.

Ramsden began to swivel on his heels, bringing the shotgun around to point it in her direction.

She moved fast, her one big advantage being that all she needed to do was twitch the pad of her fingertip on the trigger of the taser.

Which she did.

The two fine-pointed electronic darts connected to the device by thin wires shot out across the gap, propelled by compressed nitrogen. The darts penetrated the material of Ramsden's shirt around his rib cage and delivered the requisite electric shock. Some 50,000 volts shot into his nervous system, lasting just a couple of seconds, but long enough to instantly incapacitate him. He went spinning in a drunken pirouette to the floor, stunned, and inadvertently hurled his shotgun across the room where it skittered over the stone and – here Jess took an involuntary gasp of relief – did not discharge accidentally, something that had been at the very forefront of her million-mile-an-hour thinking.

She discarded the taser and with four long strides she crossed the room, having to step over the legs of the laid-out fireman before reaching down and grabbing the still twitching Ramsden and hauling the big man over on to his front. She placed her knee between his shoulder blades, twisted his thick arms behind his back and expertly stacked his wrists to apply her shiny new rigid handcuffs around his wrists.

It was only then, as she rose to her feet, did she exhale a long, unsteady breath of relief.

ELEVEN

The armed robbery in Greenwich was planned to be short, brutal, profitable and as violent as necessary.

The offenders had hoped that no customers would be in the shop and timed their entry to be just two minutes after it opened at ten a.m.

Meticulous planning aside, however, armed robbers are just as susceptible to being snarled up in traffic as anyone so they actually entered the premises at six minutes past ten which meant that when four masked, tooled-up men burst in, a couple – a man and a woman – were standing at one of the glass-topped counters inspecting a cushioned tray of expensive necklaces being displayed to them by a shop assistant who also happened to be the daughter of the owner.

She had a lovely necklace draped seductively across the palm of her velvet-gloved hand, which was valued just short of £2,000, and the eyes of the lady inspecting it sparkled as she caught her breath and made the man feel very, very smug.

Two of the robbers brandished sledgehammers and two carried pump-action, sawn-off, single-barrelled shotguns.

They burst into the shop screaming terrible threats. The pair with sledgehammers ran to the display counter where the couple was standing, rammed them out of the way, grabbed the necklace from the shop assistant, plus the display the couple had been inspecting, then began to rain blows down with the sledgehammers on to the glass-topped counter under which more very expensive items were on display, mainly watches, the theft of which was the main thrust of the robbery. The glass held, then cracked, then spidered out as it weakened before shattering completely and the robbers began to scoop up the jewellery from the display into pouch-type bags attached to their belts.

One of them then ran over to an upright display cabinet and smashed the glass before helping himself to the valuables on the shelves.

As they had entered, the two villains armed with the shotguns both fired warning shots into the ceiling, filling the smallish shop with an ear-splitting, reverberating boom. They racked their weapons again and ran across to the couple and the shop assistant, screaming, 'Get down, get down!' at them through their full-face balaclava masks.

One of them concentrated on covering the cowering couple, the other the shop assistant as all three backed off. The couple, clinging to each other, sank to their knees, completely owned and intimidated by the gunman. The shop assistant did likewise, tears streaming down her shocked face.

And meanwhile the robbers with sledgehammers continued to plunder the display cabinets.

Maybe ninety seconds of work in all.

And unbeknownst to them, the shop owner who was peering through a one-way grille from the office at the back of the shop had activated the silent alarm which had alerted the police.

Jess heard the discharge of a shotgun from inside the shop. She knew what they sounded like, had fired dozens herself. But that did not stop her moving towards the getaway van, striding swiftly along the pavement with Rigg doing the same in the road.

Then there was another shotgun discharge from within the shop.

And on the other side of the van, now out of sight, she heard Rigg shout, 'Armed police – come out of the vehicle with your hands where I can see—'

Then the shop door opened and the four masked members of the gang emerged in a line, two at a run, two backing out, looking well-drilled with the first one carrying a shotgun, two more with sledgehammers and goody bags, the last one reversing out also with a shotgun.

They saw her.

She dropped into a combat stance and screamed a warning at the top of her voice, but before she had got beyond the first two words, 'Armed police,' the first robber spun towards her and fired the shotgun.

She saw it all in slow motion, her brain computing everything.

His twist of the hip, the gun arcing around, the finger on the trigger.

She launched herself sideways and whatever the shotgun was loaded with missed her completely because the shooter was unable to control the upward recoil of the weapon. As Jess came up from the roll, she too fired upwards, a double-tap – and knew she'd hit the guy in the leg, somewhere around the outer thigh.

He screamed, dropped the shotgun, staggered backwards and fell whilst at the same time ripping his balaclava off and using it to put pressure on the wound which spurted blood.

The two men behind with the sledgehammers and the loot saw Jess nimbly roll back up to her feet – a move practised umpteen times in live firing ranges – with her gun aimed steadily somewhere between them. She completed her loud vocal warning for them to drop their weapons and, seeing what happened to their mate – still writhing around on the ground, crying in agony trying to stem the gush of blood from his thigh muscle – they must have been on the same wavelength.

They ditched their sledgehammers, turned and fled, probably praying a cop wouldn't shoot them in the back.

But the fourth gang member, armed with a shotgun, having witnessed all the chaos happening in front of him, everything going wrong within seconds, was furiously back-pedalling into the shop.

Jess wasn't inclined to pursue the two who'd downed tools and done a runner, knowing that her responsibility now lay with the man she'd shot and the fact that an armed, dangerous man had retreated back into the shop.

Rigg appeared from the other side of the getaway van, having swiftly dealt with the driver who was trussed-up, cuffed and was being bundled by the PC on to the pavement. He had done a superb job and was unfazed by the scenario in front of him: the wounded robber rolling around screaming, and the two fleeing felons who had all but disappeared through the gathering crowd of onlookers.

'Sort him!' Jess shouted to Rigg, pointing at the injured man.

Rigg nodded and forced his own prisoner face down on the pavement before dealing with the wounded man.

'One's gone back in, going after him,' she shouted to Rigg. 'Last thing I want is a siege.'

'Careful,' Rigg warned her.

She sidestepped the guy she'd shot and, still in the combat stance, edged towards the open door of the shop, continually commentating into her radio, knowing her words were now being recorded and that her bodycam footage was also – and that both would later be analysed by so many other people, the majority of whom had never faced what she was facing: split-second decision-making in life-and-death moments. She knew, even then, at the back of her mind, these moments would come back to haunt her legally and emotionally . . . but also in a humongous way she could never have envisioned as she crossed the threshold of the jeweller's shop.

TWELVE

Assisted by Samira, Jess dragged the drunken, stumbling form of Bill Ramsden out of the farmhouse and between them they ran him across to the gate where they dumped him to await transport to the cells.

Ramsden had recovered quickly from the taser but all the fight and belligerence had been sapped out of him and he sat propped up by the wall, hardly able to hold his head up or even slur two words together as he sullenly watched the fire tender manoeuvre into his yard and turn around. This was followed by an ambulance and four more police cars that had also arrived.

Jess went back to the house whilst a couple of paramedics treated Colin, the hostage firefighter. He insisted he was OK and refused the offer of a trip to A & E. Jess got the feeling he was more embarrassed at being taken by a drunk. Even though the drunk was armed and very dangerous.

As she watched, Joe Borwick sidled alongside her but said nothing. She was very aware of his presence and sneaked a glance at him.

Finally he said, 'Bit reckless' – just above a whisper – 'but thanks. Probably saved his life.'

Jess smirked. 'I'm always reckless when it comes to saving lives.'

Then she looked properly at him and he eyed her, smirking.

'You're new around here?' he probed.

'New lass in town . . . with a husband and two kids in tow.'

'Fair enough.' Borwick was still smirking.

'Sergeant Raker, I'm guessing . . . sorry to break up the chinwag.'

Jess turned towards this new voice to see a uniformed police inspector approaching her. She gave Borwick a smile then spun around to face the oncoming officer. 'Yes, guv.'

The man was middle-aged, had a paunch below his chest and a

matching chubby face with a serious expression on a ruddy countenance.

'I'm Inspector Price, your immediate line manager, although I'm based in Blackburn.'

Jess held out a hand to be shaken.

Price didn't acknowledge the gesture but said, 'It's "sir" here, or "boss", not "guv", which is a term used by the Met, I believe, and one you might like to consign to history. We suffer enough because of the actions of the Metropolitan Police, wouldn't you say? To bring their lingo up here is just one step too far; however, I'm only jumping to conclusions here because no one knows exactly where you're from, do they?'

'Er, OK, sir,' she corrected herself, but didn't respond to his implied question about where she was from.

'Good.' He nodded, his chins wobbling. 'And now, could you please explain to me why you didn't wait for armed backup?'

Jess looked up past Price's shoulder to see a liveried police vehicle pull into the farmyard. She kept her eyes fixed on it and Price followed the line of her sight as two armed officers got out of the vehicle and stretched.

Jess looked at her Fitbit watch, then the situation: prisoner secure, now being heaved into the back of a section van; a hostage relatively unharmed, other than hurt pride; no one else injured; a crime scene secure; everything done and dusted. She didn't even bother trying to explain this to Price, although she knew she would have to account for and justify her actions on paper. But now she simply looked at him with a bland expression, hoping he understood the thoughts she was having – but clearly he didn't.

'I asked you a question, Sergeant Raker.'

It looked like she was going to have to answer. 'Because if I'd waited, there might be a dead firefighter in there, not one who's just been knocked about a bit and had the scare of his life, a *dead* one.' She emphasized the word 'dead' whilst at the same time trying to keep her report matter-of-fact and her simmering emotions under wraps because the vibes she was picking up from this guy made her suspect that if she'd been a male officer, his disapproval might have actually been approval in the form of a pat on the back. 'And, as you can see, sir, the ARV has only just landed.'

Price kept his beady eyes on her for too long until he finally relented and said, 'You need to go to Whitebirk with your prisoner.

I'm sure the custody sergeant will require the fine details before authorizing this man's detention.'

'Yes, sir,' she said, 'and fine details he will have.' She had toyed with the idea of calling him 'boss', but that just seemed a bit too friendly for her liking.

Price turned away in a huff.

From Jess's right side, Samira stepped in close, having witnessed the exchange. She was about to say something into Jess's ear but stopped guiltily as Price turned back around as quickly as his girth would allow (and here, fleetingly, Jess wondered how he would fare in a bleep test). He leaned towards Jess.

'You need to watch yourself. We don't know where you came from, or what you did to get this sergeant's job . . . it's all a mystery.' He waggled his fingers to represent something mysterious. 'However, I intend to find out.'

When he was finally out of earshot, Samira said, 'He's an arse and doesn't like women cops, or PCSOs – especially if they're not to his colour coding.'

Jess blew out her cheeks and exhaled long and hard. 'I gathered.'

'However, Sarge, I can't deny that my interest is piqued. What *is* the mystery that surrounds you?'

Jess's mouth went dry as she considered that question and although she would have loved to tell all to Samira and felt mean for not doing so, what had to be, had to be.

'Maybe later,' Jess said. But in her mind, she added, *Maybe never.*

THIRTEEN

With her Glock still drawn, finger on the trigger, Jess cautiously entered the jeweller's and covered the small shop with her weapon and her eyes, again taking in everything, instantly analysing it, the dangers, the possibilities, seeing the couple huddled on the floor, cowering and embracing each other in their terror, the shop assistant next to them and the elderly man poking his head through the sturdy steel office door behind the counter. She also could not miss the smashed-up displays, all emptied; then her eyes returned fleetingly to the couple, but even though she was shocked by what she saw, her professionalism had to take over and she had to put them out of her mind.

She called, 'Anyone hurt?'

They all shook their heads, mute in fear.

The old man shouted, 'He's gone out through the back, he made me open up. Pointed a gun at me.'

Jess nodded as she moved across the shop floor and relayed the new information to the patrols descending en masse to the incident. She stepped over the outstretched legs of the couple and went through the gap in the counter to access the office door, her mind now visualizing the layout she would encounter at the back of the store which backed straight on to Greenwich Market which Jess knew was open that day, thereby giving the guy plenty of cover to use to escape as the place was always rammed with shoppers at most times of the day.

Taking each corner she came to with absolute caution, she swivelled out of the open back door of the shop, through the small yard and then into the market itself where she paused, took a breath, and lowered her gun back down her side, trying to be as discreet as possible and not induce mass hysteria. Although, presumably, a masked guy sprinting through the shoppers, brandishing a shotgun could have done that anyway.

'That way – he went that way!'

A guy ran up to her wearing a striped apron and a straw boater and a badge proclaiming he was the 'Cake Guy'. Jess recognized him as the owner of a stall specializing in fancy buns. She and Josh had wandered through the market only weeks before and bought a couple from him, devouring them like naughty kids by the Thames. That had been a good day, a good memory, but other than giving that memory a passing thought, coupled with how things between her and Josh weren't quite so rosy now, she had to move on.

'Thanks.'

Jess set off in the direction indicated which would take her out of the market into the grounds of the Old Royal Naval College set between Romney Road and the Thames.

As she jogged she maintained her commentary over the radio, asking for Comms to deploy armed patrols on to Romney Road, although she was also aware she had left PC Rigg alone at the front of the jeweller's shop to deal with his own prisoner, the wounded guy and the possibility that the two armed robbers who'd fled could return, though she believed this was doubtful. She knew he could cope and that he'd only be alone for a short period of time as other cops hurtled to the scene, but a lot could happen in just a few seconds.

It was a lot for Rigg to deal with, but Jess had weighed everything up and decided that an armed man on the loose was her priority for the moment as she emerged from the market on to the iconic central path that cut through the naval college, a favoured shooting location for many film and TV series.

She stopped.

Going right would take her up to Romney Road, left to the river. She spotted the blue lights of a liveried ARV on Romney Road outside the National Maritime Museum, so she veered towards the river although now, only seconds into the foot chase, she was slightly despairing of ever catching a running villain. People could disappear in the blink of an eye, she well knew.

Undaunted, she set off at a trot intending to get to the river then turn left and loop back to the jeweller passing the *Cutty Sark* on the way, knowing she would have to take full control of the crime scene until supervision arrived or a bunch of detectives turned up.

As much as it always seemed to be reported by the media that the public did not support the police, Jess found that, mostly, people were more than willing to help and share information, so she was pleased, yet not over-surprised, when a young man and woman who looked like holidaymakers ran up to her, looking relieved to see her.

'A man has just shoved what I think is a sawn-off shotgun into that litter bin outside Nando's.' The man gasped and pointed to the bin outside the restaurant. 'You after him?'

'You could say that.'

'Then he took his hoodie off and stuffed that in, too,' the woman added.

'Right, thanks. What's he got on, then?'

'A red T-shirt, maybe Arsenal strip,' the man said.

The woman held up her mobile phone. 'I took this of him as he walked away.' She showed Jess a photo on the screen of a broad, bulky young man with short-cropped blond hair with his back to the lens. It did look like a football shirt, though there was no number on it. He was wearing black tracksuit bottoms.

'That's brilliant,' Jess said.

'Sorry it wasn't his front,' the woman apologized.

'Can you send it to me?' Jess said and rooted out her contact card with her work number on it.

'Yes, course I can.'

'Thank you. Now I need to get after him.'

'He went up the main street,' the man said. 'Be careful.'

Jess started to jog again after that brief interlude and headed to Nando's which she knew well enough, having been a few times with Josh. They had eaten there on the day they'd mooched past the jeweller a few weeks ago.

The restaurant was on the Greenwich promenade close to the *Cutty Sark* and as she came on to King William Walk she was about fifty yards from the front of Nando's which hadn't yet opened for the day.

She ran to the litter bin the couple had pointed to but before she delved into it she did a twirl to scan the surroundings to see if she could spot the guy. As her eyes criss-crossed the wide paved apron which encircled the *Cutty Sark*, the number of people milling and meandering around the old, celebrated clipper ship was fairly light.

And there was a man.

Red shirt. Black joggers.

Sauntering. Not running. Cool guy. Scary guy.

He was, however, making good progress across the apron, with his broad shoulders hunched and his head moving from side to side, reminding Jess of a shark. Jess sprinted, holding her Glock low in front of her. The guy checked over his shoulder, saw her.

Jess shouted clearly at the top of her voice, 'You in the red top. Stop there now! Armed police. Stop walking!'

She slowed and raised the pistol.

He didn't stop but upped his pace and as he did so, Jess saw his right hand snake around to the waistband of his joggers at the small of his back and disappear under the hem of his shirt, reaching for something.

Jess knew what it was: a handgun.

'Armed police! Stop there and let me see your hands – now!' she yelled clearly and precisely.

Other people saw what was happening and started to back off.

The man did stop but kept facing away from her, his right hand still at his waistband.

Her gun was up now, and she was back in that combat stance.

'Do exactly as I say,' she ordered and took a cautious step towards him. She was aiming at the centre of his back, somewhere between his shoulder blades. There was never time for any fancy shooting, or shooting to wound. It was shooting to stop which meant going for the centre mass, heart, lungs. But only if the trigger had to be pulled, something that even in those fleeting seconds Jess knew she did not want to do. She wanted him to comply, end of. Otherwise, it would mean that if nothing else, her life would be irrecoverably changed and definitely for the worse. And his life would probably be over. 'Put both hands up now,' she reiterated, 'and get down on your knees. I will not tell you again. I will shoot you if you do not.'

The man's fingers curled around the butt of the gun in his pants, although Jess could not see this as his T-shirt covered his hands.

She saw the man's head tilt backwards.

His shoulders rose.

As if he was making a decision.

'Do not do this,' Jess warned him. 'Hands up! I am armed and I will shoot you.'

She stepped towards him again.

Then he began to raise his left hand in a gesture of submission, but his right remained on the gun and even then Jess knew this was going to end very badly for both of them.

The raising of the left hand was just a distraction, a misdirection.

A con. A move to gain an advantage.

She was about to shout more instructions to him but his head tilted forwards, his shoulders fell, his left arm seemed to act as a fulcrum and he pivoted a full one-eighty degrees, pulling the gun out as he swivelled on his heels and faced Jess, aiming the weapon at her.

She fired instantly.

A double-tap, two rounds in rapid succession. They were bang on target, entering his body mass, smashing into his chest.

He was as good as dead before his knees gave way. He staggered back a step, dropped his gun and clutched his chest which was spurting two geysers of dark red, oxygenated blood. He crumpled to the ground, dying unnecessarily under the shadow of the magnificent *Cutty Sark*.

FOURTEEN

Booking the almost comatose Bill Ramsden into the custody system at Blackburn police station took three very tedious hours; half an hour to the nick from Dead Man's Stake Farm, then a wait in the queue (where six prisoners were being processed ahead of them) and following a tussle with Ramsden – who suddenly came alive and belligerent – at the custody desk, where he kicked off by spitting at the custody sergeant (something Jess would never recommend to any prisoner), then punching Jess in the face as his handcuffs were removed, giving her a black eye, before he was pinned to the floor, searched and then dragged to a drunk cell.

Despite the throbbing eye, Jess and Samira both wrote statements whilst everything was still fresh in their minds. Then they headed back to Clitheroe with Jess's left eye beginning to close the more it swelled and turned a nasty shade of purple. Just another charge to add to Ramsden's rap sheet.

On both legs of the journey, there and back, Jess moaned about the distance and time it took to get from the sharp end to the custody office.

'I presume where you came from, distance wasn't so much of a problem?' Samira probed.

This made Jess clam up as she said, 'There were certainly more stations . . . Ow!' She touched her puffy eye and winced, quite unable to credit that on her first day in this rural backwater she'd used a taser and been punched in the face.

'Well, Lancashire's a big area and they're always shutting down police stations,' Samira said philosophically. She had driven both ways, firstly following the van containing Ramsden to Blackburn, then following no one on the way back. This conversation was taking place as she turned into the yard behind Clitheroe nick.

'Whatev,' Jess said curtly, but then with her one good eye she noticed that her slightly abrupt response seemed to have jarred with Samira, who was frowning. 'Sorry, didn't mean to be rude.' She blew out her cheeks. 'I just expected my first day to be easier somehow.'

'I know, Sarge. It is a bit out of the ordinary, I suppose,' Samira commiserated. Then grinned. 'It's usually mid-afternoon before the place kicks off!'

Jess laughed. 'Anyhow, we need to arrange for someone to go and deal with Ramsden when he sobers up, and no doubt he'll make a complaint against me which I could well do without.'

'For zapping him?'

'Police brutality.'

'Far less than he deserved,' Samira said. 'A good old-fashioned kicking would have been in order. I thought you were very restrained.'

'Maybe we should have fed him to the fire brigade,' Jess said, recalling that once Ramsden had been subdued, Colin's colleagues had let it be known that they would like to rip Ramsden limb from limb.

They entered the police station through the back door which led into the defunct small cell complex, now mothballed, which was unlikely to be used to hold prisoners again. Jess thought it all a bit sad that policing seemed to be increasingly taken away from locals to become more centralized and supposedly more efficient, although how a twenty-mile round trip to drop a prisoner off could be deemed efficient was beyond her. She had even heard the rumour that Clitheroe police station, the opening hours of which were hugely reduced, was to be closed completely and sold off, presumably to become some very nice town centre apartments, which had been the fate of other rural police stations.

She shrugged at the thought. It wasn't her problem as such. It was very much the way of the world in policing even though almost everyone, bar the bureaucrats, knew it was short-sighted. What bothered Jess as much as anything was the lack of a place of safety for anyone requiring immediate help from the police. An emergency phone on a wall would never replace access to a building. As ever, it was the public which would lose out.

Once through the cell complex, Samira peeled off to get the kettle on and Jess went into the sergeants' office which was in the same state as she'd left it several hours before with her belongings dumped and half-unpacked.

She closed the door and took a few moments to get her breath, calm down and reorientate whilst reminding herself that, actually, all she had experienced so far was just another day at the 'office':

unpredictable, challenging, exciting and truly wonderful; aka being a cop.

'Well, at least I didn't shoot anyone dead,' she said to herself, then wondered how she could bathe her swollen eye, which was hurting like hell.

FIFTEEN

Even though Jess went through the motions of trying to save the armed robber's life, she knew it was futile.

He was dead and she had killed him.

The fact she'd had no choice in the matter, that he was armed, dangerous and would have shot her stone dead if he'd been quick enough, did not make that fact any easier to bear as she holstered her Glock and rushed towards his body, sank down on to one knee alongside him whilst calling for the air ambulance, then began to put pressure on the wounds with the heels of her bare hands, trying to stem the blood flow which flooded through her fingers.

She realized it was pointless.

Blood only flowed when a heart was pumping.

For a moment she could feel pressure against her hands. But it was only a moment.

The last few desperate beats of a shredded heart.

He was gone. His legs stopped moving. His mouth drooped open as a thick gout of blood choked out of it and every muscle in his entire body relaxed never to respond to one of his brain impulses again.

Finally, with her head just a blanket of rushing noise, ears ringing and breath short, she sank her other knee to the ground and pulled her bloodied hands away from the dead man's chest. All around her was a whirring, distorted sound. Shouts. Sirens. People's faces. Screams of anguish.

She had to wait until everything came back into focus and her trained, conditioned responses returned.

Though having said that, much of what then took place was just a blur as other cops swamped the scene and an air ambulance managed to land close to the *Cutty Sark* and the on-board medics pronounced the robber dead.

Then the next eight hours were a breathless, muddled hustle for Jess.

She was whisked back to the station where her gun and body cam were seized, then all her uniform bagged up for Forensics; her hands and face were swabbed before she was allowed to wash the blood away and she was put into a forensic suit. Then, in the final act she knew was inevitable, but still felt like complete humiliation, a super-intendent she didn't even know formally suspended her from the firearms team and warned her she also faced suspension from duty.

It all hurt a lot so when she handed over her firearms authori-zation card, a small piece of laminated plastic the size of a credit card, something she treasured greatly and had worked hard to achieve and maintain, the superintendent's final words chilled her and rang in her ears repeatedly.

'Don't be surprised if you get arrested for murder.'

He left her at that point.

Following that she was allowed to shower in the changing rooms and get into a spare set of her own clothes, as she always kept a pair of jeans, a top, fresh underwear and cheap trainers in her locker.

Then she spent the next four hours being interviewed under caution by two cold-faced detectives from the professional standards department, acting on behalf of the IOPC. Though the interviews took that length of time, going over and over her story – which never wavered – it became quickly clear Jess had no case to answer. This was backed up by witnesses and her bodycam footage, plus recordings of all the radio transmissions she'd made. She knew she did not have anything to worry about as such, though the concluding words from one of the detectives interviewing her warned of a 'shit storm' that would undoubtedly fall from many directions.

She just nodded at that. Par for the course. Police haters would be out in force and social media would be an awful place.

After that she was given the details of a counsellor on a business card which she slid into her jeans pocket and completely forgot about.

Then it was time to go home and face the real world.

She did not look at any news but went home and sat in the backyard which she had turned into a wonderful terracotta pot-filled world, a small haven which caught the sun for most of the day. She sat on a wooden bench which she herself had made from old pallets and raised her face to the warmth with a mug of tea and a bar of chocolate. The temptation was to dive straight into a gin bottle but she refrained from that. Over the next few days she would be under so much pressure that she would have to be on top of her game, would need a clear head and quick mental reactions. She was under no illusions. No one would go easy on her and she refused to go under. She had witnessed a few of her firearms colleagues having to undergo lengthy, brutal investigations following a shooting. Few survived mentally intact.

But for Jess, pulling a trigger and killing a man wasn't the whole story. She knew what she had done was right and she would ride anything thrown in her direction. *Anything.*

No. There was something else.

Something much closer to her home and heart.

The one thing that *could* put her under.

That was why she was alone in her house. She'd quickly arranged for her mother to pick up the kids from school and look after them for the night.

She was still sitting on the homemade bench, the evening around her beginning to chill, the mug now empty in her hand, the chocolate bar devoured, when she heard the front door open and close quite softly.

Josh coming home.

She did not look around but was aware of the figure of her husband at the open door of the small conservatory behind her. She did not speak. He said nothing either, but Jess could hear his breathing which surprised her because her hammering heart and the pounding of blood through her ears should have drowned out everything.

Josh coughed.

Jess felt physically sick but swallowed back and turned her head slowly to look at her bedraggled, exhausted, shame-faced husband.

His eyes dropped. He could not look at her.

But now that she was looking at him, she couldn't tear her eyes away from him. She wasn't sure exactly what to say. What were the right words for this opening gambit? In the end she decided simply to go with whatever tumbled out and take it from there.

SIXTEEN

J ess placed her portable make-up box on her desk in the sergeants' office at Clitheroe and angled the mirror on the rim of the box so she could inspect her newly acquired black eye, or as she now liked to call it, purple eye. It was nicely swollen, throbbing gently, but she could actually see well enough through it and it seemed to have reached its maximum expansion, she hoped. The make-up box, described by the manufacturer as 'perfect for on-the-go touch-ups or travel', had been with her over ten years and probably needed to be replaced, but it had served her well at work, even though the lads had scoffed at her occasionally when she used it at the end of a particularly grimy tour of duty.

She groaned at her reflection and shook her head, realizing there was very little that a dab of foundation could do to disguise the injury. It would just have to be a trophy of war until it went away.

The desktop phone rang and she answered it, having to think hard not to introduce herself with her old moniker from the Met.

'Sergeant Raker, Clitheroe police station,' she said after a slight hesitation. Also, she hadn't quite yet worked out the phone system and wasn't sure whether or not this was an external or internal call. 'Can I help you?'

That doubt was immediately erased as a sharp, barking voice that Jess had only encountered for the first time earlier that day but which was already branded into her brain, snapped, 'Inspector Price . . . misper update if you don't mind.'

'Err . . .' she hesitated, hating herself for it. The term 'misper' was of course police jargon to describe a missing person, but because Jess had turned out immediately that morning and got herself into bother, she had no idea what the unpleasant Inspector Price was talking about because she simply hadn't had chance to check out what was going on in her new domain. It galled her that she wasn't on top of this. Normally she would be, and prided herself on being so. What had happened that morning was a good excuse for not knowing, but she guessed Price would not be happy with that, and nor was she. Patrol sergeants were expected to have their finger on the pulse, but just at that moment, Jess felt more like she had her thumb up her arse.

'Got to admit it, guv – sorry, sir – I have no idea what you're talking about,' Jess said.

'We have a vulnerable missing person on your patch, so maybe you would like to acquaint yourself with the details, where we're up to with it, ensure the log is updated and then get back to me, please,' Price said snootily then hung up, making Jess wince and scowl at the phone.

She replaced the receiver, muttering, 'I don't even know your extension number . . . prick!'

'That would be Inspector Prick.'

Jess swivelled quickly to the door where Samira had appeared bearing two teas in large, old mugs, typical of those often found in police stations which, if scientifically inspected, would probably be deemed germ-laden death traps, although Jess did not know of anyone who'd ever been adversely infected.

Samira placed one of the mugs on a beer mat – another regular feature in police stations. The colour of the brew reminded Jess of her terracotta garden pots and that memory jarred her slightly.

Somewhere down the corridor a locker door slammed shut.

'Thanks.' The tea tasted amazing. She gestured at the phone. 'He wanted an update on the missing person.'

'Ah . . .' Samira was about to say more when there was a sharp rap on the office door and a uniformed constable popped his head in. He was perhaps mid-to-late thirties.

'Hi, come in.' Jess beckoned.

He stepped in. Tall, broad-shouldered and pretty good-looking was Jess's first impression, and smart as could be in a modern police uniform. Jess stood up and extended her hand. 'I'm Sergeant Raker, new in today.'

'I know,' the PC said curtly. He shook her hand just as curtly and Jess wasn't impressed by the inflection in his voice or hand-shake, nor the slight sneer on his face when he spotted the make-up case on the desk or the smirk when he looked at her black eye. He seemed to achieve quite a lot in those few seconds, putting Jess on her guard.

'And you are?'

'PC Dave Simpson.'

'Pleased to meet you, Dave.' She smiled.

He did not return the smile but did acknowledge her with a nod. 'I'm attending the report of a body in a reservoir, thought you might want to tag along, Sarge . . . and you, Sam,' he added, turning to Samira who was watching him with a neutral expression.

'Oh, right . . . Inspector Price has just called me about a misper . . . could this be the one he was on about?'

Simpson shrugged. 'Dunno.'

'Let's find out then, shall we?' Jess said, took a mouthful of tea and stood up thinking there seemed to be little chance of getting anything sorted today and grabbed her hat.

'Audley Reservoir,' Simpson said to Samira. 'Know the one?'

'Off the fifty-nine, near Pendleton?'

'That's the one. See you up there.' He turned and was gone before Jess could utter another word.

Jess blinked. 'Bit rude.'

'You don't know the half of it,' Samira said. 'Looks like we're going up together.'

'Looks that way,' Jess said, unimpressed, though not by the prospect of going with Samira but by what felt like a forewarning of insubordination from Simpson.

SEVENTEEN

Jess regarded Josh standing at the conservatory door and said, 'I shot a man dead today, yet you're the one who's got the explaining to do.'

Her husband nodded. 'Yeah.' He stepped out of the conservatory and came to Jess's homemade bench with the intention of sitting next to her until she held up a hand and said, 'Don't.'

He was taken aback. 'Jess . . . honey,' he mewed feebly, about to beg. He was on the verge of tears.

She knew her own face had turned to granite or ice or whatever, and was glad he could see that. 'Don't even think of using any term of affection with me,' she cautioned him.

Her nostrils dilated with anger and she allowed herself to glare contemptuously at the forlorn figure now standing, quaking before her.

'I . . . I,' he stuttered, unlike the guy, the businessman, normally full of bluster and confidence that he usually was.

Jess raised a warning finger at him. 'Let me just say this: do not lie to me in any shape or form, Josh. I *demand* the absolute and honest truth to come out of your mouth, do you understand?'

His nod was meek.

'Right.' Jess sat upright and braced herself. Then she said, 'Now you are going to tell me what the *actual fuck* you were doing in a jeweller's shop in Greenwich High Street this morning buying jewellery for another woman who, guess what, wasn't your wife? No bullshit, please.'

EIGHTEEN

PC Simpson didn't even wait for their arrival. By the time Jess and Samira made it on to Pendleton Road which ran along the western edge of Audley Reservoir, he had already parked the Land Rover tightly to the side of the road underneath a hedge, and as Jess climbed out of the passenger seat of the police car she could see him making his way up the track leading to the water's edge.

Jess frowned. 'What's his beef? I get the impression he doesn't like me much?'

The expression on Samira's face told Jess the PCSO knew exactly what Simpson's problem was, but still she said, 'Not for me to tell you, Sarge.'

'After what we've just been through together?' Jess quipped. 'Facing a mad gunman?' She set off towards the stile which she had to negotiate to get on to the track. 'Don't worry, no doubt I'll find out myself.' She lifted one leg over the slightly rickety wooden structure and dropped over the opposite side.

Samira followed her on to the narrow path and they began the short ascent up to the reservoir.

Over her shoulder Jess inquired, 'So are you going to tell me, or what?'

'All I can say is this – he was the temporary sergeant until you landed.'

'Gotcha,' Jess said, her mouth twisting at this news. Although she had literally only just met PC Simpson she understood instantly his chilly attitude towards her, because maybe her arrival on the scene had just screwed up his promotion prospects. From those few words said by Samira it seemed that Simpson must have been holding the fort by acting up a rank from PC to sergeant, probably in the expectation he would eventually be given three stripes substantively. Though that was just an educated guess, Jess thought, she also believed she wouldn't be far off the mark. It was a regular thing, a not very pleasant thing, in the police. Officers were expected, often seduced by false promises, to 'act up' and often did the job for long periods and then found they were just being used to plug a gap in the hierarchy, only to be busted back to their original rank. The service had many dissatisfied officers because of this practice, which was very wrong. It had happened to Jess a couple of times too and the sense of deflation could be overwhelming and demotivating. So without knowing the full details surrounding Simpson, Jess was pretty certain this was his 'beef' with her, and was a problem that needed to be addressed as soon as possible.

With these thoughts in mind, she scrambled to the top of the track on to the path surrounding Audley Reservoir, closely followed by Samira. About a quarter of the way around the perimeter of the water Simpson was talking to a man holding a fishing rod.

She shaded her eyes and with her one good one and one not so great, she scanned the very still water and in the centre of the reservoir saw what looked like a big bundle of floating rags, rising gently with the ripple of the surface.

A body. Face down in the water. Even from this distance, Jess could tell it was a man.

Behind her Samira gasped and clamped a hand over her mouth and said, 'I'll bet it's Bart Morrison.'

'Bart Morrison?' Jess queried.

'Old guy, often goes missing from an old people's home in town, goes walkabout and then hands himself in, if you will. Usually sneaks out in the morning, then by the time staff notice and tell us, he's usually back at the home, no harm done.'

Jess set off towards Simpson and the angler with Samira in tow.

Speaking – again over her shoulder – Jess asked, 'So this guy hasn't been reported missing yet?'

'Not that I know of,' Samira admitted.

'So who would Inspector Price be on about when he phoned me, expecting me to know? Do we have other missing persons I should know about?'

'A woman went missing last week, early thirties, bit of an odd job,' Samira said. 'Maybe that's who. I don't know of any others.'

Jess nodded and continued to make her way around to Simpson, whilst keeping her good eye on the body floating in the water, unmoving apart from with the gentle surface movement of the reservoir.

They reached Simpson and the angler.

'Bart Morrison?' Jess asked the constable.

'I reckon so,' he replied.

Jess turned to the angler. 'I take it you spotted him?' He was a small man, mid-fifties, with a collection of rods at his feet.

'Yep, and it probably is Bart . . . this is one of his routes, strolls around the res.' His right forefinger did a circle.

'You've seen him here before?'

'Few times.'

'We'll need a statement from you,' Jess said, gave the angler a nod, then took a look at the width of the path encircling the water. A couple of feet, maybe wider at some points, made of pressed gravel and quite flat. Jess jerked her head at Simpson. 'Let's take a stroll.'

'I think we can pretty much see everything we need from here, don't you?'

Jess ignored the less than subtle defiance. 'Maybe we can ascertain where he went in.'

'For what reason?' The PC continued to be stubborn.

'Did he fall or was he pushed? Let's go look.' Her tone, coupled with a no-nonsense glare brooked no dissent. Already she could tell that problems with this man were simmering and she would have to stomp on him . . . in a nice way to begin with, then maybe not so nice if he didn't respond. He needed to understand who was boss here.

Because she was. And Simpson had to accept that whether or not he felt pissed off by her stepping into the role he had been doing for a while now.

He followed her along the path with a miserable expression on his face.

Once more calling over her shoulder, Jess said to Samira, 'Can you contact the care home, see what they think the current position is with Bart Morrison? Cheers.'

Jess pushed on with Simpson following her for maybe fifty yards or so before she halted and turned abruptly. They were far enough away from the angler and Samira to be out of earshot.

Simpson almost collided with her.

With a dead body floating on the water nearby and a black eye, Jess was in no mood to mince words. She'd taken the snap decision to confront the officer now because she would never accept dissent and questioning from him, particularly in front of a member of the public. She didn't have a problem being challenged in the right environment. 'Let's get this straight from the get-go, Dave, whether you're happy or not with any of my decisions, I've got three stripes and you haven't.'

Simpson's mouth popped open like a goldfish.

'I'm aware you might feel a bit peed off because you didn't get promoted, and I get that – been there, done it, got the T-shirt on several occasions – and it's tough, but you've got to deal with it, OK? But never' – and here Jess's voice dropped an octave and became ultra serious – '*ever* question me in front of a member of the public. I'm not averse to anything I do being scrutinized, believe me, I'm still living with a huge decision I made, but it's done out of earshot of Joe Public. Got it?'

Simpson literally seemed to wind his neck in as he saw that this new, female sergeant was not going to be the pushover he might have assumed.

Jess noted his body language, satisfied her message had been understood. 'Right, let's see what we can see.' She spun and continued along the footpath, a grim expression on her face.

NINETEEN

'No bullshit?' Josh said quietly, as though he had been considering it.

'No. Whatever you do, don't take me for an idiot.'

Josh's eyes closed for longer than a blink, then he slowly opened them. He sat down on a garden chair set at an angle to Jess on the bench. He interlocked his fingers, clearly trying to construct the words in his brain to be relayed out through his mouth.

Finally . . . *finally*, he spoke.

'I . . . er . . . I've been seeing her for about three months.' He swallowed. 'She's a secretary.'

Jess's heart was beating quickly now, hammering relentlessly against her rib cage like some sort of trapped alien trying to burst out in a blood-soaked fountain. She held herself back from blurting, 'I know who she is!' Because she did know the woman. The dark-haired, pretty, slim, flirtatious younger woman who'd been Josh's secretary for about a year. Ali, or something short and sweet like that. Jess had met her in passing at a couple of Josh's work events but had never once imagined he would be so stupid as to . . .

'And? Do you love her?' Jess demanded.

The breath seemed to leave Josh's body. 'No . . . no, it's over. I promise. It was just a stupid fling.'

'Don't you mean it's over because you got caught up in an armed robbery and your actual wife and' – she could not resist this bit – 'the mother of your two children just happened to turn up and, y'know, shoot two of the robbers?'

'I know, I know,' Josh admitted feebly.

'Josh, I killed a man today.' Jess tilted her head slightly as she looked at him. 'And what I wanted most after that . . . because God knows, being a firearms officer, it's one of the things that continuously plays through the back of your mind . . . y'know? Will it ever happen to me? Will I have the courage and grounds to pull the trigger and shoot someone? And if so, how will I face all the fucking shit that'll come my way after that bullet leaves the barrel, even if I'm one hundred per cent justified in what I did? Well, guess what, matey boy, my answer was yes, course I can face it, the fact that my life will be turned upside down, I can face it because at the end of the day I will have my family behind me. That's what I wanted most: my kids, my mum and most of all you, my husband in whose arms I can melt into every night and feel safe and reassured that you will always be there for me. And fuck me – guess what?'

'You didn't need to be a firearms officer,' Josh said.

'You dimwit! Of course, you're right . . . however, you would still have been in a jeweller's shop buying expensive . . . *stuff* . . . for your fancy piece. And you'd still be coming home, facing me and trying to explain why you're screwing your secretary.'

'Things haven't been right between us for a while,' Josh said defensively.

Jess licked the tip of her forefinger and made an 'air' tick. 'Excuse number one, the old chestnut, you predictable divvy! Next one – we haven't had sex for a couple of months? Am I right?'

'It's true.'

Jess had to stop herself from giggling. 'What's the next one? It meant nothing?'

'It didn't.'

Suddenly Jess was overwhelmed by the whole thing: the robbery, the shooting, the questioning, the deceit . . . essentially her whole life crumbling around her and with absolutely nothing to cling to in order to prevent herself from pitching headlong into a black hole.

She stood up, her legs unsteady.

Josh got up too and tried to reach for her.

'Don't touch me.' She backed away. 'I'm going into our bedroom and I don't want you anywhere near me, understand? If you're sleeping here and not at her Putney flat – yeah, I know where she lives, I've met her, remember? – then you're on the sofa. Mum's going to sort the kids overnight. I'm going to ring them and hear their voices, then I'm going to have a long hot soak accompanied by wine and then I'm going to crash out. Alone.'

She left Josh in the garden and wondered just how the hell she was going to deal with all this without going into a mental vortex and then, probably, insanity. However, one thing she did know was that whatever was thrown at her she would deal it somehow, because that's what she was made of.

TWENTY

'He could have gone in here,' Jess said. She and Simpson had walked the path around the reservoir. She had gone slowly ahead of him, searching for clues like a bloodhound, as to where the old man might have entered the water. Once or twice she had glanced around and seen Simpson's annoyed face and the fact he wasn't putting any effort into finding the spot. He was beginning to infuriate her but any showdown would have to be put on hold for somewhere more private, although at one point she did snap, 'You could humour me and at least pretend to be looking!'

'Yes, Sarge,' he replied sullenly, adding something indecipherable under his breath Jess didn't quite catch but which was probably for the best, she thought.

They circled around the reservoir with Jess keeping an eye on the floating body as they came back around. She felt guilty about not taking immediate steps to recover Bart, but she did not want to put anyone in danger either. As they came back round Jess noticed some scuffmarks on the outer edge of the path in the grass where the ground angled away down into a marshy bog. She stopped and went down on her haunches, wondering if this was significant or was it just her imagination running riot to shoehorn a half-baked idea into the meagre facts available.

However, she stuck to her guns.

'What do you think?' she asked Simpson.

He was looking over her shoulder. 'Doubt it.'

'Mm.' She raised her eyes from the marks, half-wondering if they could be where a struggle had taken place. She looked down the slope to the marsh.

At first she saw nothing, so she stood upright and did a 360-degree scan from where she was standing, her mind working, eyes roving over the water. The bank of the reservoir was quite steep here right down into the clear water and there were no reeds or weeds at any point where the concrete plunged into the water.

Simpson watched her impatiently.

'You knew this old guy, didn't you?' she asked him.

'Came across him a couple of times.'

'When he went walkabout, did he use a walking stick?'

'I'm sure he did.'

'So where is it? I haven't seen it in the water, have you? I'm assuming it would probably float, even if it was made of metal.'

'Or not.'

'Or not . . . but if it did float, it would be possible to see it on the water, would you agree?'

'Suppose.'

'But we haven't seen it.'

'Nope.'

Jess stopped rotating and faced away from the water, down the slope to the marsh. Sidestepping carefully so as not to disturb the marks in the grass she had spotted, she slowly eased herself down inch by inch until her shoes sank into the mushy wet area of the marsh where she steadied herself. And looking over the reeds she immediately saw a silver-tipped, dark wood walking stick and what looked like a flat cap. She crouched down, took out her mobile phone and took a few photographs from where she stood, plus shots of the slope down to the marsh from the footpath.

She didn't touch the items, left them in situ, then carefully clambered back up to the path on which Simpson was regarding her with a pained look. Jess refrained from being smug, just said, 'A cap and a walking stick and what could be scuffle marks here' – she pointed to the edge of the path – 'and a body in the water. Thoughts?'

'Needs looking at,' Simpson acknowledged ruefully.

'So much so that I want a crime scene investigator to record all this and I want CID here, too, and I want to get Bart's body properly recovered by divers, OK? Let's treat it as a murder scene and if it turns out to be just a tragic accident then at least we won't have scrambled egg on our faces.'

'Your face, you mean? Out to make an impression?'

'No. Just out to do a bread-and-butter job of being a cop . . . so, CSI, CID and divers, can I leave that to you to sort?'

He nodded.

'I'll go and see what Samira's learned from the care home.'

'What do you reckon, Sarge?' Samira asked Jess, who was more used to being called 'skip'.

'Better safe than sorry . . . just a couple of things that don't add up in my highly suspicious mind. What does the care home have to say?'

'They confirmed Bart did sneak out but also that they contacted him by phone and he said he was on his way back, so they weren't too concerned.'

'Right.'

'Something troubling you?' Samira asked of the puzzled expression on Jess's face.

'Er, dunno. We need to go and speak to the home but I also want to stay here and protect the scene until the specialists arrive.' She looked over to Simpson. He was on his mobile phone. Jess hoped he was starting the process of getting the aforementioned specialists contacted and turned out.

'I can stay here and do that,' Samira volunteered. Then cheekily added, 'And keep an eye on him.'

'Appreciate that but on balance I think scene management is my first priority, so maybe we'll all stay here until the circus has arrived.'

TWENTY-ONE

E ven though Jess and Josh had been involved in the same incident at the jeweller, their evidence did not really overlap as such. Josh was in the shop with his 'lady friend' (as Jess continually referred to Abigail, as she was called, with an accompanying, disapproving roll of her eyes) when the gang burst into the shop, robbed it, and Jess had subsequently thundered through, weapon drawn, in pursuit of the escaping villain who she confronted and shot in a different location, out of view of Josh. This made things a little simpler, evidentially speaking, and there was no need to keep the pair, as witnesses, apart from each other.

Even though they did spend most of their time apart.

After the revelation concerning Josh's office-based 'shagathon' (as Jess called the affair with his secretary, again with an accompanying roll of her eyes) she finally insisted he 'do one' from the marital home.

This demand resulted in the biggest shouting match the couple had ever had because Josh insisted he had nowhere to go. When Jess pointed out, not for the first time, that his 'lady friend' had a flat, he assured her the fling was over and by making him exit the house he would effectively be homeless.

Jess wasn't even sure why she conceded on that point, but instead she was the one who left and took the kids to live with her widowed mother. This pleased the older lady no end. She had never liked Josh much (too flash) and being a fairly recent widow, and having a hard time adjusting to life as a singleton, the influx of Jess and the two children was a lifesaver for her.

In terms of the internal police response to the shooting, Jess was quickly removed from all operational duties and stuck in an office in the New Scotland Yard building on the Thames embankment which was about as far away physically and symbolically from front-line policing as could be.

It felt like a massive punishment for simply doing her job but she knew it was par for the course. It was also to protect her as much as possible from the scrutiny of the press, the public outcry that any police use of firearms generated and to keep her safe from any reprisals that any villains related to, or friends of, the robber might wish to vent on her. Also to achieve this, her identity was never publicly revealed at any stage.

All in all, her life became very complicated. She felt as if she was at the centre of a swirling storm over which she had no control, and which made her physically sick on occasions as everything seemed to vie for her attention. Although she believed her focus should be on keeping her family together, the process of justice was the thing that compelled her the most and demanded attention.

It was horrible.

The round of accusative interviews on the day of the shooting was just the start with detectives and interviewers from the IOPC mashing her head with constant questions, mostly designed to steer her from her story and portray her as a trigger-happy cop out to murder anyone who crossed her that day.

However, she didn't even need to think about 'sticking to her story' because her story was a true and honest recount of events.

Eventually, months down the line, came the inquest. She and her colleague Mark Rigg were allowed to give their evidence via a video link. The only disquiet Jess had about this was that her voice was obviously that of a female – which was not a secret as such – but female firearms officers were a bit of a rarity and if anyone wished to ID her for a nefarious reason, it probably wouldn't take too much digging.

The inquest, with a jury, lasted, on and off, two months. Long, drawn out, draining for all concerned.

Jess spent three days on the stand – via video link – being questioned and keeping, unwaveringly, to her story, not being fooled by clever barristers to ever question her own, crystal-clear recall of a day which would live with her forever.

She was in her office at New Scotland Yard when the coroner's jury reached its verdict – lawful killing – much to her relief. That, however, did not mean her ordeal was over. Although there would be no criminal proceedings against her, she knew that the IOPC were waiting in line with bated breath to have their bite of the cherry.

Shortly after hearing the coroner's court verdict, Jess was in the toilets, vomiting back her lunch, not having realized how much on edge she had been. As she looked at her pale, sickly reflection in the mirror, about to apply lipstick, her mobile phone rang. The number was listed as unavailable and having become ultra-cautious about answering calls from unknown numbers, she merely said, 'Yes.'

'Sergeant Raker?'

'Who's calling?'

'Sergeant Raker . . . you may or may not remember me. I'm DCI Costigan, National Crime Agency. I was present when you received the briefing on the morning of the Greenwich robbery.'

'No, I don't remember you.'

'No probs. I was skulking about in the shadows, which is what I do.'

'Okaaay?'

'We need to speak,' the man said.

'About what?'

'Not over the phone. Face-to-face. And soon. Like within the next half-hour.'

'Come to my office. I assume you know where I work?'

'No, look, we need to talk now, away from prying eyes. You choose a location, maybe somewhere in walking distance of your office.'

'Err . . . why?'

'Look, Sergeant, please don't hesitate. I'm genuine – check me out, ring the NCA if you like, I get it, you're wary. But we must speak. This is a vitally important discussion. Bring someone along with you, if you like, though whoever you bring will not be party to our talk.'

'Look, what the . . .?'

'Choose a location, see me there in half an hour,' the man called Costigan said.

Jess made the decision. 'The café in Waterstones on Trafalgar Square.'

That café had become a bolthole for Jess since being uprooted and 'dumped' as she called it, in a back office at New Scotland Yard.

When she had been a firearms officer (as she still was, technically) there was rarely time for formal meal breaks. Everything was on the go, hurried, guzzled down and unhealthy. Office life was so much different and took a lot of adjustment: same start time every day, a coffee break, a lunch break, even time for a brew in the afternoon. This was a whole new world for Jess, a real eye-opener and truly not for her but for the time being – until she was completely exonerated for her actions by the justice system and the IOPC – she was stuck where she was.

And though it went against the grain, she decided to take full advantage. Although as a police officer she was only supposed to take three-quarters of an hour for a refreshment break, she took an hour, figuring she was just reclaiming what she had put in over the years of frequently having no breaks at all.

No one challenged her about it. In fact, most people in the office hardly ever raised their eyes to her, even acknowledged her presence as if by doing so they might somehow become infected by her situation – or shot by her.

However, the life of a pariah suited her.

It gave her time to think, even at her desk, and the extra-long lunch break which occasionally stretched to ninety minutes, was lovely.

Following the mysterious phone call she grabbed her coat from the hanger behind her desk, shrugged it on and left the office. No one spoke.

Jess grinned, shook her head and just about stopped herself from saying, 'Arseholes.'

This *so* wasn't her world. She needed to get out of this place and get back to the sharp end of policing, even if it meant being without a gun.

She emerged into nice sunshine on the embankment, gave a slight nod to the world-famous rotating sign outside the building, turned up Richmond Terrace and on to Whitehall, more or less opposite Downing Street. As usual the street on which the official residence of the British Prime Minister was located was under siege from several hundred very vocal protesters demanding immediate action for various causes, none of which seemed directly linked to the UK as far as Jess could see. But she wasn't great with politics. She turned right and headed up towards Trafalgar Square and Nelson's Column. Waterstones was located in the Grand Building on the corner of Northumberland Avenue, but Jess crossed over Whitehall before she reached it and did a slow circle of Nelson's Column where she paused by one of the lion plinths from where she could see over to the bookshop.

The day was hugely busy as always; buses, taxis and thousands of other vehicles of all shapes and sizes and swarms of people bustling around so that keeping a steady eye on the shop front wasn't easy. She didn't completely know why she was being so suspicious, probably the innate nature of an experienced cop: testing the lie of the land, not wanting any nasty surprises.

She tried to visualize DCI Costigan, but couldn't bring him to mind, and she had just about given up and was going to go into the café in the bookstore when a voice close behind her made her jump.

'I assume you're looking for me?'

Jess spun round so fast she almost fell over, again that inbred nature of a cop expecting to be attacked, but that wasn't going to happen as Costigan stood there leaning against the plinth, smirking and with a cigarette dangling from the corner of his mouth. He looked cool and amused and despite herself, Jess liked what she saw – with the exception of the cigarette, a foul habit she had left behind twenty years ago.

'You made me jump,' she accused him, now recognizing him from the briefing at which he'd been doing a bit of lurking around.

'Sneaky beaky stuff,' he conceded. 'It's in my nature to creep up behind folk.'

'Even when they're on your side?'

'Especially then.' He grinned, then extended a hand. 'Dave Costigan, DCI.'

They shook. 'Shall we?' He gestured towards the bookshop, mashed his cigarette into a bin, then the two of them negotiated the traffic and entered the shop, making their way up to the first-floor café where they found a table by a window. Nothing was said until the coffees arrived, then he reached across and proffered his hand again and said, 'Dave Costigan, NCA . . . we haven't been formally introduced.'

They shook hands again and he also gave her his ID card, which she inspected carefully then handed it back. 'Sergeant Raker, as you know. So, what's this about?'

'Straight in, I see,' he said appreciatively, then took a sip of his brew, keeping an eye on her across the rim of his cup. 'But first, how are you?'

Jess frowned. 'Me? I'm OK,' she answered cautiously, half-wondering if this was some sort of welfare visit and she was being set up as a nutjob.

'You got caught up in a perfect storm, I hear. The shooting, your family . . .'

'Whoever coined that phrase clearly never got caught up in a storm.'

'Probably not.'

'So, what gives, as they say?'

Costigan placed his cup carefully down and his whole demeanour seemed to change, his body language and eye contact now very serious. Not that Jess expected anything less from a meeting like this, whatever it was about.

Costigan pursed his lips. 'The guy you shot . . .'

Jess stiffened. 'Terry Moss, remember him well.'

'What do you know about him, other than he finally got cremated?'

'What I heard and read and saw on social media. Quite some coverage for a toerag.'

'Yep.'

The funeral really had hit the headlines about a week ago, just a few days before the verdict of the inquest. One of those over-the-top celebrations of a gangster's demise on the streets of London with the obligatory horse-drawn hearse strewn with garlands and Moss's name written in white roses on the coffin lid; and the claims he was such a good boy, life and soul of the party, never did no one no harm. Jess had tried not to look but had been inexorably drawn to the media coverage, the photos and videos of the crowded streets, and also repulsed by it, in particular the statements made by Moss's family about wanting to make the trigger-happy (a phrase which had come to haunt her) Met police pay for shooting an innocent, law-abiding man despite overwhelming evidence to the contrary.

Justice will be done, the family threatened.

'Good riddance, I say,' Jess muttered through gritted teeth.

'Hear, hear. He was an all-round bad boy,' Costigan agreed.

'Although shooting a man dead will live with me forever, good or bad, justified or not.' She took a shaky drink of her latte.

'Of course it will,' Costigan said sincerely.

For a moment Jess suspected he was mocking her and his sincerity was fake, but a glance into his deep grey eyes and a check of his body language told her his words were for real and she almost lost her poise and defence system then. She had been through the wringer so many times over the past months and most of what had been launched in her direction had been attacks or mealy-mouthed platitudes, mock sympathy and sincerity, even from the useless counsellor she had finally opened up to. She clearly remembered him rolling his eyes when she had started to snivel during a session. None of these responses would have mattered so much, she believed, if she'd been able to return to the bosom of a loving family.

However, in the here and now, in a coffee shop in central London, she tried to shrug away those negative thoughts that hounded her mental health and continued to regard Costigan who appeared to know exactly what was tumbling through her brain.

He said, 'Don't get me wrong, I've never been in your position. I've never shot anyone. I did shoot at a guy once and missed, thankfully.' He smirked at the memory. 'Even that stayed with me for a long, long time. But I have supported a couple of guys who have done the deed and, though it's a different kettle of fish for me, I'm also the handler for three deep undercover officers whose lives are constantly on the line . . . anyway, I digress. Point is, I kind of know what you're going through.'

'Thanks,' Jess acknowledged. 'But we're not really here to discuss my mental state, are we?'

'No.'

'So, what exactly?'

'Background first,' Costigan said. 'Moss Bros.'

Jess half-grinned. 'Moss Bros' was the nickname of the Organized Criminal Gang (OCG) Terry Moss had been part of, according to what Jess knew, the moniker coming after the famous men's clothing retailer.

Costigan also grinned at the name. 'Probably the only slightly amusing thing about them,' he said. 'The only made-to-measure suit they're likely to put you in is a concrete one.'

Jess knew their reputation well enough. She sipped her latte, her hand now slightly steadier. Like most cops in the Met she'd heard of the gang but hadn't knowingly had any direct dealings with them. Up to now.

'They've been in existence since the 1940s,' Costigan said. 'Usual kind of London gang back then – razors, clubs, prostitution, protection rackets, black market goods, that sort of thing. They've continued to evolve and expand, mainly by supporting other OCGs and remaining on good terms with them, until the relationships go wrong.' Costigan grimaced but did not expand, though Jess could guess what he meant. 'So normally, they're pretty much behind the scenes with legit businesses fronting the illegal stuff. But I assume you know all that?'

She nodded. 'South London, mainly?'

Costigan confirmed that with a nod and added, 'But with sticky tentacles all over the capital and beyond. The business started post-war but only really got going in the sixties when Jack Moss, ex-paratrooper and all-round hard man, got into bed with the Krays in the East End, then expanded south. It was a pretty brutal time, lots of blood spilled. When Jack was gunned down in an ambush his son Billy took the reins. He's still in charge but more as a figurehead and his sons mostly handle the day-to-day stuff. Mostly low profile, lots of fake goods, cut-price ciggies and booze often from very slick heists, but they are very nasty when needs be. Plus they're into the usual drugs trafficking, people trafficking, et cetera.'

'Four sons?'

'Tommy, Trevor and Theo are the ones who run the show. Number four was Terence – Terry – the youngest and, irony upon irony, the one who went off the rails, if it's possible to go off the rails when the whole effin' family is criminal. Anyway, Terry was the untame-able black sheep who did whatever the hell he liked and seemed to have no interest in the family business.'

'Like robbing jewellers?'

'Yep. And while old man Billy indulged him – you know, typical family stuff, the youngest son being the favourite and all that and gets all the free passes, armed robbery is really a thing of the past for the Moss gang so this job was unsanctioned.'

'Really?'

'Apparently, even though he got a big send-off, Terry was running with a gang who just like hurting people for fun and enjoy robbing them, too, and apparently Billy is fuming at them and wants them dealt with.'

'Dealt with?'

'Y'know, dealt with!'

'I can imagine.'

'However, whilst Terry was a wild card, he was still a member of the family.'

'And at his glorious send-off, he's suddenly lauded as a goody two shoes and a hero, taken down by the brutal cops?' Jess guessed.

'Which is why I'm – we're – here,' Costigan said gravely.

TWENTY-TWO

It wasn't long before the police diving team arrived at Audley Reservoir. They had been on a training exercise in the River Ribble at Ribchester, the site of the old Roman fort, so they were close by and quick to pack up their gear and head over. They were there within half an hour. Minutes later they launched their small dinghy on to the water and not long after they were respectfully pulling the body of the old man on to the boat and video recording the process.

The local detective, DC Dougie Doolan, arrived at much the same time and watched the body recovery with Jess, Samira and Dave Simpson, which was also videoed by a crime scene investigator who had also managed to get there in fairly quick time.

DC Doolan had introduced himself to Jess. 'Straight into the fire,' he commented, his assessment on her first day on the new job.

'Tell me about it,' Jess said.

Dougie Doolan looked like an old lag and though Jess didn't want to stereotype, he looked like a jack from the Morse era, smart, slightly careworn and maybe a great fit for the Ribble Valley. He was perhaps in his mid-fifties possibly on the verge of retirement with a craggy face and an aura about him Jess quite liked, one which said he was a detective *who knew* – knew his stuff, knew people. She got the feeling he would be an invaluable font of knowledge, one she intended to tap when she got the chance.

'I'm not totally convinced this old fella just tripped and slipped into the water,' Jess said. 'Hence why I called you.'

'Why?'

'Follow me.'

She led him around the path to the point where she believed Bart had gone in and indicated the scuff marks and the fact Bart's flat cap and walking stick were in the marshy area and not in the water with him.

'Not conclusive, obviously,' she admitted. 'But maybe there could have been some sort of scuffle here.'

'I take it you've asked CSI to photograph all this and get any samples?'

'I have. What do you think?'

'Open-minded, I suppose.'

'I agree it needs more for it to look really sus,' Jess said, 'but I would have thought he'd have gone into the water with his cap on, stick in hand if he'd tumbled in accidentally, rather than have left them behind. Dunno.' She shrugged.

'Well, let's ensure that everything's properly recorded, get the old guy down to the mortuary for a PM as soon as possible and see where that takes us,' Dougie suggested.

'Once he's gone I'm going to head down to the care home and have a chat with them about him.'

'Good idea and don't forget to inform the coroner.'

'I won't.'

They walked back to where the diving team had placed Bart's sad-looking body on a plastic sheet on the path, with the CSI recording the event.

'What a shame,' Jess said. She gave Dougie a knowing look.

'What?' he asked.

'Until we know for certain . . .' she began.

He finished for her, 'Think murder?'

'Exactly.' She was glad they were on the same wavelength. Then she looked at the time and said, 'Shit!'

Her mobile phone rang.

TWENTY-THREE

'As I mentioned,' DCI Costigan reminded Jess as they reached the end of their coffees in the café in Waterstones on Trafalgar Square, 'I'm the handler of three very deeply imbedded undercover officers, two of whom, shall I say, are closely connected to the discussion we are having right now, and even by saying that I've probably told you too much.'

Jess did not say anything. Best not, she thought. She knew,

however, what Costigan meant and realized he might have admitted too much, vague though it was. She knew that people in his position held the lives of others in the palm of their hand and that knowledge wasn't for sharing. Without gilding the lily, lives would be at risk.

'I didn't hear a thing,' Jess reassured him.

He gave a short nod of understanding. 'Maybe just best to say that some intelligence has filtered my way and although it's just chatter at the moment, I thought it best to share it with you.'

'OK,' she said, a strange feeling of dread wafting through her whole being.

'Word is, and I stress it's only "word"' – Costigan did the air speech marks, a gesture which usually infuriated Jess – 'but word not to be taken lightly.'

'Go on.'

He took a deep breath. 'It's rumoured that Billy Moss has put a contract out on you for killing his son, Terry.'

'A contract as in . . .?' Jess probed, knowing the answer and fearing it.

'Information leading to your identity and location which can then be given to a hitman, or woman, to take you out.'

TWENTY-FOUR

'Mum, where are you?' The harsh, accusative voice of her angry daughter Lily made the question seem like a threat. 'You said you'd pick me and Jase up from school and here we are, da-da-da-dah-dah-dah, still waiting for you like two homeless street urchins, one hour later.'

Jess glanced at the time on her Fitbit and castigated herself: her baptism of fire first day in a new job had shot by in an instant and it was now after five p.m.

She grimaced at DC Doolan, seeing the flicker of a smile on his craggy face, and turned away to speak to Lily.

'Oh God, look, sorry . . . been a—'

'What? Bit busy?' Lily cut in savagely.

'You could say that.'

'So why make a promise you were never going to keep? We could have got a taxi home.'

'I had every intention,' Jess began defensively even though she knew for sure she would have been delayed picking them up anyway. Both had been at the new school for almost a month now – while she had been on a local procedure course – so Jess knew the school day ended at three thirty p.m. but both kids attended after-school activities which would have taken them to at least four thirty. Jess's shift that day was nine to five p.m., even though she'd started at eight thirty a.m., and she knew she'd keep them waiting for half an hour at least, which she could have smooth-talked her way out of.

Over an hour, however, was totally unacceptable.

'Look, I got caught up with a suspicious death,' she began again, realizing the futility of her words. Nothing would wash with Lily, or Jason, although he was younger and more laid-back and forgiving, the type who just went along with the flow, whereas Lily was more in-your-face, which Jess thought reflected herself.

Someone tapped her on the shoulder.

Dougie Doolan.

'Mute your phone,' he said, pointing to her mobile.

'One second, love,' Jess said, knowing this would wind up Lily no end. Snubbing her. She thumbed the mute button and looked at Dougie.

'Sorry, I overheard,' he said, indicating the phone. 'I'll take over here. I'll accompany Bart's body to the mortuary and arrange a post-mortem, and then go to Blackburn DHQ and see where we're up to with Bill Ramsden and try to sort him out. He should be sober by now.'

Relief flooded through Jess, very visible in her body language.

'Thank you so much,' she began to say to Doolan, only to be interrupted by Samira who said, 'And I'll stay here and help Dougie, if you like?'

'But you've been on since this morning,' Jess said.

'No worries,' Samira assured her.

'Thank you,' Jess said, swallowing back her emotion at the generous nature of her two new work colleagues, but then glanced at Dave Simpson who was in hearing distance. He pulled a face and said, 'I should be off duty now so don't ask me to do anything.'

Jess did not rise to that. She clicked the unmute button and spoke to Lily. 'Give me fifteen minutes, lovey.'

*   *   *

Samira drove Jess to Clitheroe nick and dropped her off. She scurried through the building, divested herself of her uniform jacket, grabbed her civvy coat, headed out of the back door, got into her car and sped out of the car park.

A few minutes later she drew up outside the school gates on the hatch-marked area in which parking was only permitted outside school hours.

Lily was in deep conversation with another girl whilst Jason was, as ever, doing keepie-uppies in the school yard. On seeing Jess he immediately caught his football and rushed to the car, looking as bedraggled as ever from his day at school – tie askew, shoes scuffed, satchel slung over one shoulder, a sports bag over the other – and a huge grin on his face at seeing his mum. He was so easy to read, Jess thought; wore his heart on his sleeve and just got on with life, almost without question. He jumped in the front passenger seat and gasped as he saw his mum's black eye.

'Mum! Are you OK? Who did that to you?'

'I'm OK, love. You should see the other guy.'

Lily, however, was a different kettle of fish to Jason. A young girl on the cusp of maturity, she kept secrets, said little, clammed up a lot, was quite angry at times and seemed to despise her current existence, uprooted from London to the sticks.

Although she'd glanced at the car when Jess had pulled up, all her attention was focused on the girl she was talking to, who looked almost like a Lily clone in her appearance and dress.

Jess lowered her window. 'C'mon, love,' she called.

Lily continued to talk to the other girl, obviously just to get her own back on Jess and keep her waiting for being late.

'Who's the girl with Lil?' Jess asked Jason, who had already got his phone out and was busy shooting things in outer space.

'Dunno,' he muttered.

Helpful, Jess thought and took a breath – *keep calm, gal* – then looked forwards as a sleek black Range Rover drew up, nose-to-nose in front of the Citroen. Being a street cop, Jess knew cars well and could appreciate this one was a top-of-the-range motor, costing probably on the north side of a hundred grand. It was driven by a woman who blipped the accelerator pedal to make the big engine emit a throaty growl. Although Jess knew her cars, she was fairly ambivalent to them, but this beast did quite impress her.

The girl with Lily gave her a hug and skipped towards the Range

Rover, got into the front passenger seat and the car slid smoothly away from the kerb.

Jess watched the woman at the wheel, assuming it was the girl's mother, who in turn seemed to be looking closely at Jess as the car passed. Jess frowned, wondering if there was a glint of recognition, something vaguely familiar about the woman although she could not be certain.

Her attention returned to Lily who, unlike her friend, slunk across, almost dragging her feet, looking totally miserable, around to the passenger seat of the Citroen, stopping abruptly when she saw Jason was already occupying it.

She banged on the window.

He didn't even look sideways.

'Shift,' she told him through the glass.

He just kept playing his game.

'Hate you,' Lily said and as though it was the worst thing in the world, got into the back of the car, giving her brother a slap on the back of his head, drawing an 'Oi!' from Jess. 'Less of that.' She twisted around in her seat and looked at Lily, presenting the side of her face and saying, 'No peck for mum?'

'Nope.' Lily didn't even look at her.

Miffed, Jess put the car into gear and set off. 'Who's your new friend?'

In the rear-view mirror, she saw Lily shrug but say nothing, not even about the black eye which she must have seen.

'Like that, is it?' Jess asked, tight-lipped and annoyed.

'Yep.'

And that was the last word she said on the way to Bolton-by-Bowland.

TWENTY-FIVE

Costigan's words gut-punched Jess hard. 'A contract on me? You can't be serious,' she whispered harshly, suddenly feeling disconnected from the world as though this was happening to a third person.

'It's only whispers,' Costigan stressed, 'but yeah, I am serious.'

Jess ran her hands nervously over her face, pulling at her features, trying to find her way back from that sense of unreality.

'So . . . what now?' she asked.

'Maybe a form of witness protection.'

Jess scoffed at the thought, the ridiculous idea, immediately seeing the practical and emotional pitfalls of that. 'What, a new identity? A new place to go and live? Stacking shelves in Aldi?'

'It happens,' Costigan said.

Jess snickered at the idiotic prospect of that, then laid both hands palms down on the table. 'I have a career, possibly with prospects. I have two kids at school, both of whom have a wide circle of friends and very busy lives. Can you even imagine dealing with their reactions to being uprooted? I have an ageing mum living nearby. Is she going to get protection too? And I have a husband – just – with a mega job in the city. Yeah, OK,' she admitted, 'my family is a bit fractured right now and I'm trying to keep my shit together, but up-sticking would just break its back. So, initial reaction? A no from me.'

'It's been done before. It gets done all the time and all those points you make quite rightly will be addressed.'

'Nope,' Jess said stubbornly.

'The plus side of it, as I understand from the intel, is that they haven't actually identified you as yet,' Costigan said. 'You gave your evidence incognito, so no one knows who you are for sure so we could whisk you away, rub out any HR trail . . .'

'And that's supposed to reassure me?' Jess snarled, affronted. 'With due diligence and a bit of hard work, anyone could probably find out who I was . . . not hard.'

'We'd obliterate personnel records.'

Jess almost laughed in his face. 'And the social media accounts of my kids? Mine, even?'

'OK, OK, I just wanted to run this past you, Sarge, because I think it's something you should seriously consider, OK?' Jess nodded glumly in answer to that question. Costigan continued, 'In the meantime I'll try and get a message to my U/C guys to find out more, find out just how serious the threat is.'

'You do that,' Jess snapped. 'Are we done here?'

'We are.' Costigan slurped the last dregs of his coffee. 'I'll walk back down with you.'

'To protect me?'

He chuckled. 'I'm going to the NCA office near Westminster Abbey.'

'Through the back door?'

'Of course.'

They made their way out of the café into the bustle of Trafalgar Square, crossing Northumberland Avenue on to the slope that was Whitehall, having to weave between numerous other pedestrians going up, down and crossways, but they did manage to stay side by side, more or less.

'How serious is it, really?' Jess asked, having to raise her voice above the sound of the streets.

'Old man Moss is rumoured to have put a few people into early graves, nothing ever proven.'

'Bad guys just disappearing?'

'Something like that.'

'Rumour clinic?' Jess asked.

'There could be some of that,' Costigan admitted. 'Myths and reality, but we really don't want to take the chance with you, Jess, so really – really – give this some thought,' he begged earnestly, having to step sideways as a couple of Japanese tourists barged between them, putting perhaps two yards between him and Jess.

Jess angled towards him just to catch the last few words he was saying – but suddenly it wasn't the words that were the problem at that moment, it was the expression on Costigan's face because he was looking beyond Jess, seeing something over her shoulder. His face contorted into a scream of warning as he heaved the Japanese tourists to one side and lurched desperately towards Jess, his hands outstretched, his fingertips reaching for her.

She frowned, unable to comprehend this unexpected move and began to say, 'What the actual . . .?'

But that was as far as she got – an open mouth – because Costigan managed to grab her and spin her sideways at the exact moment Jess heard gunfire from somewhere behind her.

Two shots. Double-tap.

As she teetered sideways, propelled by Costigan's shove, the DCI's face seemed to implode horrifically and then the back of his head exploded. He had been shot in the face and the two slugs from the double-tap had taken out the back of his skull on their bloody trajectory.

Jess kept stumbling, but also felt the hot splatter of Costigan's blood across her own face.

Costigan, fatally wounded, took a crazy step back, then collapsed.

Jess twisted down on to one knee, seeing the DCI hit the pavement with a loud thud and the instant spread of thick blood pouring out of the horrific exit wound.

Around her, people screamed, as she pivoted as best she could to see where the attacker was, trying to remain cool and focused, maybe ID him or her, but all she saw was a cluster of pedestrians, some blood-flecked, all shocked, screaming, terrified. Then she was up on to her feet. A glance at Costigan's body confirmed there was nothing she could do for him, so she forced her way through the wall of onlookers, even though she knew she might be revealing herself to be shot as well, but sticking to that decision as her mind dealt with a myriad of thoughts (obviously putting the emotional ones right to the back) and knowing this is what had to be done there and then: identify, confront and capture the shooter. There were no second thoughts, no hesitation.

She screamed, 'Move, move,' as she elbowed through the ever-thickening cluster of people in the hope of seeing someone either fleeing from the scene, or waiting to get her in their sights.

Gasping and wiping blood from her face as she emerged into a space of sorts, she stood still, her sharp eyes roving, probing, but there was no one obvious.

The shooter had evaporated into the ether.

TWENTY-SIX

His name was Assistant Commissioner Amir and it was the first time Jess had ever met the man, a big, broad-shouldered guy who she knew was a highly respected boss in the Met because he got things done, no messing. Street cops loved that because they got little enough of it from most high ranks.

Amir was at his desk in his office high up at New Scotland Yard which, unlike the one she had been ensconced in since her enforced move from firearms, had a great view across the Thames to the slowly revolving London Eye. On a chair to one side of Amir was a dapper but slightly frayed-looking middle-aged man in a nice suit. Jess guessed this guy was a high-ranking detective.

Sitting on Amir's other side was Maureen Cook, acting head of the Human Resources Department, a frazzled-looking woman who had a job Jess did not envy in the least. Even to Jess's limited knowledge of that department, she knew Cook was the fourth head in less than two years, each of her predecessors having had massive meltdowns. Crap job, Jess thought.

As Jess entered the plush but functional office, the three of them stood up and Amir came out from behind his desk and greeted her with a warm handshake and a shoulder pat.

'Sergeant Raker, please take a seat,' he said, and steered her gently to a leather sofa by the wall. 'May I get you a drink of some description?'

'I'm fine honestly, sir.'

'OK.' Amir sat on a comfy chair set at an angle from the sofa and gestured for the other two to join them. The man sat on the other comfortable chair and Maureen Cook sat at the opposite end of the sofa to Jess. Amir said, 'I assume you know Maureen Cook?' to Jess.

Jess gave her a nod and a tight smile. 'I do, sir.' Knew *of* her more than anything.

'And this is Detective Superintendent Jack Marsh, currently seconded to the National Crime Agency from the Met.' Amir indicated the man who nodded solemnly at Jess. 'So, Jess, firstly, how are you? I know yesterday was hugely traumatic for you.'

'More so for DCI Costigan and his family,' Jess answered brusquely.

'Oh, absolutely. He was a family man first and foremost and also a professional, dedicated police officer. His family have lost a wonderful man.'

Detective Superintendent Marsh grunted something in agreement.

Amir blew out his cheeks and it seemed to Jess that his body language gave the impression he did not quite know where to start. His facial features tightened up and he blurted, 'We seem to be in quite a situation.'

'A quandary,' Marsh added.

'Very much so,' Maureen Cook put in.

Amir gave them both a withering, shut-up look and they averted their eyes.

Amir went on, 'I realize yesterday was very difficult for you so soon after the incident in Greenwich. I know you've been interviewed several times already about DCI Costigan's death and have given a very detailed statement, which I don't particularly want you to cover again for us here. However, we're not sure where that leaves us as there seems to be something missing from your account.'

'Which is factual, one hundred per cent true and accurate,' Jess said, wondering already where this was going.

'I don't doubt that, and without any subjective conjecture which is good and how it should be – a blow-by-blow account of the incident.'

'Yes, it is,' Jess agreed, now beginning to second guess where this might be headed.

'DCI Costigan was a man who played a very long, tight game, kept his cards close to his chest, you might say, and he was allowed to do so because he was very good at his job and the way he ran things is imperative in the area in which he worked. Loose lips and all that. However, I did know he was running three high-profile but very hush-hush investigations at this moment,' Marsh said.

'OK,' Jess said.

'One of which,' Marsh continued, 'was into the OCG controlled by the Moss family, a member of which you . . . shot dead next to the *Cutty Sark*.'

'Which I'm well aware of,' Jess said with a chill in her voice. The pulse in her temple began to throb.

Marsh nodded and raised his grey, unkempt eyebrows. 'I know you are, but the thing is, Sergeant Raker, as you can imagine, since DCI Costigan's murder, everything is in a complete mess, a real tangle, and though your description of the shooting is very detailed, there's a huge gap in your story that we need filling urgently.'

Jess did not say anything. Now she knew what was coming, although she then could not stop herself from exclaiming, 'Perhaps you should tell me what I've neglected to tell you.'

Marsh sighed irritably. 'The gap is this: why were you with DCI Costigan?'

Jess regarded the three people in the room, one at a time. 'I'm not sure I want to say.'

'I really don't think you have a choice, my dear,' Marsh said condescendingly, then glanced worriedly at Maureen Cook, obviously aware of his patronizing, sexist remark made in the hearing of an HR specialist. He gulped.

'I'll tell you why,' Jess said after a short period of consideration. 'It's because I'm not sure who I can trust.'

'I beg your pardon?' Marsh said, taken aback with shock.

'Like you say, DCI Costigan played his cards close to his chest because of the line of work he was in and that people depended on him to keep them alive when a careless word could cost a life . . . oh, the irony of that,' Jess said.

'I can assure you, you can trust every one of us here,' Amir told her with an inclusive sweep of his hand.

Jess let her eyes move from him to Maureen Cook and then to Marsh, knowing fully that their appearance of innocence could be deceptive. Fraudsters, rip-off merchants and corrupt cops banked on it. She knew Amir and his fine reputation and did trust him; she didn't know the other two and though she had no reason to doubt Amir's reassurance about them, she did.

Jess took a breath, feeling she was being bullied into a corner and she either came clean and filled the gap they wanted her to fill or clammed up and claimed the trauma of the shooting had made her recollection just a fuzzy haze. She knew she could pull that off no problem, but it would not do her personal situation any favours. She made a decision.

'My statement is one hundred per cent true, as I told you,' she said, addressing Amir.

'We know that.'

'DCI Costigan and myself arranged to meet in Waterstones café on Trafalgar Square, though I didn't know the purpose of that meeting.'

'How did he contact you?' Marsh wanted to know.

'Mobile phone.'

'OK, go on,' he said.

'So I met him. I didn't know the guy, though I'd seen him in the briefing before the shooting. He told me that information, intelligence, whatever you want to call it, had come to light which indicated that a contract had been put out on me.'

An uncomfortable silence descended on Amir's office.

It was a chilly one, broken only by the sound of Maureen Cook swallowing rather loudly.

'Did he say what or who the source of this intelligence was?' Marsh asked.

'No. Only that a contract had been taken out on me by the Moss gang because I shot Terry Moss dead, and now they want their pound of flesh.'

'Shit.' That was Marsh, slumping back into his chair.

'That's exactly what I thought,' Jess said.

'And he didn't say where this information came from?' Marsh asked.

Jess's inbred suspicious nature made her say no again. Costigan had revealed to her it was from someone working undercover in the Moss gang and that the identities of such people are closely guarded secrets and only a handful of people ever knew who they were and this handful could easily exclude an assistant commissioner or a detective superintendent and certainly the head of HR.

Marsh said unguardedly, 'He must have U/Cs in the gang. Jeez!'

His words made Jess feel her reticence to divulge anything was well-founded.

Marsh looked at Maureen Cook, the HR lady. 'Do you know anything about this? From an HR point of view?'

Maureen Cook looked completely out of her depth. 'No,' she squeaked, possibly on the verge of vomiting.

Amir, who still looked very cool, said to Marsh and Maureen Cook, 'No offence, but I would like a word with Sergeant Raker alone, please.'

Maureen Cook didn't need a second invitation. She grabbed her belongings and scuttled out of the office without a word or backward look.

Marsh, however, hesitated. 'Whatever you are about to discuss concerns me,' he stated.

'Go. Give us ten minutes,' Amir told him, countenancing no argument.

The detective superintendent nodded unhappily and left.

Amir waited for his office door to close behind Marsh before allowing himself to lean back in his very comfortable-looking leather chair, rub his face and regard Jess who sat there numbly, a bit like a rabbit in the headlights.

'Do you think the shooter was after you or after DCI Costigan?' he asked her bluntly.

Jess, too, sat back, closed her eyes and revisualized the scene again – not for the first time. She'd had the chance to see some street CCTV footage from various security cameras the police had managed to seize, but it was mostly blurred and certainly did not tell the whole story of an incident that lasted maybe a dozen seconds.

The whole story, Jess knew, was in her head.

'Not sure,' she admitted. 'But I think it would be too much of a coincidence that he tells me I'm a target one minute and next there's a gunman behind me.'

'I know what you mean. For what it's worth, I'm speculating that DCI Costigan himself could have been the target. He is very unpopular with the London underworld with a lot of top-class crim scalps under his belt and good coppers have been targeted many times in the past.'

'I was thinking that,' Jess agreed. 'If they were after me, I could be dead now, *should* be dead now.' She shivered at her words. 'He did try to push me out of the way, but maybe that was just him being brave or something. We'll never know.'

'I think there could well have been a contract out on him we had no inkling about, which means that if what Costigan was warning you about is an actual fact, then we are duty bound to provide you with some means of protection, Jess. Did the DCI cover this at all?'

'He mentioned some sort of protection programme.'

'I can tell from your tone of voice it's not something that appeals to you,' Amir said.

'Not remotely. Too complicated. Family, et cetera . . .'

'I understand. I also understand that being threatened by criminals is an occupational hazard for us and mostly it's just hot air, but in this case, as unfortunately DCI Costigan has shown, it's real and deadly.'

'I just don't want to drag my family through the mire.'

'I'm afraid you may have to,' Amir warned starkly.

TWENTY-SEVEN

Jess vividly recalled those words she'd spoken to Amir as she drove the kids out of Clitheroe that afternoon. She recalled them vividly because in the end she had dragged them through the mire and even the beauty of the Ribble Valley was no compensation either for the children or Josh.

Lily found scenery boring. She much preferred built-up areas. Jason didn't mind as long as he had a football and an Xbox to hand.

Josh, the brooding Josh, was altogether a different matter.

She drove through Chatburn, then out on to the A59 towards Skipton for a short spell, then came off into and through Sawley and beyond that village through narrow, twisty country roads into the undeniably beautiful village of Bolton-by-Bowland where she and the family now lived in a rented cottage on the Main Street within sight of the old church and, more importantly perhaps, the Coach & Horses pub.

Lily surveyed the cottage with a turned-down, disapproving mouth. It was much smaller than the one they owned in South London which was now in the latter stages of being sold. They planned to use the equity from it which would almost cover the asking price of a house near Clitheroe they had their eye on, even though Jess was already feeling settled in Bolton-by-Bowland although here they were squeezed into a three-bedroomed cottage in which the rooms were much smaller, tighter and lower than their London home. It felt like they were living on top of each other at the moment.

However, Jess loved the village, which brought back pleasant if slightly vague memories from her childhood and early teens.

A long time ago. A lot of water having flowed along the Ribble since then, although only a stream – Kirk Beck – ran through Bolton-by-Bowland which Jess could hear when she switched off the engine and opened her car door.

'Home!' she announced cheerily.

Lily gave her a killer sidelong squint which said it all, but Jason jumped out and immediately started his keepie-uppie practice in the middle of the deserted road. Lily stalked to the front door and Jess swallowed, trying to hold back a tear, then turned to the village and inhaled a deep breath to fill her lungs with cold, crisp air from the surrounding hills and wondered if she had the wherewithal to pull off this new life.

TWENTY-EIGHT

To be fair to her hastily assigned protection detail – Jess didn't even dare guess how much it was costing – they did keep a pretty low profile and only she could spot them. They protected her house in London during the times she was there – after work and overnight – and stood down when she was in the office at New Scotland Yard. Just to be on the safe side, she'd been told.

Nothing happened.

Life, as much as was possible having shot someone dead, having had someone standing next to her have his brains blown out and living under the murky cloud of threat, went on as normal, albeit with the extra burden of the heartache of a fractured marriage and two very savvy kids, one of whom – Lily – made her life even more uncomfortable.

She couldn't seem to get any answers from above or sideways and she began to fear that the remaining years of her police career were going to be spent in limbo in a grim office, pushing paperclips, loading stats on to spreadsheets, instead of being on the front line.

She hated it.

Hated the job. Hated the inertia of it all. The not knowing.

One morning, almost a month after that meeting with Amir, Jess was sitting at her desk staring numbly at her computer screen, trying to hold herself back from playing patience, when she placed her elbows on the desk, put her hands together and dropped her face into her palms for a moment, then raised her face and uttered the word, 'Crap!' at the exact moment someone clasped a big hand on her shoulder and made her almost jump out of her skin.

She spun aggressively. 'What the . . .?'

Amir stood there and jerked back slightly at her reaction. 'Sorry to startle you, Sergeant,' he apologized.

Jess caught her breath. 'No problems, sir.' She spun her chair around to face him. 'Just having a moment.'

His apologetic face turned serious when he said, 'Pardon the drama, but my office – now.'

Jess shot to her feet, the words, 'What's going on?' on her lips,

but Amir was already out of the office door. Jess followed. He led
her into the lift, saying nothing, and Jess thought better not to ask.
She could sense tension emanating from him and knew she would
find out sooner rather than later what this was all about. And then
the palpable tension coming out of Amir's body seemed to infect
her so by the time the lift reached the corridor of power – as it was
known – her knees were jelly-like.

It didn't help when, as she passed through Amir's outer office in
which his secretary was located, the woman behind the desk gave
her a very concerned look.

Then she was in Amir's office, where as before, Detective
Superintendent Marsh from the NCA and Maureen Cook, temporary
head of HR, were waiting. Maureen Cook looked as though she'd
plugged her fingers in a mains socket, she seemed so frazzled. Marsh
looked as untidy as ever.

Amir waved Jess to a chair between the two, then sat down at
his desk.

Not the comfy sofa today, Jess thought.

There seemed to be a lot of swallowing and gulping going on,
plus averted eyes and Jess's immediate thoughts were that something
had happened to her family.

'What is it?' she demanded. 'Is it my family?'

'No, no,' Amir said, holding up his palms. 'Your family's fine.'

'So . . .?' Jess flung her right hand in a gesture to include Marsh
and Maureen Cook.

'Things have moved on somewhat,' Amir said, and nodded to
Marsh to take the obviously unpleasant reins here.

'Firstly,' Marsh began after clearing his throat and squirming in
the chair, 'in spite of the large investigation into DCI Costigan's
murder, we are no nearer to solving it.'

'I know that,' Jess said impatiently. She had been keeping an eye
on the investigation from the sidelines.

'OK, but since our meeting here some weeks ago, I did discover
that the DCI did have two undercover officers working in the Moss
crime organization and I felt it prudent to extract them somehow
without arousing any suspicion from the gang. The only problem
being that it's not always simple. However, I managed to pull one
out and debrief him; the other' – he cleared his throat again –
'seemed to have gone missing.'

'Seemed?' Jess said.

'Mm, no contact, no responses to messages from his handler, that kind of thing,' Marsh said.

Jess waited, sensing this was not going to end well.

Marsh sighed heavily, clearly troubled and emotional. 'Two days ago our divers pulled a body out of the Thames on the marshes at Gravesend.'

'Shit,' Jess said quietly.

'Not just a drowning victim, a murder victim who seemed to have been in the water quite some time and a certain amount of decay had taken place but not enough to disguise the fact the man had been brutally murdered as well as having been tortured.'

'This man being the undercover cop you could not contact?' Jess asked weakly.

Marsh nodded. His face was gaunt and grey. 'He was a detective constable from Lancashire Constabulary who had been deep in the Moss Bros set-up for some time.'

The fact he was a DC from Lancashire was no surprise to Jess. Local cops were never used undercover for obvious reasons.

'Other than he was working the Moss gang, unfortunately we do not have any actual evidence that points to the gang for his murder, even though we know it's down to them and we are working flat out to prove it.'

'Same old, same old,' Jess said tiredly. Knowing and proving were two completely different entities. 'OK – so why tell me this?'

Marsh looked at Amir, then at Jess. 'Because we now feel the need to better protect you, more than just a cop car sitting close to your home. We now believe that your life is in imminent danger and going into some sort of protection scheme, we believe, is now something you must do.'

'Sir.' Jess looked levelly into Amir's brown eyes. 'No fucking way.'

Amir sighed. Jess could tell he was weary of her intransigence.

'I've looked into it and we could relocate you to the Midlands,' Marsh said but before he could finish, Jess guffawed and almost choked at the same time.

'No way to that, either. I don't have a Brummie accent to start with. We'd stand out like sore thumbs.'

Amir grinned. 'We thought that would be your reaction.'

His eyes flicked from side to side, reminding Jess of Jason's Action Man, as he looked at Marsh and Maureen Cook in what was clearly a pre-arranged signal and they both stood up and left the room. When the office door closed behind them, Amir rose and crossed over to the window with a view, perched his backside on the ledge and folded his arms.

'The danger you are in is very real, Jess,' he said. 'Just because no attempt has yet been made on your life doesn't mean it won't happen. The Moss gang operate a very long game.'

'I know. I've done my research.' She had – via the Met's intel database (as far as she was permitted with her low security access) and also with the news media and Wikipedia. None of it made pleasant bedtime reading.

'I thought you would have,' Amir said and then paused. 'The undercover detective whose body was recovered was, as mentioned, a detective from Lancashire and as a result I've spoken almost continually over the last couple of days to members of the chief officer team up there. Also, you may or may not know, I did four years up there as an ACC before taking on my current role here.'

Jess nodded as if she knew. She didn't, mainly because she was uninterested in the butterfly-bouncing the higher ranks did from force to force, like some sort of elite men's club with the occasional woman allowed in to play along at promotion tag. Mostly she despised them, but Amir seemed nice enough and did have a decent reputation.

'Obviously I've also read your personal file too.'

She shrugged.

'I see you spent your childhood and teenage years in Lancashire.'

'I did.'

'Thing is, my discussions with the chiefs in Lancashire obviously involved you as a subject.'

'Right,' Jess said, drawing out the word in a cautious way.

Amir unfolded his arms, returned to his desk and opened an unmarked folder on his desk, which he spun around and pushed in Jess's direction.

'What do you think about this?'

TWENTY-NINE

B efore setting off for her first day at Clitheroe, Jess had put on the slow cooker and with the addition of microwaved jacket potatoes, she fed her two ravenous children that evening with a chicken casserole to die for, and after they'd scoffed this followed by an ice cream each, all three of them seemed to chill out and some sort of harmony descended on the little village cottage.

After deciding not to face a rebellion about who did the washing up, Jess did it and the kids went off in different directions, Lily to her bedroom and Jason outside with his football.

Jess relaxed in the lounge as much as she could, churning everything through her mind that had happened on this auspicious first day in her new job, from the brief but terrifying hostage situation to the sad death of the old man in the small reservoir. She hoped she had made a good fist of everything, but even so early she could see problems ahead with PC Simpson, whose promotion had been scuppered by her arrival into a job he wanted, and with Inspector Price, who she hadn't quite fathomed out yet. However, she liked the look of the PCSO, Samira, and DC Doolan, who seemed like a decent jack.

The day had been unexpectedly busy and she guessed that what had happened was pretty unusual. But everywhere had its moments. Jess just hoped that Clitheroe had had its moments for a day or two so she could establish herself.

She found herself nodding off and also thinking about Joe Borwick, the firefighter. Fireman Joe as she now thought of him with a wry smile which disappeared the moment her mobile phone rang with a shrill ringtone; she wondered why she persisted with it as it grated her nerves no end. She shot upright on the settee and answered it.

Before she could speak, her husband Josh said harshly, 'I thought this place was supposed to be effing crime-free!'

'Why, what's happened?'

'You're going to have to come and pick me up from the railway station – someone's nicked my motorbike! God, I miss the Underground.'

Josh hung up.

THIRTY

Jess had to admit that Amir's proposal had some merit and for the remainder of that day in London she mulled it over, did the pros and cons thing, some actual research and had a lunchtime stroll along the Thames with a baseball cap pulled down over her face and collar up just in case.

Finally, at three p.m., raising some eyebrows from her work colleagues (most of whose names she hadn't even bothered to learn) she closed down her computer and declared, 'I'm done and if you want to report me to Assistant Commissioner Amir, go ahead.'

Ten minutes later she was on the tube to Canary Wharf for a meeting with Josh she'd arranged, insisted upon, via a terse email exchange.

She made her way to a Starbucks, bought something hot and milky for herself and an Americano for Josh who turned up looking harassed a few minutes later.

He sat across from her, leaned forwards and hissed, 'I was in an important meeting.'

Unimpressed, Jess shrugged and said, 'Too important to duck out of, see your wife and try to save your marriage?'

Those words had a salutary effect on him. He breathed in, tried to stay calm and picked up his coffee.

Jess watched him sip it, then teased him, 'Or have you got used to the bachelor life?'

'No. I miss you. I miss the kids. I miss our life,' he stated. 'You're the one who's doing all the blocking.'

It would have been easy, and was tempting, for Jess to launch into another bitter tirade of recriminations, but she resisted. There had been too much of that from both of them and she'd had enough. Now all she wanted was her life back, some normality, nothing special, and despite the fact Josh had cheated on her big style and she was secretly convinced (although he denied it) he was going to shack up with his secretary, she still wanted to give the marriage a go, even if he'd been caught in the act of buying the woman more expensive jewellery than he'd ever bought her.

Not that it rankled. Much.

But to move on would require some major upheaval from both and just possibly Amir might have come up with a feasible option.

Jess unfolded a piece of paper and slid it across the table.

'What's this?' Josh asked suspiciously.

'Don't worry, it's not a decree nisi. You can touch it,' she said.

'Hm,' he muttered and with just a fingertip he swivelled it around so he could read it, continuing to mutter as he read it aloud, paraphrasing as he went. 'Lancashire Constabulary . . . applications invited . . . post of uniformed sergeant . . . Ribble Valley Rural Team . . . blah, blah, blah.' He raised his eyes. 'And? What about it? How does this concern you or me or us?'

'Given our circumstances I can walk straight into that job so long as I have an interview and an assessment and convince Lancs I'm not a complete tosspot.'

'Why, though?' Josh's face was screwed up.

'A normal life?'

'Normal? Two hundred and fifty miles north of here? How would I commute?' As he spoke, the last word faded out weakly as it dawned on him and he said, 'No chance!'

Jess had been expecting this response. 'Hear me out,' she said.

'If I have to,' he said reluctantly.

She sighed and rubbed her brow. 'First off, you do know my life is under threat, don't you?' She knew he did. They'd been over it many times, but he'd been sceptical mostly.

'Nothing's happened, though.'

Jess blinked and did an exaggerated double-take and half considered launching her now lukewarm latte over him, walking out, forgetting him and making a future with just her and the kids.

Quietly she said, 'The body of an undercover cop has been pulled out of the Thames, murdered. He was working on the Moss gang.'

'Shit,' Josh said.

'So you're right, Joshua, nothing's happened to me yet but I can't afford to take the chance that they won't come knocking sooner or later.'

'So what are you saying – moving up to Lancashire will keep you safe?'

'I'm not saying that as such. What I am saying is that I want my life back in some shape or form. If I stay here, that is not going to happen because I'll spend the rest of my service in a back office somewhere, occasionally coming up for air and blinking in the sunlight like one of those blind worm things. I want to be on the front line. It's what I do, what I love, what I'm good at.'

'Are they going to give you a gun up north?'

'No. The job's' – she tapped the advertisement – 'basically a patrol sergeant but with a lot of other responsibilities.'

Josh read it again, then begrudgingly admitted, 'You'd be good at this.'

Their eyes met.

Jess tried to see if there was something still there, something between them that could be saved. She thought there was. It was a complex mix. Having met at university in York, they'd moved to London, then had the kids and a lot of tough but happy times when each had the other's back; thick and thin and all that. Ups and downs. A relationship forming and meaning something, but only recently that the cracks in that structure had begun to show. She was sure it wasn't too late, but maybe Josh wasn't.

'What about me?' he asked.

'You know you could walk straight into any job in Manchester, any big company up there would have you like a shot.'

'Manchester?' he queried.

'You'd still have to commute, obviously.'

'From where?'

'Clitheroe, maybe.'

'By train? Is there even a railway station there?'

'Yes, and I've looked. You could get a train to central Manchester easy.'

'And we'd live in Clitheroe? Wherever that is.'

'Until we sold the house we could rent. What we get for the house here would probably buy outright a decent house in the Ribble Valley.' She was warming to the idea, becoming quite enthusiastic even.

'You've really thought this through, haven't you?'

'Look at me. Course I have. I'm me, you know what I'm like. So, what do you think? I know it's huge but it's doable.'

There was a silence. Josh closed his eyes and rubbed them. 'I've got to get back to work.'

*   *   *

Despite Josh's chilliness at the prospect of being uprooted, Jess submitted her application for the role of Rural Police Sergeant at Clitheroe with responsibility for the whole of the Ribble Valley. Even though it was virtually a done deal, she knew she still had to impress an interview panel and pass a psychometric test. That meant preparation work, research and not taking it for granted she would be offered the job even though it was two police forces trying to help out one of their own. She knew Lancashire would not want to take on anyone who didn't come up to standard.

It also meant a trip north, a two-hour plus train journey to Preston, then a taxi ride to police headquarters situated at Hutton Hall about five miles south of the city. Going in through the entrance barriers, Jess immediately liked the more open feel to the campus, having been accustomed to tight, concrete police yards and grotty stations down in the Met. She hadn't expected to have such a pleasant inner response to just turning up at an out-of-town HQ, then paying off the taxi driver, and stepping out to inhale fresh, cool air.

After presenting herself to the receptionist she was given a voucher and directed to the dining room, told to grab a cup of tea and something to eat if she felt peckish. Someone would come along to collect her for interview shortly. The dining room looked out across playing fields towards the police training centre and as she sipped a coffee (she was too jittery to eat anything) she thought she might be in heaven.

When she noticed a neat middle-aged lady in smart uniform enter the dining room, she recognized her as the chief constable, the second woman to hold that rank in Lancashire.

Chief Constable Gail Newby. Although Jess didn't expect to be asked any questions from the interview panel about Ms Newby, she had done some background on her just in case. Newby had a very impressive CV which included spells on various serious crime squads and important uniformed operational roles along the way. She had a good reputation by all accounts and was a doer.

Neither did Jess expect Newby to be on the interview panel.

Or – in fact – to be the only member of it!

And for the interview to take place on a three-mile stroll in the sunshine.

Jess watched Newby negotiate her way between the tables, a broad smile on her face and finally her hand reached out.

'Sergeant Raker . . . I'm Gail Newby, Chief Constable of this parish, and I believe you might want to join us?'

'Y-yes, ma'am.' Jess rose and shook the hand.

'How was your journey?'

'Good, good, thanks. Nice to get out of London for a change.'

'I'll bet. I once worked undercover there.' Newby tilted her head and regarded Jess with narrowed eyes. 'The Moss Brothers mean anything to you?' she teased.

'You were after them?'

'Oh yes, almost twenty years ago now. Even then, back in the day, they were savvy and dangerous and I had a little success until I got wind that my cover was possibly blown and, if you'll forgive the terminology, my arse was a very big target and I had to do one.'

'Really?'

'Yeah, so I kind of know what you're facing, which is why when Mr Amir told me the awful news of the murder of one of my officers who was undercover, I was only too willing to offer you something if it was in my power to do so.'

'Hence . . .?'

'Hence you being here today and us going for a stroll and a chat. I am your interview panel and assessment rolled into one. Welcome, Jess.'

A mile and a half later Jess was offered the job and accepted it. An hour after completing the stroll-stroke-interview she was back on a London-bound train, buzzing with excitement. There was a long way to go practically and emotionally speaking, not least of which sorting out Lily and Jason, but the fortunate plus in that respect was it now wasn't too far off the summer break which would give the family some breathing space.

On the walk with the chief constable, Jess and Newby brainstormed how it all would work out, and Jess admitted that her husband wasn't too enamoured by the idea at all, and, of course, at that stage, the kids knew nothing, which made her feel guilty.

One thing was decided, though: the transfer would be done quietly and without fanfare. No press releases or interviews about a new sergeant in town. She would simply slide into the role and it would be up to her to present a viable backstory to her new colleagues if need be. Although her accent was likely to hint at her local roots, she was strongly advised to err on the side of caution and keep any discussion of her background and personal details as vague as possible. Reverting to her maiden name – Easterby – as an extra precaution was also discussed, but Jess thought it would make life too complicated for the children who would be stressed out enough as it was. Telling them wasn't something Jess was relishing.

At the end of the walk, back at HQ the chief stopped and looked seriously at Jess.

'I understand why you want to keep to a normal life, Sergeant, but you must understand that the Moss gang has a very long memory and you cannot ever let your guard down. They're not the mafia, maybe a sixpenny version of the Cosa Nostra. You may well live a long and happy existence but one day down the line they might come for revenge, retribution, whatever. You need to be ready for that, always. I make no apology for saying this.'

'I get it, ma'am,' Jess had gulped.

THIRTY-ONE

And now Jess and her family had made the transition to live in one of the most stunning areas of Britain and her first day at actual work had gone with a bang and, to cap it all, she was about to collect Josh from the train station because his motorbike had been stolen sometime during the day.

On top of that, it had started to rain torrentially.

And to make a point, Jess suspected, Josh was standing in said rain in his snazzy work suit, letting himself get saturated with his motorcycle helmet in one hand and work briefcase in the other.

He looked thoroughly miserable, but no more than he had done for a long time now. Jess drew the Citroen alongside him and he dropped in with a big, wet squelch and confirmed everything by saying, 'I am so miserable.'

No kiss. No smile. No 'how are you?'

Jess winced, flicked the windscreen wipers on to clear the deluge off the screen, then set off into the night.

'How the heck am I going to get to work tomorrow?' he moaned.

'I'll drop you off for your train.'

'You do know I catch the six twenty, don't you? Changing at

Bolton, et cetera, et cetera?' he said in a whiney voice that grated with Jess.

She winced again, flicked the wipers on to the very fastest setting and gripped the steering wheel hard.

THIRTY-TWO

It rained hard overnight but by morning it had cleared and although dawn was reluctant to appear it was very beautiful. Standing at the front door of the cottage munching a piece of wholemeal toast and sipping hot coffee accompanied by the rushing sound of Kirk Beck, Jess relished the view as the moors to the north cleared of low-hanging cloud to reveal their majestic glory.

So far there had been few moments like this.

The last few weeks had been a miasma of rush, bluster and arguments, but here this morning, toast in one hand, mug in the other, a chill in the air – admittedly – Jess was almost overwhelmed by the beauty of it all and the picturesque village she now lived in. Deep down she knew the move had been the right one, even if it had been driven by circumstance.

The plan was to buy a larger house closer to Clitheroe but she was suddenly enveloped by a desire to live here in Bolton-by-Bowland, although property coming on to the market was rare, expensive and quickly snapped up.

From inside the cottage she heard the sound of Josh clattering around, getting up, muttering. She knew he wouldn't have breakfast at this time of day. When in London he always liked to grab the early tube to Canary Wharf and have a coffee and croissant whilst strolling to his office. A ritual he loved, part of London life, and had tried to recreate it here but the best he could do, depending on whether his train was on time (often not), was to grab a coffee as he sprinted down the slope at Oxford Road station in Manchester and sip it as he hurried to his new office in a high-rise block close to the Midland Hotel.

He hated it and Jess knew.

But at least he had made the move north and easily managed to get a job in Manchester. His skills were in demand so he could easily relocate anywhere, but the money was only about two-thirds of what he had earned down south. Still good and double what Jess earned but he was doing it under sufferance. London was his dream.

Jess finished her toast and went inside as Josh came down the narrow stairs, having to dip his head under a beam, into the living room.

Their night had been one of back-to-back in bed. Not particularly friendly, plus his drenching seemed to have given him a severe cold and he sneezed dramatically as well and whined about his stolen motorbike. Jess had reported it via an online link but she doubted it would ever turn up again, unless dumped in the Ribble.

Josh shrugged himself into his overcoat and said, 'Ready.'

She dropped him off at Clitheroe railway station and he trudged off with a muted 'Goodbye' but no backwards glance.

Jess lowered her window and called, 'Phone me when you're on your way home and I'll pick you up.'

That got a dismissive wave from him, but not a look.

She put the window back up. Her contentedness from earlier had disappeared and she wondered if there really was a future for her and Josh. She was prepared to hang in there. She wasn't so sure about him.

The police station was quite close to the railway station, so Jess drove up and parked in the backyard. It was 6.10 a.m. and she noticed that four police vehicles – two cars, the van and the Land Rover – were still parked up and her assumption that no one on the early turn was out on patrol yet proved correct when she peered around the door of the tiny kitchen and found three uniformed cops – two constables and a PCSO – were huddled around the table having a brew and some toast.

Her unscheduled appearance had about the same effect as a lightning bolt. All three shot to their feet, guilt etched on their faces.

Jess grinned as she peeled off her civvy jacket and said, 'A brew for me, too, if you don't mind and a slice of toast if there's one going. I'll contribute to the tea fund if someone tells me how.' Then she looked at the PCSO – it was Samira Patel – and said, 'Don't you go home?'

'Occasionally,' she admitted.

'OK . . . anyway, good morning, guys,' she addressed the two still-standing, very erect young constables. 'Don't worry, I'm not here to catch you out. I've had to drop my hubby off for an early train, so I thought I'd start early myself and try to get through some of the stuff I thought I'd do yesterday, on my first day. Blimey, is this only the second day? Feels like I've been here months. Anyway, chill guys, bring me a brew and toast and come and introduce yourselves when I've got my feet under the desk. Milk, no sugar, by the way.'

'Yes, Sarge,' they said in unison.

Jess gave them a cheeky wink and went to the sergeant's office which was in the same state she'd left it in the day before. She knew that supervisory cover overnight was from Blackburn so there was little likelihood of anyone else using the office. Somewhat different from her time in the Met where sometimes sergeant numbers exceeded constables. Up here it was a very different matter – both were thin on the ground – and it was an entirely different form of policing, mainly based on self-preservation by skilled communication and not relying on backup to help out.

She logged on to her computer and accessed the overnight incident logs to see if much had happened. It looked a relatively peaceful night: a domestic dispute, some straying animals in the town centre – and here Jess had to do a double-take as she read the log: straying llamas! Four of them. It took over an hour to get the owner to round them up. Then there was the report of Josh's stolen motorcycle from the railway station, which could have been nicked any time from Josh getting yesterday's six twenty a.m. train to when he returned in the evening. A very big window of opportunity and Jess once more thought it was unlikely ever to reappear.

One of the young PCs came in bearing a mug of tea and a slice of toast. He was a gawky lad with an ill-fitting uniform on his spindly frame. Jess guessed that his helmet would look like a bucket on his head. He had a kindly face.

'Tea and toast, Sarge.' He slid the mug and plate on to her desk.

'Thanks . . . er?'

'PC McKinty, Vinnie McKinty.'

'Pleased to meet you. Sergeant Jess Raker in case you didn't already know?'

'Pleased to meet you, Sarge – and welcome to the mad house.'

'Thanks.' She picked up the steaming hot tea which singed her tongue as she sipped it. 'I didn't see you around when I came yesterday,' she observed.

'No, I was over in Blackburn at an inquest.'

'Oh, anything of interest?'

'Well, yes and no. A fatal hit-and-run from about a month ago.'

'And you're dealing with it?'

'Yep.'

'Not the traffic department?'

McKinty winced. 'Nah, they're generally too busy in Blackburn and mostly what comes our way out in the sticks, we deal with. Like this one.'

'Did you nail the driver?'

McKinty sighed heavily. 'Still looking for him – or her. The inquest was just for ID purposes and for the coroner to see where we're up to. It just dragged on a bit.'

'Any ideas? Lines of enquiry?' Jess asked.

The youngster scratched his head and blew out his cheeks. 'Not really,' he admitted, 'but I'll keep trying. It'll be somebody local.'

'OK, thanks. You got anything more on this morning?'

'If it's OK I'm going to head to Dunsop Bridge for an hour. We've got a woman missing and there may be some connection that way out.'

'Good stuff. Let me know if you turn up anything,' Jess said, making a mental note to familiarize herself with that one.

'Will do, Sarge.'

'And we'll have a proper chat as soon as we can.'

He took the hint and turned to leave. As he did Jess asked him to send Samira in, then returned to her computer screen to check the duty state system which recorded the booking-on and -off duty times for all staff. She saw there should have been three PCs on duty at six a.m. that morning – PC McKinty, the other PC who was having a brew and one more, PC Dave Simpson. The first two had booked on duty, but Simpson hadn't.

'Oh, where's Dave Simpson, by the way?' Jess called after McKinty who stuck his head back around the door with a strained expression on his face.

He said, 'Err . . .'

Jess understood and said, 'No problem.' She saw relief flood into McKinty's face that he didn't have to discuss Simpson's absence.

Jess glanced at the duty states again and saw that the entry relating to Simpson's tour of duty had just updated to show he had booked on duty at six a.m. Jess checked the Fitbit on her wrist – which she also used as a watch: six thirty-five a.m. Simpson had booked on from another computer. She noted it.

Samira came in, bearing her own mug of tea and Jess motioned her to take a seat.

'Anything to report?' Jess asked her.

Samira screwed up her nose. 'Don't think so.'

'Have you contacted Blackburn custody office to see how Bill Ramsden's faring?' the sergeant asked, referencing the violent, drunkard from Dead Man's Stake Farm.

'Not yet. Should I?'

'Let's find out what's happening to him, shall we?'

'Let's,' Samira agreed.

'And when we've done that and I've done a bit of admin, say in about half an hour, let's go out in the sergeant's car for a spin to familiarize myself with the town and you can point out any trouble spots and after that let's see where we're up to with the unfortunate Bart Morrison and his post-mortem. Then, if we can, let's visit the old people's home for a proper chat and look into any relatives he might have who need to know about his death.'

Then she added she would need to nip home about eight a.m. in order to get Lily and Jason to school.

Bill Ramsden had been so completely inebriated that he had spent most of the previous day in an alcoholic stupor-cum-coma in a drunk cell at Blackburn and was unable to be interviewed. He'd been given fifteen-minute visits, placed in the recovery position and the police surgeon had also checked him out and declared him fit to detain. He had only just sobered up enough this morning to be interviewed. That meant his first twenty-four hours in custody were almost up and his continued detention had been authorized and extended up to thirty-six hours by which time, hopefully, decisions would have been made as to his disposal: charged and released or bail refused and put before magistrates.

Jess was on the speakerphone to the custody officer with Samira sitting alongside her.

'He's just had an early breakfast,' the custody sergeant was saying. 'He looks pretty bad but isn't remotely remorseful and he's very bad-tempered.'

'What's the likely outcome?' Jess asked.

'Have to wait until he's interviewed. One of your detectives is due to sort that.'

Jess asked, 'Who?'

'Dougie Doolan.'

'Oh, that's good.'

They ended the conversation. Jess said to Samira, 'Early start for Dougie?'

'He's a man who never sleeps,' Samira said.

Jess stood up. 'Right, let's go for that drive. Admin can wait.'

The morning after the storm was fresh, the streets of Clitheroe washed and clean. There was a pleasant feeling in the air as the two law enforcement officers tootled around their patch.

It was years since Jess had spent any length of time in the area. She had gone to primary and secondary school in Clitheroe, but on getting a place at York University she had never returned nor wanted to other than for her father's funeral.

Back in her teenage years, boys had been a bit of a problem for her – one in particular – and she'd been relieved when she went to uni because it disentangled her from a messy situation with him which included jealousy, threats and the possibility of violence. Not from her or the lad (who was a weak-willed wimp, easily led by his raging testosterone levels), but from the other party involved in a push-me pull-you scenario which got nastier and nastier even when Jess backed off, hands raised in submission, not wanting further involvement. That 'other' person, a young woman, had become a ferocious, scary individual as the scenario panned out and Jess had become terrified by the change in her, from acquaintance to monster.

That had all been during the summer whilst waiting for A level results which couldn't come quickly enough, and when they did, Clitheroe didn't see Jess for dust.

But now all that past was like water under Edisford Bridge and if she played her cards right, this was a new beginning even if she had to keep one eye over her shoulder.

In the early morning the town looked good as the sun continued to rise, framing the old Norman castle spectacularly on the edge of town, built high on a hill to keep a lookout for invading armies, something which resonated with Jess as she drove up Moor Lane and dropped down the main shopping street. She hadn't had any recent updates about the threat from the Moss gang and she didn't know if this was good or bad, no news and all that. Yet she knew she still had to keep her wits about her but not allow it to shroud her life, otherwise she would become a nerve-shredded wreck, neither use nor ornament to anyone.

Although Castle Street hadn't changed structurally, Jess did notice a proliferation of charity and pound shops, which was unfortunately the way of the world, but didn't detract from the prettiness of the ancient town.

She turned down King Street, drove past the police station, then left on to Station Road where the market was getting underway, as it had been doing so for hundreds of years, a history that moved Jess in a strange way.

There was one last thing she wanted to have a look at before returning to the station, so she drove west along Edisford Road and managed to park the car snugly just before reaching Edisford Bridge.

'Just want to have a look-see.' She smiled at Samira before getting out and walking on to Edisford Bridge itself where she leaned on the wall and took a few moments to watch the River Ribble flowing underneath her feet. The water was quite high and running force-fully because of last night's deluge. Jess loved the river and as a kid she had played here in the river in summers past, obviously when water levels were low and safe, and she had many cherished childhood memories of these days.

Samira joined her, leaning next to her. 'I love this river,' she said. 'It's seventy-five miles long, you know?'

Jess did know, but then suddenly the prospect of the whole of the Ribble Valley slightly overwhelmed her. Fairly sparsely popu-lated, maybe, but in terms of area was huge with two other substantial rivers flowing into the Ribble, the Hodder and Calder, and if Jess was correct, she was the only sergeant across the whole shebang. Yet whilst feeling overwhelmed, she felt completely confident in her ability to handle it, despite it being a big responsibility, maybe in some respects even more than in the Met, where she was a small fish in a big pond, whereas here she was one of the few and under much scrutiny.

'So.' She turned to Samira. 'Who's the biggest, baddest, best criminal in the Ribble Valley?'

Samira drew a sharp breath. 'Ooh, take your pick. So many to choose from.'

'Who do you think?'

'Well, there are quite a few organized drug gangs, but even so I'd say they are quite low level, really.' Samira held out her hand, palm down about waist high to give Jess a visual representation. Then she raised her hand so it was level with her chest and said, 'And these guys are controlled by some higher-level crims, some we know, some we don't.' She paused. 'Then we have our more traditional criminals such as burglars, high-volume thieves, those linked to rural crime, which of course is rife around here and very profitable, and, of course, as is the way of the world, most of this is associated to the drug trade. I'm not sure if there's any link to human trafficking, but never say never. Just because we're a bit detached from the urban world doesn't mean that sort of stuff isn't happening out here.'

'It will be,' Jess assured her grimly.

'But it's mostly run-of-the-mill stuff.'

'No Mr Bigs? Or Mrs Bigs?'

'Not at the level I work,' Samira said.

'Don't knock your level,' Jess said. 'What you do is vitally important. I think it's the bedrock of coppering, community level. As a service we seem to have forgotten that. Anyway, coming back to my original question, give me a name of who you think is a big, bad crim.'

Samira's mouth twisted as she thought. 'OK, then. Micky Roach. Lives on High Moor estate. Tough nut and dealer. Intimidates folk left, right and centre. Once punched my lights out.'

'Really?'

'He was involved in a pub brawl. I broke it up, with help obviously, but Micky landed a right hook into my face.' She touched her temple gingerly, the blow still a memory. 'Went down like the sack of spuds, I did.'

'And what happened to him? Jail time?'

'Didn't even get charged. Not enough evidence. Dave Simpson was there but said he didn't see it happen.'

'That's not good.'

'I agree.'

'And he's still out and about?'

'Cock of the town.'

As Samira spoke, Jess found herself getting hot under the collar, furious that a cop could get assaulted and the offender could get away with it.

'Hm. How about we make Micky our little hobby?' Jess suggested.

'What do you mean? We're not detectives.'

'So what? Let's do to him as he'd like to do to us, metaphorically speaking. Disrupt him. Annoy him. Stop and search him. Let him know we're watching him. Arrest him if we have evidence, that sort of thing.'

'That really would annoy him.' Samira smiled.

'Hopefully.' Jess checked the time and said, 'Oops – kids to sort.'

They were at an age when, mostly and with a bit of butt-kicking, they could be trusted to get up on time and sort out their own breakfasts, which they had been briefed to do that morning. When Jess arrived outside the cottage she was pleased to see they had complied with all instructions and were up, washed, dressed, fed, ready. A small miracle.

For a moment or two on entering the cottage and seeing them at the dining table, Jess was overcome by her love for them and wanted to hug them both. The other emotion she felt was that of guilt at having brought them kicking and screaming out of their comfort zone without being able to tell them the whole truth as to why she and their dad were moving. The reason given was for her career and the chance to bring them up in a rural environment for the remainder of their teenage years.

What they didn't know and what was kept from them was that their mum had shot and killed an armed robber and was now under threat herself.

To keep it from them had been a tough decision justified in that the less they knew, the safer they would be.

It wasn't that they were terribly interested in her job but – and this had been discussed earnestly between Jess, Josh and Assistant Commissioner Amir – to expect them to keep something like that secret would be too much of a burden for them and was excessively unfair.

But it still made Jess feel bad.

'Hi, you two,' she said, holding back her mother's urge.

Lily said nothing, didn't even look up from her cereal.

Jason grunted something unintelligible but did give her a half-grin.

'We need to move,' Jess said.

It took ten more minutes to load them into the car – she had come back in the Citroen – and get them on the road to Clitheroe to drop them off at school and despite her best efforts Jess was unable to prise anything out of them about their day ahead. Lily was too busy concentrating on her phone and Jason was munching toast.

As she drew to the side of the road outside the school, Lily looked up suddenly and blurted, 'Caitlin!' then leapt out and ran towards the girl she'd been chatting to the day before, the girl whose mum had the big, eff-off Range Rover which was just pulling away from the opposite side of the road.

It drove past like a huge black bear and Jess got a good side profile view of Caitlin's mother. The woman did not turn to look; her nose was pointing upwards.

And Jess's stomach did a backflip and she went cold all over as her mouth sagged open as she recognized the woman.

THIRTY-THREE

With her head feeling like she had got some sort of post-Covid brain fuzz, Jess entered the nick to be faced by Samira scuttling along the corridor towards her with a worried expression on her face which puzzled Jess, particularly when Samira gesticulated to the locker toom, urgently mouthing, 'In here!'

Then just to ensure she hadn't been misunderstood, Samira grabbed Jess's arm and steered her in and when they were face to face between two rows of lockers, Samira brushed the sergeant down saying, 'Sorry, sorry.'

'What's the matter, love?' Jess asked, confused and amused at the same time.

Samira jerked her head. 'Just a warning, just a warning,' she said, keeping her voice hushed.

'About what?'

'Inspector Price . . . in your office . . . got a "mad-on" for some reason.'

'About what?'

'You.'

'Oh, OK.' She was unfazed.

Samira's lips pursed tightly. 'I don't want to speak ill, especially of the supervision, and it's only rumour-mongering but . . . watch him.'

'OK,' Jess said again.

'He's a nasty piece of work . . . and he's a toucher . . . bra-strap twanger, too.'

Jess began to smile. 'Just my sort,' she said, and laid a hand on Samira's arm. 'I'll be fine.'

'And Dave Simpson's in with him . . . They're like . . .' Samira crossed the first and middle finger of her right hand.

'Thanks for the heads-up.'

'Oh, by the way – Dougie left me a message to pass on to you saying Bart's post-mortem has been arranged for later today, asks if we can cover it.'

'OK.'

'Morning, boss . . . Dave,' Jess said at the threshold of the sergeant's office. She had actually sneaked along the corridor and spent a few seconds discreetly listening just to check if there was anything incriminating being said, but the men were speaking in whispers so she couldn't hear anything, and she also felt stupid by sinking to this level, so she stood upright and swung innocently in through the door and greeted them pleasantly. Price was in her chair, Simpson perched on the edge of the desk itself.

Both reacted like they'd sat on cattle prods before regaining their composure.

Jess smiled sweetly. She seemed to be making a habit of making people jump.

Price checked his watch. 'Time do you call this, Sarge?'

Jess looked at the clock on the wall. 'Eight thirty-five, sir.'

'I like my officers to be early for their shifts, sergeant,' he said formally. Price eyed her.

'Which is why I was in at just after six this morning,' she said. Then she looked at Simpson and added, 'Me, I'm just happy if members of my shift turn up on time.'

Jess was unable to prevent a twitch of her mouth when she saw Simpson swallow something the size of a brick.

Price coughed and stuttered, 'I . . . I didn't realize.'

'But to be fair, I have just popped home to give my kids a lift into school, obviously not in a police car.'

'Ah,' Price said. Then to Simpson, he added, 'We'll speak later, Dave.'

'OK, boss.' He slithered off the desk and, looking through the corner of his eye at Jess, he left.

Price remained lounging in her chair, looking at her with narrow, suspicious eyes. He waved her to the seat on the opposite side of the desk.

She almost folded her arms and stood her ground but thought better of it. If he wanted to play petty psychological games, then let him. It might be her office but he was a rung above her, so she sat.

'Quite a busy first day,' he said.

'Yes.'

'You know that your use of the Taser has been referred to the IOPC, don't you?'

She nodded, but didn't know. Just add it to the shooting dead of an armed robber. She was getting used to being a bad girl.

'Any comment?' Price asked.

'Not specially.'

'Cool lady.'

'Not specially. I just know there's no case to answer.'

'Hm,' he muttered. Then his eyes played over her, head nodding as if in appreciation, lips pursing as he gave her an evaluating once-over and Jess felt the chill that prey must feel under the scrutiny of a predator.

Except, of course, Jess Raker was no one's prey. She'd pretty much weighed Price up the day before and nothing Samira had said this morning came as any sort of a shock to her.

'I'm intrigued,' Price said after what seemed an age.

'By what, sir?'

'Your past history, Sergeant Raker.'

Jess remained silent.

'Y'see, all I know for sure is that you came from nowhere, were foisted on me by the powers that be without any explanation.' He sucked in some saliva as he spoke, turning Jess's stomach. 'You're given a job which really should have gone to Dave, yet no one knows shit about you. I've been into your personal file, except of course it still says "pending".' He did air speech marks to emphasize that last word. 'So yeah, curiouser and curiouser. Care to fill me in? I mean, you called me "guv", which is Met terminology, so I'm guessing you're from down there, yet your accent is northern.'

Jess wondered how to play this. She was severely uncomfortable by this unnecessary examination, but cops, even shitty ones like Price, liked to know things, liked to piece things together and make sense of puzzles.

'I've no idea why my personal file isn't updated, but to be honest, I'm surprised you have access to such things.' She watched his reaction to that and saw him squirm a little. She knew she'd struck a chord, one maybe worth knowing about. She knew it was easy for supervisors to get access to personal records if required, but GDPR legislation was usually a barrier and permission had to be authorized by the HR department. Unless you had a mate in HR . . .

'Anyway,' she went on, 'whatever my origins, I applied for this job legitimately, went through an interview process and was successful and that's all you need to know – sir. Shit happens. But I will let you into something, I've got almost twenty years' service, ten of them as a sergeant and I know my job, OK?' she concluded.

'OK, for the moment, but I'll be keeping an eye on you. I backed Dave for his stripes. He's a good lad and deserves 'em.'

'Your pal in other words?' Jess guessed cuttingly.

Price sucked in saliva again. 'I'll let that one go for now.'

'So, can we get down to do some actual police work, boss? Oh, by the way, maybe you'd like to have a whisper in Dave's lug hole for me, save me a job?'

'About what?'

'Coming in late, but booking on duty early . . . bit fraudulent and I won't have it. But if you don't want to upset him, I really don't mind getting him in here and laying down the law.'

She gave Price a nice smile. He sucked up more saliva.

Jess couldn't be sure if Simpson had been earwigging her conversation with Price but as she left the sergeant's office, he was scuttling away down the corridor. She wasn't bothered. She hoped he'd heard if she was honest.

'Dave?'

Simpson continued walking as if he hadn't heard her, but her second, louder and more strident iteration of his name gave him no choice. It was little short of a bellow, so he stopped and turned as Jess walked up to him. His expression was bland.

'Yes?'

'Yes, *Sarge*.'

'Yes, Sarge?'

'I was wondering if you'd be able to cover Bart Morrison's post-mortem later?' she asked sweetly.

'Hadn't planned to, not for an accidental death.'

'Don't you mean a suspicious death?'

Simpson's bland expression morphed into one of contempt. 'No, I mean accidental and anyway, I don't do post-mortems. They give me nightmares and affect my mental health. All that blood and guts.' He did an exaggerated shiver.

Jess got the message and wasn't about to argue. 'Fine.'

'That it, *Sarge*?'

'Yeah, that's it.'

He spun away on the heels of his Doc Martens. Jess was aware of a presence behind her, accompanied by the wet slurp of saliva being sucked up. Another creeped-out feeling slithered down her spine as she turned to see Inspector Price there, leaning on the door frame of the sergeants' office. He said nothing, just pushed himself upright and walked towards her.

They were alone in the corridor and Jess didn't like it.

Price slurped again, rolling thick saliva around his mouth, making Jess feel nauseous.

Price was a big guy with a fat gut, one of those cops who would never pass a fitness test and from the way he was approaching her, Jess knew he wanted to do a 'corridor pass', something she'd experienced all too often in her service, particularly in the early years. The deliberate move to pin her against the wall on the pretext of there not being enough space to squeeze by without physically brushing against her.

She geared herself up for it: fight or flight?

Should she stand her ground and make it plain that any trespass into her private space would not be tolerated but then risk the accusation that she was responsible for the contact?

Or maybe just punch him in his wattle-like throat?

Suddenly they were face-to-face, maybe eighteen inches separating them.

Price slurped, grinned.

The fist in the Adam's apple seemed like a good option but then Jess found herself rooted to the spot.

From nowhere, the slim figure of PC Vinnie McKinty came from behind Jess and somehow installed his slim frame between her and Price, driving a wedge between them. 'Boss,' he said close up to Price, 'can I have a word?'

The tension was instantly broken by this intervention and Price backed off a couple of steps. 'Yeah, sure, Vinnie. What can I do for you?' His eyes, however, went across the young cop's shoulders and glared at Jess. Who glared back.

'Could we talk in the sergeants' office?'

Price nodded, about-turned and led the PC away. Just before entering the office, McKinty glanced knowingly at Jess and gave her a surreptitious thumbs-up.

Without realizing she'd been holding her breath, Jess exhaled a lungful of air, with mixed feelings about McKinty's no doubt well-meaning intervention. Jess could fight her own battles and needed no help from anyone when confronted by people like Price.

She decided to speak to McKinty later.

Next job was to find Samira who, keen as ever, had left the station and was out patrolling the streets of Clitheroe, mingling with the town centre community.

Jess made a couple of quick phone calls using a phone in the report room, then hopped into the sergeant's car and picked up Samira on York Street.

She plonked herself in beside Jess who asked, 'Ever been to a post-mortem?'

Samira could hardly close her mouth at the question. She shook her head.

'Fancy going to one? Well, not fancy as such: do you want to and add some valuable experience to your CV?'

'Er . . . um, yes and no,' the PCSO said cautiously. 'Do you mean Bart Morrison?'

'I do.' Jess paused. 'Look, I know that normal police practice these days is not to go to most PMs unless they're suspicious or unusual deaths. On the face of it, Bart's death is probably a tragic accident, and it might turn out that way, but it's niggling me for some reason and I think a cop needs to attend the PM. I'm going to cover it and if you want to come along, you're welcome.'

'Let me get this straight: I'm welcome to go and watch an old man get sliced up good and proper?'

'That's about the long and short of it,' Jess confirmed.

THIRTY-FOUR

B illy Moss sat brooding in the portable cabin situated by the entrance gate to an immense industrial park in the shadow of an M25 flyover, covering over 150 acres (which Billy owned) and home to 130 companies of various sizes, half a dozen of which Billy and his family also owned.

Although he was literally watching money roll in in the shape of huge, heavily laden heavy goods vehicles coming and going, twenty-four-seven, to this multimillion-pound enterprise, Billy was not a happy man. Not even when the latest chilled transporter turned up containing several hundred thousand pounds worth of stolen avocados imported from Mexico, courtesy of one of the drug cartels Billy did business with and which made more money for him than drug- or gun-running, and without the risks.

Just another facet of the business portfolio of the Moss brothers, the organized criminal gang Billy headed, though which was run on a daily basis by his three sons.

Over the course of his life and criminal existence, Billy had been responsible either directly or indirectly for the brutal murders of dozens of people, usually business rivals. He'd strangled a couple of men himself and found that to be a deeply satisfying experience, watching, feeling the life ebb out of a person close-up, hearing their gagging breaths, pinning them down as they wriggled and struggled for life. Much better than shooting or even sticking a knife into someone's heart, methods he had also used to bring about the demise of bitter, nasty people.

He had done such things many times but beyond the euphoria of the moment, that incredible heavy power and surge of adrenalin, he had never given much afterthought to his victims, other than to ensure that evidence, including bodies, were destroyed and obliterated and there were no scraps for law enforcement to get its teeth into.

Of course he had been arrested numerous times, but mainly on bullshit, speculative lock-ups by the cops and for him they had usually been occasions to sit tight, say nothing and watch desperate detectives flounder like flatfish trying to get him to confess. Never happened because they never had any concrete evidence against him.

He had often chuckled at that phrase: concrete evidence. Because there were a couple of rivals encased in the stuff who had been on the seabed of the English Channel for many years now, from a time when concrete coffins were all the rage. Not so much now.

Billy pushed himself up from the desk and stood at the window of the cabin to watch the avocado lorry enter the industrial park under the raised barrier.

This was followed by three separate vehicles. Two were driven by two of his remaining sons, the third by a chauffeur who drove his third son Theo because Theo had been banned from driving for being four times over the limit which got him a ten-year ban for his third drink-drive conviction.

They were all high-class cars, Tommy the eldest in his Aston, then Trevor in some obnoxious, OTT four-wheel-drive beast and then Theo in the back seat of a Mercedes. All reflected the wealth generated by the Moss bothers but, Billy thought, none had any real style to them. Just outrageous displays of bling, which he despised.

Billy watched them arrive, a brooding anger welling from deep within him.

Yes, Billy had murdered people, had arranged to have others murdered, and never thought twice about it.

But now things were very different.

Things were on the other foot.

Someone very close to him had been murdered. Despite how it might be phrased in legal gobbledegook, to Billy it was cold-blooded murder. Not lawful killing. Not justified. Just murder, pure and simple.

And it had hurt him so much.

He had been surprised by this.

Even the death of his beloved father – who had been shot to pieces in a gang-related ambush – hadn't affected him as deeply as that of his youngest, uncontrollable son, Terence.

Terry.

And he wanted something done about it.

All that bollocks about 'closure'. In the past he'd thought that phrase was worthless, made up by snowflakes who just wanted an excuse to moan and cry. Now he realized it was different.

Because there would be no satisfaction for him in any way through the criminal courts or by any other legal means, even if he had just begun to pursue a civil claim against the Met police even though his lawyer had advised him to drop it because it would be wasted money. That little exchange had ended up with Billy crashing a thick glass ashtray into the fat guy's sweaty face, even if he acknowledged that would be the reality of pursuing such a case. He just didn't like being told what to do by someone he employed.

Now he wanted to pursue a more direct avenue which he was certain would give him that closure he required.

Or was it revenge?

His sons had driven on the estate and parked in a fenced-off compound with security cameras which contained two identical two-storey office buildings. One was purely offices and a boardroom, whereas the other was a series of rooms, including five ensuite bedrooms, a large, shared lounge and a well-equipped kitchen which was rarely used but kept well stocked-up. This latter building was for when any large-scale operations were underway and could be used as a safe refuge for the family if it was necessary to go to ground. In it were also rooms with basic facilities and bunk beds in which enforcers could crash. The block also had a hidden armoury as well-stocked as the kitchen, plus an underground escape tunnel under the fence which would lead any escaper to the M25 underpass and a garage containing a couple of well-maintained getaway cars.

So far, other than for an occasional operation, none of these facilities had been used in anger.

In fact, the main use of the ensuite bedrooms was as shag-pads for Billy's sons, each of which, Billy knew, was playing away to some degree or other from their official partners.

Billy watched the lads walk into the office block and gave them time to settle. Today was supposed to be an accounts day, the bimonthly get together when business was discussed, legit and criminal, and profits were counted and projected.

When Billy left the cabin he strolled towards the high fence surrounding the two buildings and entered the one where actual business was carried out and made his way up to the boardroom on the first floor. His trio of sons were seated, spaced out around the large, oval, highly polished mahogany table which was far too big for their purposes but the lads liked it because, like their cars, it made them feel grand and important.

Billy would have been happy to cluster around a green baize card table. In fact, that is how it had been for many years for him, meeting business partners in smoky back rooms in boozers he then owned south of the Thames. Days that were long gone.

As he entered the boardroom, a door at the far end opened and a good-looking young woman entered with pouting lips and tight clothing.

She was carrying a tray of mugs and a coffee percolator.

Billy noticed her glance slyly at Theo, the youngest and horniest of the remaining sons and Billy knew this lass would be Theo's latest conquest despite a wife and a couple of rugrats at home. As the woman passed him, Theo gave her a pat on the backside which made her chuckle throatily, pout and almost drop the tray.

Billy regarded it all with disdain and seated himself at one end of the table.

He waited for the woman to leave and close the door before he announced, 'Business.'

Billy listened to the reports submitted by each of the brothers for the different areas of the overall business.

It was booming.

Billy had seen the possibilities of the Covid pandemic to prise money from the authorities for free and not ever repay it. This cash, in turn, went to shore up and start up other lines, in particular the illegal transportation of people into the UK from across the globe. Billy had seen the possibilities of combining that with drugs trafficking, essentially a no-brainer with hardly any risk to the Moss family. Illegal immigrants carried the drugs, usually heroin from the Middle East, then simply handed them over when their boats or containers landed on British soil and they themselves were jettisoned into cities far and wide.

In the last month, the Moss gang had grossed in excess of twenty-four million pounds.

Finally, after covering other areas, such as the clubs, pubs, localized drug dealing and county lines, prostitution and other traditional forms of criminality, the briefing was over. Then it was time for AOB – any other business.

None of the sons had any.

Just Billy. And they all knew what was coming as they folded away their paperwork, ready for the shredder.

Theo made to stand up.

'Sit,' Billy ordered him tersely.

Theo plonked himself back down. Though younger and physically able to overpower his father in a fight, he trembled, still quietly terrified of the older man.

'Daaad,' Tommy moaned.

Trevor just looked down at the tabletop and tapped his ballpoint pen irritably.

'Where are we up to?' Billy asked. He looked pointedly at Tommy.

'With what, Dad?'

'Don't screw me around, Tom. Answer me.'

'OK – nowhere. That's where we're at – nowhere. We just can't find her,' Tommy said. 'I've tried all my contacts and no one seems to know a thing and the firearms lot are tight-lipped, even though I know one or two of them.'

'Thomas, people don't just disappear unless I disappear them,' Billy explained. 'So, what have we got? Terry's out on a fucking stupid job that I knew nothing about . . .'

'With those rag-tag gyppos, the Skeltons,' Theo cut in. 'Bunch of dangerous wankers!'

'Right, and on that note,' Billy said, staring grimly at Theo, 'I want those lot dealt with for leading my boy astray – get it, get my drift? *Dealt with.*'

Theo blew out his cheeks. He knew what 'dealt with' meant and as much as it would be a pleasure to put a few of the Skeltons underground, he didn't relish the task. They were like a swarm of rats.

He nodded.

'Back to the subject in question,' Billy said. 'So Terry's out on a job I know nothing about . . .'

'None of us knew,' Tommy stressed.

'Whatever. He gets wasted by a fucking female cop who we can't even find now. We don't even know her name, other than Officer X two two three which was how she was referred to by the coroner. How is that possible, guys?'

'Even that undercover cop couldn't answer any questions,' Theo said, referring to the detective who'd been discovered, tortured and dumped in the Thames.

'It should not be that hard to find her,' Billy stated.

'Well, fact is, Dad, so far, zilch,' Tommy said. 'She's definitely not on the firearms branch any more, no one seems to know where she's gone, there's no trail.' He shrugged. 'I mean, fuck me, Dad, we're not private investigators, we don't trace missing people . . .'

'No, we make missing people,' Billy growled.

'And not only that,' Tommy went on after the interruption, 'we really don't want to fall foul of the law. We don't want the filth breathing down our necks at this moment in time. We've been lucky so far – we took out that Costigan guy who was coming for us and we dealt with the undercover cop. Now we need to let it lie, Dad. The money's flowing in. Our organization is more profitable than it's ever been. We have a few cops on the payroll who'll keep their noses to the ground for us, so it's going well.' Tommy was the voice of reason.

'And?' Billy raged suddenly and ferociously slammed the side of his fist on the tabletop, making his three sons jump like a mini-Mexican wave.

'Daaad,' Theo whined, 'is this all worth it?' But he shut up quickly when Billy turned his attention to him with menace in his eyes.

'Dad, he's got a point,' Tommy said, coming to Theo's rescue.

'In what way exactly, do tell?'

Tommy sighed deeply as he plucked up courage but knowing he was probably the only one of the three 'remainers', as they called themselves after Terry's death, who had Billy's ear. 'It was only a matter of time, Dad.' Here Billy started to rise slowly from his chair and Tommy knew he was on the verge of one of his huge, uncontrollable temper tantrums. Tommy patted the air and said, 'Dad, hear me out. Please. For once.'

Reluctantly Billy lowered himself, but his jaw rotated and his fingers curled and uncurled into fists.

'I loved Terry. We all loved Terry,' Tommy said and glanced at his two brothers, glad to see they were nodding solemn assent. 'You know that and we all miss him like mad. He was our baby brother for goodness' sake. We brought him up when Mum passed. We gave him everything.'

Once more the two other brothers nodded.

'But the fact of the matter is this: he wasn't interested in the family business and he was a loose cannon, a dangerous guy who loved the thrill of armed robberies. He did things unsanctioned, off-grid. He was a danger to himself and others, Dad. Jeez' – Tommy shook his head despairingly – 'I wanted to do a shit sandwich here, but the filling is dropping out. He had more cons than pros and you know it. Yeah, we loved him, still love him and his memory, but what happened, happened.' Tommy's voice dropped low. 'We all know he got what he deserved. He drew on a cop and wasn't quick enough. Even I see that evidence is overwhelming. Sorry, Dad, but that's how it is . . . and we know how deeply upset you are . . .'

'After all, he was your favourite,' Theo muttered, but not quietly enough.

Billy moved quick, came up like a cobra and shot around the table before Theo could react and before the son knew it, his face was being squished into the polished mahogany top by the flat of Billy's right hand and Billy's face was up close to his squirming son who gasped for breath through his distorted, flattened features.

'I love you all, dammit,' Billy snarled, then with a show of contempt he pushed Theo aside, causing him to tumble sideways off his chair on to the carpet from where he glowered up at Billy through furious eyes. 'Now then, I want this: the Skeltons need putting down for leading my lad astray and getting him killed and I want two bullets putting into the bitch's brain who shot my son dead. *Do you understand?* And with regards to her, I want someone brought in to do it, OK? And you know who I'm talking about here, don't you?'

By this time Theo had dragged himself back into his chair and as Billy made his demands clear, all three brothers exchanged worried looks.

Because they knew who Billy was talking about and who he wanted brought in.

Tommy closed his eyes and hung his head despondently.

The Saint.

THIRTY-FIVE

Although Jess would not have known this being new to the patch, and although she could have guessed it, all post-mortem examinations for sudden deaths in the Ribble Valley would historically have been performed locally. Until now, of course, since everything about policing had become centralized. That meant she and Samira had to head to the mortuary at Blackburn hospital on another inconvenient journey two days running, and which again gave Jess a very good idea of just how remote the Ribble Valley was in terms of self-sustenance.

She tried to make small talk with Samira as she drove east along the A59 but could tell the PCSO was feeling uptight about something. Jess hazarded a guess. 'Are you bothered about the post-mortem?'

'Very,' Samira admitted. 'My stomach is churning at the thought.'

'Understandable, but you don't have to watch if you don't want to. Honestly,' Jess said.

'But . . .'

'I won't think any less of you,' Jess promised. 'They're not pleasant, obviously, but they are necessary in some cases and police attendance might not be needed usually but any questionable death should have the investigating or reporting officer present in my opinion. It's one of those things that if something goes wrong somewhere down the line and the chain of evidence is questioned in a court, for example, then at least that side is covered.'

'Have you been to many?'

'Quite a few.'

Samira exhaled nervously.

'The thing is, Samira, the best way to approach a PM is to be interested in what's going on. If you go in thinking you're going to vomit, you'll vomit for sure. But if you go, "I'm going to be interested in this", it does help. It's a very unique insight into the workings of a human body and I haven't come across a pathologist yet who won't gladly explain what's happening and show you things . . . but, yeah, it's gruesome, but there's no way around that.'

'Have you ever spewed?'

'No, I haven't,' Jess chuckled, 'although I've been close. Some bodies that've been dead for a while have an overpowering odour and that, combined with the sight in front of you, can get to you; plus if the body is, shall I say, not in one piece, it can affect your equilibrium.' She glanced at Samira who gulped and stifled an urge to be sick and wafted her face with both hands. 'Like I say, you don't have to watch,' Jess said.

'Wasted journey otherwise.'

'I don't want you to say you were forced.'

'I won't.'

They carried on the journey, turning off the A59 at Copster Green and heading up towards Blackburn through Wilpshire.

Samira cleared her throat.

'What?' Jess asked.

'Hope you don't mind me asking again, Sarge, but what is your background? Where are you from? It does all seem to be a bit of a mystery.'

'Mm, all I can say is this: I've transferred from another force. I'm an experienced sergeant with a very clean record and I'm here for the duration. I don't take shit from anyone and I know my job inside and out. Beyond that, and please don't think I'm being funny, you don't really need to know.'

'OK, fair enough,' she said brightly. 'That'll do for me, Sarge.' Then she clearly made a decision. 'Let's go to a post-mortem.'

Three hours later, following the post-mortem, they found a table tucked away in the corner of the busy café near the hospital entrance, ordered coffees and waited for the pathologist to join them.

Jess watched Samira out of the corner of her eye. She'd had some delicate moments during the procedure and on a couple of occasions Jess thought she was going to cut and run, but she didn't. She had gone extremely sickly-looking several times but was now back to normal.

'How do you feel?' Jess asked gently.

Samira placed her coffee down and considered the question. 'You know what, oddly privileged by being there for him. And proud to be some part of the investigation into his death and knowing we'll be there for him when, possibly, no one else will be, even if it turns out to be a tragic accident and nothing sinister. But it was a tough call, admittedly.'

She smiled at Jess who nodded, understanding this, then looked across the café to see the pathologist walking towards them now changed into fresh medical scrubs. Jess pretty much knew what she was going to be told but it would be good to spend a few minutes chatting to her. She knew how valuable the input was from an experienced pathologist.

She sat across from them. Jess pushed an Americano towards her.

She thanked them and guided the large cup to her mouth.

'Wonderful,' she said appreciatively then eyed them. 'Well, cause of death is drowning, that's indisputable.'

'But?' Jess ventured, picking up on the slight hesitation.

'You told me his walking stick and flat cap were found down a banking on the other side of a path the deceased was walking along?'

'Yes.'

'And you thought this was odd?'

'Still do. I would've thought these items would have been in the water with him or at least on the bank of the reservoir where he went in.'

'You would think that,' the pathologist agreed.

'But it doesn't necessarily prove anything,' Jess admitted.

'No, but I have taken samples from underneath his fingernails and although I have yet to analyse them, I know enough from what I can see that they are skin, hair and blood samples as though he may have been struggling with someone trying to force him into the water. There are also some indentations at the back of the deceased's neck which may suggest he had been held under by a shoe, possibly.'

'In other words, someone's foot?'

'Could be.'

Jess slumped back, slack-jawed and exchanged a look with Samira who looked equally shocked.

'I'm only hypothesizing based on what I've found,' the pathologist said, 'but I think he was pushed into the water, struggled with his assailant, grabbed the person's arm or hand and may have been held under the water by a foot.'

Jess was still slack-jawed. She rectified this by closing her mouth. 'I wasn't happy about the walking stick and hat thing.'

'In which case your instincts are spot on, Sergeant,' the pathologist said. 'This should be regarded as a murder investigation until proved otherwise, though it's not up to me to tell the police how to do their job. Meanwhile, I'll analyse the samples I've taken and send some off for DNA profiling. Maybe your footwear specialists could have a look at the marks on the deceased's neck.'

'It's murder,' Jess said. She was on the line to Dougie Doolan who was still dealing with Bill Ramsden at Blackburn DHQ.

'You're sure? Let me get out of here . . .' There was a rushing and rustling noise, the sound of a door opening and Dougie came back. 'That's better. Murder, you say?'

'Yeah – skin under his fingernails, possibly a shoe print on his neck. Looks like he fought, struggled, and explains why his walking stick and cap weren't in the water with him. Probably lost them in the fight, poor guy.'

'Right, OK. Pathologist's report?'

'She's doing it now, then emailing it to me and you.'

'Right, OK,' Dougie said again, obviously gathering his thoughts. Jess could almost hear the cogs whirring in his brain as he put all this together. 'What are you doing now, Sarge?'

'On the way back from the mortuary and I want to go and have a chat with the manager at the old people's home. I think we need to push things along here, Dougie. We're already behind the curve.' Jess was acutely aware of those crucial first few hours at the beginning of a murder investigation.

'Yeah, I know. I'll speak to FMIT while I'm here. They have an office.'

'FMIT?'

'Force Major Investigation Team,' he explained.

'So glad I took the scene seriously.'

'Yeah, good move,' Dougie said. 'Look, Sarge, I'm not hopeful of a lot of resources on this. I've already been asked to help out on an overnight murder here, a shooting. I've said no, but I'll be under pressure.'

Jess felt her heart drop.

'There's a lot of detectives been drafted in for this,' Dougie said. 'A gangland thing, a bit sexy, y'know. An old guy pushed into a reservoir doesn't come close.'

'I get it. Do your best not to get roped in and we'll get the ball rolling in the valley. Looks like it's down to us.' She shared a pissed-off glance with Samira, who was listening in to the conversation. 'How have you got on with Ramsden, by the way?'

'Charged, bail refused, though the court might allow him out.'

'OK, whatever,' Jess said, having no great confidence in the courts these days.

'Golly, I've never been involved in a murder investigation before,' Samira said worriedly.

'It's mostly dull, box-ticking, making sure everything's done, collecting evidence and, most importantly, talking to people, door to door, social media posts and all that,' Jess said, reeling a few things off the top of her head. She'd been involved in countless murder investigations in London, most recently related to the surge in knife crime which was rife across the city. Her roles had mainly been leg work for the murder investigation teams and the arrest of, often, quite dangerous individuals usually with a gun in one hand and a ballistic shield in the other. She had lost count of the number of forced entries she'd led through battered-down doors, along grubby unlit corridors and into weed-reeking bedsits. She had shouted a lot and although she was naturally softly spoken, she had learned to project her voice to great effect. 'And if we are going to be short of staff for this, then we're going to have to improvise, multi-task and use whatever, whoever we can.'

'I'm up for it,' Samira said and wriggled on her seat. 'I'm invested now and want to be there for Bart, right to the end.'

'Good. So do I, so unless we're told differently, we get on with the job and first things first, let's go visit the old people's home.'

Less than twenty minutes later Jess was turning off the A59 and heading towards Clitheroe.

'You seem to know your way around pretty well, Sarge,' Samira commented.

'Mm,' Jess said vaguely.

'You're so not going to tell me, are you?'

'Like I said, best you don't know.'

'Mystery woman.'

Jess continued driving for a few moments, thinking hard, trying to come to a decision. She checked her mirrors, pulled safely into the side of the road and stopped the car, her fingers still gripping the wheel, looking ahead.

'What is it, Sarge?' Samira asked, slightly worriedly.

Jess turned to her. Samira seemed to cower slightly, perhaps worried she was going to get ticked off for asking awkward questions she wasn't entitled to know the answer to.

Jess made her decision. She wasn't one hundred per cent certain why she was about to do this, but there was some sort of necessity inside her to open up to someone, plus the very good feeling she had about Samira, even in the short space of time she had known her. Jess somehow knew that she could trust Samira, a trust which would be reciprocated.

Jess was also a tad weary of feeling mean-spirited by not telling

Samira about her past and why she was now here in the Ribble Valley. But it was a slightly selfish thing too, because there was a simmering inside that she had to get off her chest.

'Mostly, I think, I'm a pretty good judge of character, Samira. And I'm looking at you thinking you're a good, honest trustworthy person and colleague.'

Samira's mouth pursed.

'Am I right?'

Samira nodded. Hesitantly.

'So what I tell you now must remain just between us and this car.'

'Right, Sarge.' Samira's throat had dried up considerably.

Jess told her everything in a quick summary: her Clitheroe roots, her life in the Met, the fatal shooting (which made Samira almost explode with shock), DCI Costigan's murder, the subsequent threat on her life followed by the move north with a reluctant family and the necessity to be evasive about all this, with the blessing of the Lancashire chief constable, who had sanctioned everything.

'And that's about it,' Jess concluded, smiling at Samira's dazed face. 'Now you know.'

'Oh my— I didn't expect that,' the PCSO gasped.

'Your word,' Jess reiterated.

Samira nodded again, this time without hesitation. 'You've got it.'

'Which means you'll have to unload some of your secrets to me,' Jess said mischievously.

'I . . . I don't have any, I don't think.'

'Maybe later then,' Jess said, back in business. She checked the mirrors and pulled onto the road. 'For now, just direct me to the old people's home.'

Which Samira did.

The Pendle View Care Home was situated on Pendle Road, appropriately enough, and Jess quite liked what she saw: a nice, refurbished, double-fronted old house that could once have belonged to some long-forgotten mill owner, surrounded by well-tended gardens with lots of mown lawns, wide paths and outside seating areas.

There was a large car park at the front on which Jess pulled in close to wide steps leading up to the main entrance.

'You know anything about this place?' she asked Samira as both got out.

'Expensive and popular and has a good rep, but that's about all.'

Jess jogged up the steps and thumbed the intercom, looking up at the security camera over the door and giving it a wave. The door clicked open and both officers stepped into a large, impressive foyer.

A reception desk was set to one side and a young lady emerged from an office behind it, looking pale and shaken.

'We've come to speak to Mrs Dean, the manager, please,' Jess said.

Elsie Dean was a smart, middle-aged lady oozing care and professionalism and Jess, who thought of herself as a decent judge of character but without ever jumping to conclusions, took to her right away.

'Mrs Dean, I'm so sorry I couldn't make it to see you yesterday,' Jess apologized after introducing herself as the new cop on the block. They had moved into a large, comfortable office with a bay window overlooking the front gardens.

'That's fine. PC Simpson came and explained everything. We know him quite well – he's always been very helpful when there's been any concern relating to the residents – so getting the news about Mr Morrison from him slightly softened the blow, if you will.'

'Oh, that's good,' Jess said, slightly annoyed she did not know about this visit.

'Such a tragic accident,' Elsie Dean said. 'But Bart was an independently minded man and liked to wander.'

'So it seems,' Jess said. 'It was early in the investigation when PC Simpson came to see you, so we didn't have all the facts to hand then.'

'Oh, I see,' Elsie Dean said.

'So, as you know, because of the circumstances of Mr Morrison's death the coroner ordered a post-mortem to be carried out which is usual in sudden deaths like this and I'm afraid to say the examination revealed that Mr Morrison was drowned, as suspected, but deliberately pushed under the water.'

Elsie Dean looked at the officers blankly, not really understanding.

'Mrs Dean,' Jess said firmly, 'Bart was murdered.'

It took a few more gentle passes to get the message across but Jess stuck with it. In her experience most people automatically raised a mental barrier to news about death and the word often had to be said clearly and forcibly but with compassion.

Jess sipped her tea and observed the now distraught Elsie Dean who had moved across to the bay window with her arms folded across her bosom, having finally accepted the news.

'No, no,' she said sadly in answer to one of Jess's questions, 'he had no one, no living relatives. He was alone in the world. Didn't stop him being cantankerous and mischievous though. But he wouldn't hurt a fly. He was just playing games to keep himself amused and sneaking out was one of them. He could look after himself, so we were never too worried about him. He was poorly in several ways, but not up here.' She tapped her temple.

'Had he fallen out with anyone?' Jess asked.

'He fell out with most people, but as far as I know, no one took it too seriously.'

'Anything physical, ever? Fights, argy bargy?'

'Not that I know of.'

'OK. We need to have a look through his things.'

Elsie Dean led them through the home, smiling and acknow-ledging other residents and members of staff they encountered on the way to Bart's room. It was a quiet place, Jess thought, and everyone seemed smiley and pleasant and Elsie Dean had a moment for all.

Finally they reached Bart's room with a brass plaque on the door with his name etched on it and a ceramic tile underneath it with a painting on it of hills and countryside entitled 'Bowland Knotts'. The door was locked and it took Elsie Dean a moment to fiddle with the keys, giving Jess time to look at the tile, which took her slightly by surprise. She didn't have time to dwell, however, as the door swung open and Elsie Dean stood aside as the two officers filed in to find a neat, tidy and spacious apartment rather than just a room.

'It's nice,' Samira commented. 'How much?' she asked bluntly.

Elsie Dean blinked at the directness of the question.

Jess hid a smirk and walked over to the French window leading on to a small balcony overlooking the inner square.

'It varies, according to the package,' Elsie Dean said after clearing her throat.

'Ball park?' Samira prompted pleasantly.

'From seven hundred pounds a week.'

'Holy something or other!' It was Samira's turn to blink.

'What was Bart paying?' Jess inquired, then spread her arms to indicate the room. 'Smart place, all meals included presumably?'

'A thousand a week,' Elsie Dean admitted.

'Wow!' Jess said.

'Partly state-funded, obviously.'

'Absolutely.'

'But we provide luxurious accommodation, great food, great atmosphere and our waiting list stretches for miles.' Elsie Dean sounded very proud.

'So someone's ready to come in and fill Bart's shoes, so to speak?' Samira asked.

'Oh yes, been on the list for months.'

Jess and Samira caught each other's eyes fleetingly, both having the same thought.

'Maybe we need to check out that person.' Jess voiced the thought. 'To see if Bart was bumped off to make room on the waiting list. Not unknown.'

Elsie Dean seemed stunned and almost apoplectic at the suggestion. She folded her arms under her bust again and said, 'I really don't think so.'

'We'll have to follow any leads as it's a murder investigation,' Jess warned her. 'I need to see the waiting list . . . I presume there is an actual list with contact details?'

'The lady at the top of that list, who will shortly be moving in, is eighty-seven years old. She isn't capable of murder,' Elsie Dean assured Jess.

'Her younger, spritelier relatives might be,' Samira suggested.

Elsie Dean's face tightened disapprovingly. 'I'll send you the list.'

'Thank you. You do understand where we're coming from, don't you? Just a line of enquiry,' Jess said more softly. Then: 'Right, let's have a looksee.' She turned her attention to the apartment. There was a small writing desk, like a posh dark wood version of a school desk with a hinged top in which were documents, including bank statements, a will and accompanying letter in a legal envelope which contained Bart's after death wishes.

Jess and Samira pulled on disposable gloves and Jess handed the PCSO the bank stuff whilst she read Bart's will and the handwritten letter regarding the cremation.

The will was simple: half his estate was to go to an age charity, a quarter to a local cancer charity and a quarter to a local hospice. There was no mention of any relatives which aligned with what

Elsie Dean had told Jess, but that didn't mean there were none, just that they weren't getting a dime.

Samira then did a low whistle as she read a bank statement, one of several.

It showed a savings balance of a quarter of a million pounds.

Another was a printout of Bart's current account showing a monthly income of around six thousand pounds and a direct debit to Pendle View of four thousand per month.

Bart clearly hadn't been short of a bob or two.

Jess read Bart's cremation wishes again to herself and how he wanted his ashes disposed of, feeling her insides churn a tiny fraction. She looked at Elsie Dean. 'Right, what I'd like you to do is keep this apartment locked and I'll arrange for a proper search team and scenes of crime to come and have a look through everything.'

'Highly inconvenient. We need to prepare it for the next guest, as we like to call our residents.'

'Have to wait, I'm afraid. I'm sure it'll be sorted within a couple of days at most, then your next guest can step into a dead man's room.'

Dougie Doolan was waiting when Jess returned from her travels.

'Managed to avoid being involved in that Blackburn murder, juicy though it looks,' he said as Jess bustled in and slid behind her desk. 'That said I'm probably too old for that kind of thing – kids with knives and guns and all that police hatred.'

'You mean you're better off dealing with old fogeys' murders?'

'Exactly, more my pace.'

'Like a cosy murder, if there only was such a thing.' Jess laughed.

'Yep. Now, where are we at?'

There was a knock on the open door and Samira poked her nose in hesitantly and gave Dougie a little wave. Jess beckoned her in and pointed to a seat and began to regale the detective about the day, the post-mortem and the visit to Pendle View.

'So maybe there is a line of inquiry as regards the possibility of residents being bumped off prematurely to free up spaces for those on the waiting list. By all accounts competition is fierce to get into the home, although I suspect it's a non-starter to be honest,' Jess concluded, 'as Bart seems to be the only victim.'

'Well, it certainly wasn't a robbery gone wrong, either,' Samira said.

'Why do you say that?' Doolan asked.

'I've been through Bart's property that came back with us from the mortuary and booked it all into the system and did a good search of his pockets and everything. His wallet was still in his jacket.' She held up a clear plastic evidence envelope in which was a sodden leather wallet. She held up a second envelope which had a wad of wet twenty-pound notes in it. 'Five hundred and twenty pounds, plus his debit and credit cards.'

Dougie's face twisted. 'Which makes you think Bart might just have been in the wrong place at the wrong time?'

'Possibly, although I do hate that phrase, Dougie. However, maybe he did bump into a psycho, an opportunistic killer who just happened to meet Bart and had a laugh by killing him.'

'We need to keep that in mind,' Dougie said. 'I'll get a list of our most violent offenders who are currently out and about who might have done something similar or who have the potential to do something like this.'

Jess eyed Samira who in the less than two days she had known her had mightily impressed her. 'One thing we need to work on, Samira, is the timeline from when Bart was last seen alive to when his body was discovered.'

Samira nodded. 'OK.'

'And also,' Jess continued, 'to try to work out the route Bart took, as best we can, from the home to the reservoir, and once that's done we need to go knocking door to door and maybe put out a social media plea for witnesses.'

'Door to door?' Samira said excitedly. 'How exciting . . . count me in.'

'OK, that and the timeline are your jobs, at least until we can get some reinforcements drafted in.'

'I've got pro formas to fill in,' Dougie said. 'They tell you what details you need from each household, including any doorbell or security camera footage which might be of use.'

'I'll get cracking,' Samira said.

Jess looked at the pair. 'So, we're the murder squad?'

'Looks very much that way,' Dougie said.

'Yay!' Samira uttered. Then shut up quickly.

THIRTY-SIX

'Oh, you really are a saint,' Mrs Belcher said with a cheeky grin as though she'd said something original when she opened the delivery door at the back of Sunny Common Old People's Home which was situated close to Wimbledon Common in South London to find Joseph Saint there with his van drawn up and the rear doors open. Mrs Belcher could see past Saint's shoulder into the van, inside of which were four new, luxuriant hanging baskets which she knew he'd made himself and brought down to the home to replace the rather bedraggled ones hanging out back. These new ones would brighten up the place immeasurably and she knew Mr Saint would not expect a penny in payment.

Because he liked old people.

Such a good man.

'No,' Joseph Saint said. 'My name may be Saint, but I'm not really that good a person. Sometimes I'm a little sinner.'

'Oh, you are good, you really are,' Mrs Belcher insisted. 'And' – she raised her eyebrows and indicated the flowers – 'am I correct in assuming they are all for us?'

'You assume right, my darling.'

Ten minutes later Saint had replaced the old hanging baskets and once he'd washed his hands he walked into the communal activity area where over a dozen elderly residents had gathered, reading, chatting or watching TV.

'Hello, everyone,' he announced.

They turned at their own pace and waved or said hello back.

Joseph Saint was a well-known visitor and a couple of times a week, even without flowers, he would come in and spend some time with them, playing games and organizing activities.

That afternoon he thought he might try a bit of karaoke, just to get them going, get their thin blood circulating through their narrow arteries. They liked a good old sing-song.

Saint's birth name was Vernon Venator, which he had loathed. As soon as he'd reached an age when he could, he'd changed it by deed poll to Joseph Saint, which he knew, suited him very nicely.

Because Joseph was the patron saint of the dying and happy death.

But though quite a few people had died at his hand, none had experienced a happy death.

Not even his mother.

The old people's version of the Neil Diamond classic 'Sweet Caroline', now used as a sing-along at England soccer matches, was not bad, Saint thought, as he led the song with enthusiasm following a very piss-poor rendition of 'Mama Mia' which hit the skids quite quickly.

The whole room had reached one of the 'dah-dah-dahs' when Saint clocked Tommy Moss leaning on the door frame with a look on his face which was a combination of disbelief and rank amusement.

At least this was the last song for the moment.

It had been a pretty good, impromptu party, but now it was time for the old dears to get their breaths back and go to the loo.

By the time Saint had wound up the session he found Tommy outside leaning on his car, smoking. Saint strolled up to him.

Before anything else, Tommy demanded, 'Why do you do this?'

'I enjoy it.'

Tommy knew he was speaking to a psychopath, even though Saint's response was, on the face of it, sensible. There was just something lurking under the veneer that was 'off', something too many people had found out to their mortification too late on several occasions. However, being a psycho didn't mean that Saint wasn't intelligent, a good planner, a man with excellent contacts and above all, a good executioner. He'd done a few very dirty jobs for the Moss gang over the years, often involving torture and extreme pain, and even though Tommy actually hated Saint with an intensity, he reluctantly realized he might be the right man for this job.

After all, he'd done the last one for Billy Moss. The one involving the undercover cop who had been exposed and then brutalized just for the sake of it. Saint had strapped the unfortunate guy to a chair whilst he sliced slivers off his flesh like carving a turkey. He made him squeal, especially with added splashes of vinegar, as Billy watched. Finally, with the man never revealing a thing, a knife in each hand, Saint double-stabbed him in the eyes, gouging them out and piercing his brain by twisting the stilettos up into it. By all accounts, that killed him instantly.

Saint grinned at Tommy, knowing he made this big, hard guy very uncomfortable. Weirdos, Saint thought with glee, sometimes had great powers.

'My dad wants you for a job.'

'What sort of job?'

'The kind you like.' Tommy threw down his cigarette and crushed it out.

THIRTY-SEVEN

T he phone call was unwelcome.

Jess, Samira and Dougie had spent a couple of hours plotting an investigative strategy for Bart's murder; always at the back of their minds was the possibility that if the real murder squad stepped in they would probably have it all whipped away from under their feet. Such was life but if – when – that happened, they wanted to be able to hand over something good and worthwhile.

It was all fairly basic stuff based on the location of the killing, what was known about the victim and the offender and establishing any links that connected those dots.

Unlike the murder which Dougie had described in Blackburn, this little backwater, Ribble Valley murder, was not 'sexy' and did not have a huge murder team to throw at it, but at least the trio could get the ball rolling and Jess would use other officers in Clitheroe when she could.

Based on what time Elsie Dean at Pendle View believed Bart had sneaked out and what time his body was discovered, the three cops made an educated guess at the probable route he had taken, which included taking his life in his hands crossing the treacherous A59, then up to Pendleton.

Dougie rooted out a large-scale street map of the area which he tacked to the wall of the sergeants' office which they had declared would be their own incident room for the time being. It was handy and everyone had access all day, every day, but could be locked if necessary.

It was four p.m. by the time they were happy with what they'd achieved.

It didn't feel like much, but they knew it was and were all three eager to arrest the person who had killed Bart Morrison, a fate he did not deserve.

However, there was still normal life to contend with.

'I need to do a school run,' Jess announced, determined that today she would not miss it.

'Understood,' Dougie said.

'I'm going to grab a plant-based sandwich, then the door-to-door forms and head up to Pendleton, if that's OK, knock on a few doors and let residents know there's been a murder on their doorsteps and that we'll be around for a while,' Samira said.

'Plant-based, yummy,' Dougie said. 'I'm more of a carnivore.'

'Each to their own,' Samira said.

The pair left the office. Jess sat back in the creaky chair and had a quick look at her black eye using her make-up mirror. The swelling had waned, but the colour was a lovely shade of puce which would require judicious use of foundation. 'Damn,' she muttered.

Her personal mobile phone rang, number withheld.

She half-expected it to be Inspector Price, harassing her about something or other.

'Sergeant Raker, can I help you?'

'Bit formal.'

'Oh, darling, there was no number.'

'Phoning from the office,' Josh said.

'Oh, how's it going?'

'OK, I suppose.'

'Oh, very good. Me, I'm running a murder investigation.'

'Oh, fancy,' Josh said. 'Each to their own,' he added, the second time Jess had heard that little phrase in the last few minutes. It was unusual for Josh to phone at any time during his working day and despite the lightness of his tone Jess was apprehensive, so she asked the next question with a degree of trepidation. 'To what do I owe this unexpected pleasure?'

That pause, the one between question and answer, instantly told her this was going to be bad news.

'Look, babe,' he began – two words which filled her with dread, 'I'm not gonna be able to make it home tonight. I've got to meet a client at the Hilton up on Cloud 23, then I'm staying there for the night.'

She knew she could have bombarded him with worried, wifely

questions: what about a change of shirt, underwear, teeth cleaning? But she didn't want to annoy him.

'Right,' she said shortly, and her level of being unimpressed was all over that word.

She also backed off from other, more serious questions, such as who the client was, did they really exist, because they would have painted her as a jealous harridan when all she was, genuinely, was a worried wife who had been cheated on and was suspicious of it happening again.

'I know what you're thinking,' Josh cut in smoothly. 'The client's a big retailer from Munich, his account is important and I need to butter him up, OK?'

'OK, OK yeah.' Jess wiped a tear away from her good eye. She knew what he was telling her was probably true. It was what he wasn't saying that bothered her. 'You fix the deal and I'll see you tomorrow night.'

'Yeah. Love you.'

'Love you, too.'

They hung up.

Her phone rang almost immediately. 'Sergeant Raker.'

'Ah, Sergeant Raker . . .' This time it was the dreaded Inspector Price.

Jess thumbed the end-call button and said, 'You can sod off,' although she wasn't one hundred per cent sure if she'd said the words before or after she'd ended the call.

Fortunately for Jess, Lily and Jason were once again attending after-school activities. Lily was in a Shakespeare appreciation class (although Jess did not know why) and Jason was playing volleyball – no surprise there.

This time Jess was the one waiting for them to come out.

She parked across the road from the school but needed some air so she crossed to the school gates and did a bit of pacing. She had noticed the big Range Rover that belonged to Caitlin's mother who was suddenly now Lily's best friend who she assumed was also in the Shakespeare class. Jess wasn't really thinking about it until she heard a harsh voice behind her.

'I bloody thought it were you!' The woman's voice was accusatory. 'Jess Easterby, the bitch who stole my boyfriend from me all those years ago.'

THIRTY-EIGHT

S aint finished off his karaoke spot with a rousing rendition of 'You'll Never Walk Alone', despite the moans and groans from the non-Liverpool fans, which were all the old folk. However, when they got going, swaying their arms in unison eventually, and their voices lifted, Saint left on a high.

He liked old people. Quite a few had left him considerable amounts of money in their wills over the years following untimely, but obviously non-suspicious deaths.

He packed up his gear into his van and drove down into Wimbledon where he had his shop, a florist he'd owned for several years.

He liked flowers too.

Even he admitted that he was an oddball.

He lived in the apartment over the shop and once he'd unpacked his gear, had a shower, he settled himself down for a while at his laptop feeling it would be an easy enough task to find the where-abouts of the police officer Billy Moss wanted dead.

His first port of call was to unearth all the media reports of the shooting at the jewellery shop in Greenwich where Terry Moss had been shot by the cop. He noticed that all the reports managed to keep the gender of the cop who'd pulled the trigger unknown. 'Gender neutral,' Saint scoffed.

Then he spent time sifting through the subsequent social media and political point-scoring outrage that followed the shooting. Although the cops got it in the neck, the outpouring was a bit muted because the feeling was that Terry had clearly got what was coming to him. Armed robbery. Drawing on a cop. Getting shot. Tough shit.

Still, Saint thought, he was not there to pass judgement or be all moralistic, he was here to do a job.

Kill a cop.

Didn't need a rhyme or a reason.

Just like a plumber fitting a new toilet bowl in place of one that was perfectly useable. The customer wanted one, the customer got one.

Saint's next port of call was to the online reporting of the inquest into Terry's death, which throughout referred to the cop who had pulled the trigger as 'Officer X223', again gender neutral. The officer gave evidence via a secure video link and was never caught on camera anywhere. Saint did wonder how Billy knew it was a female cop, but he answered his own question because other members of the robbery gang would have seen her – one had even been wounded by her – and she would have been audible over the video link.

If the cop had been a male firearms officer it would probably have been more difficult to identify him as most AFOs were male – only a few females in among them, which should make it much easier to track her down. In theory.

The thought that then occurred to Saint was this was a bit like closing the stable door after the horse has bolted. All official reports had been extremely cagey about identifying the firearms officer as they always were and, Saint agreed, with good reason.

However, there could be the possibility that her name might well have been mentioned in news reports prior to the shooting.

He sat back and said to himself, 'I mean, cops are always visiting schools and colleges to give talks, aren't they?' His thought was that these visits often resulted in news items in local papers or on school Facebook pages and they often named the officers.

It was a lead worth following, he thought. Just the beginning of my journey.

THIRTY-NINE

J ess clamped her teeth tight as she watched Maggie Horsefield emerge from the back door of the Coach & Horses pub in Bolton-by-Bowland and teeter across the covered terrace with two pints of 4 Mice lager, which was brewed on site, plus two bags of crisps clenched between her very white teeth. She placed the glasses down on the table where Jess sat and let the crisps drop from the grip of her teeth.

Her maiden name was Goss – or, as Jess frequently used to refer to her in flat-out hatred for the girl she was way back, 'Gozzer'. Or 'Mags the Gozzer', which was pretty appropriate because 'gozzing' was an unpleasant northern term for spitting and Mags Goss did quite a lot of it whilst living up to her nickname.

'Only right we should have a chinwag, a catch-up,' Mags said. 'After all these years . . . gosh, look at you!' she said in mock admiration as she parked her slim backside on the chair opposite and made her overlarge boobs wobble on purpose, Jess thought. 'Jessica Easterby, well I never!'

Jess made a muted noise at the back of her throat and hoped it was masked by the rushing sound of Kirk Beck, which ran alongside the terrace. She reached for her lager and glugged a few mouthfuls. It tasted amazing. Helped to wash away the grime of the day as she could still almost taste the post-mortem from this morning. It also relaxed her nerves for this girlie catch-up.

At the school gates Mags had immediately said, 'I'm just joking,' after her heartfelt remark when she'd called Jess a bitch, which Jess knew she definitely meant, and was back-tracking. 'It's really nice to see you, Jessica . . . let's have a snifter and a bit of a reminisce.'

Jess was taken aback. 'Maybe some other time?'

'No, no, today. Now. Let's do it. Girlie catch-up. We could go to the Coach and Horses. I know you live up there.'

'You do?'

'Yeah, course.' She pointed to the school door out of which Lily and Caitlin were coming, laughing and joking, arms draped around each other as though they'd been friends forever.

'Our kids are besties, they've really hit it off. C'mon, you know you want to. I'll give Lily a spin in the Range Rover – she'll love it. And we'll see you up at the Coach in about ten minutes. Oooh, by the way, nasty-looking eye!'

And so it was, with Jess now looking across at her old adversary-cum-love rival from twenty years ago who clearly still bore a grudge even if she denied it.

Jess had managed to drop Jason off at the cottage and quickly scrambled into a change of clothing – jogging bottoms and a baggy T-shirt – before dashing over to the pub.

Lily and Caitlin were already on the terrace, sitting at a table in one corner, heads down, giggling at their phones.

'Not Easterby any more,' Jess said.

'I know, Raker must be your married name, but just look at you,' Mags said again, then took a sip of her drink. 'Dowdy mum of two and a cop to boot.'

Jess's anger began to simmer instantly. 'No need to be nasty, Mags. I've been at work all day.'

'And so have I, my dear,' Mags responded.

Jess regarded her sceptically: still slim, smart, coiffured, tits to die for, and very much a stunner whereas Jess thought of herself as a stressed-out frump, hair scraped back from her forehead into a tight ponytail.

'Well, you look good on it,' Jess said, deciding it was best to stick to compliments.

'Thank you,' Mags said as if it was her due. She sat back and looked down her long, fine nose at Jess with a pair of piercing green eyes (at which point Jess realized she was wearing contact lenses). 'Hell, doesn't time fly? What have you been up to since you stole my Ted Bear away from me and I had to use all my female wiles to lure him back?'

Ted Bear was her pet name for the boy back then who was bouncing back and forth between the two competing females. Real name, Edward Janus.

Jess screwed up her face. 'You and I both know it wasn't as clear cut as that, don't we?'

It wasn't.

True it was a sordid triangle of teenage angst, lust, love and raging hormones, but the reality was that Ted Bear was enticed away from Jess at the start of it into the arms of the larger breasted, obviously more overtly sexy and exciting Maggie Goss, who then paraded him around the pubs of Clitheroe and beyond like a prize stud and effectively rubbed Jess's nose in it.

Which hurt. A lot.

It was Ted who finally saw the error of his ways and scuttled back, tail between his legs, to Jess, who kept him at arms' length at first, then crumbled; the sex was new and fun at that age and to be honest that was mostly what she was interested in. Ted's personality was as flat as a plank, even though he was a very good looker.

Then the stalking began. The criminal damage. Jess's parents were dragged into ugly scenes on their front doorstep. Name-calling in pubs escalated into a nasty brawl between Jess and Mags from which Jess emerged scratched and bleeding and deeply traumatized and told Ted Bear to fuck off back to Mags. Jess had had enough drama and was relieved to get that place at York University and never came back to the Ribble Valley to live.

'I married him, you know,' Mags said. 'Ted Bear.'

Jess didn't know. *Married Ted Bear?*

'Eight months, then I kicked the useless git out.' Mags chortled at the memory. 'Pity you weren't around to have him back between your legs.'

'Mags!'

'Not sorry. I hated you but he just couldn't get you out of his dim skull no matter how many times we did a sixty-nine.'

'I think that's enough,' Jess said, already weary of the exchange and half-expecting Mags to tip her drink over her like she had done years before. Her drink and two others.

'Yeah, yeah, maybe you're right,' Mags conceded. 'We're not kids any more. Now we're both being driven by a completely different level of hormones, aren't we?'

Jess laughed.

'So, cop, eh? I'd heard you went to uni, met a guy, moved to London then joined the cops. Not heard of you for what, must be fifteen plus years, then suddenly you're back here and I hear it through Caitlin.'

'Yeah, back here,' Jess said dully.

'Why?'

'Why not?' Jess didn't want to expand.

'I'll bet you're gagging to know about me.'

Jess bit down on the urge to say no, not really. Even before Ted Bear she and Mags hadn't been friends. It wasn't like Ted had ruined a good friendship, just an indifferent relationship. 'Yeah, course I do,' she lied, but still wracked her brain about what she knew of Mags' family. Something to do with scrap metal, she seemed to recall. 'You look like you're doing well if the car is anything to go by.'

'More than well. Own businesses. Biggest scrap dealer this side of Manchester, a bloody good haulage business and motor vehicle sales businesses too – heavy plant and all that.'

'Wow,' Jess said, genuinely surprised.

'Took on Dad's business, gave it the butt-kick it needed and now . . . mega rich.'

Jess's thoughts unkindly added the rhyming word 'bitch' to 'rich' but she chastised herself for that and said, 'Good on you. And your parents still around?'

'Mum dead, Dad a silly old git.'

'Oh, OK.'

'And you're a cop?'

'Yeah, I am,' Jess said in such a curt way as not to encourage more prying. She'd already had her fill of Mags and was wondering what tactics she would have to deploy in order to extract Lily from her new friendship with Caitlin. Or was that just selfish?

'And you're re-married?' Jess asked sweetly, then sipped her lager, quite a lot of which had already gone down. It was tasty and moreish.

'Once more. Kicked that idiot out, too, money-grabber. Kept his name and our daughter. Now I'm just playing the field and loving teasing slobbering guys.' Then she went slightly dreamy-eyed. 'Except there is one . . .' Her voice tailed away and she jerked herself out of the short reverie. 'You should try it. Hey! We should go out, night on the town . . . I own a couple of pubs, too.'

'Crikey, but no thanks.'

'Have it your way.' Mags shrugged. She looked at Jess across the rim of her pint glass. 'We should've been mates, you know, me and you.'

Jess almost choked on the swig of lager she was taking. She cleared her throat and wiped her lips.

'We still could be,' Mags said enthusiastically.

'I don't think so. Friendly acquaintance will do for me. No offence.'

'I could benefit you and you could benefit me.'

They were words that sent a warning shiver zinging down Jess's spine and put her on full alert. 'It's OK, Mags.'

'I think we should seriously look at it.' Mags' whole tone had changed.

'You make it sound like a business venture.'

The half-grin that came to Mags' face confirmed that Jess was thinking along the right lines.

'Anyway, let me know, Jessica. I'm away tomorrow on business.' Mags raised her tattooed eyebrows a couple of times in a 'you know what I mean?' sort of way. 'Plus other pleasures. We'll chat when I get back.'

It was an actual physical relief to watch Mags leave in the Range Rover, so much so that when she was out of sight, Jess dashed straight to the bar and bought another pint of 4 Mice, half of which went down almost immediately, watched in awe by Lily who just scowled but said nothing.

It was a rushed tea for herself and the kids but one of those the kids scoffed and loved – microchips, chicken dippers and beans.

Afterwards Jess watched TV although her mind wasn't on it and she went to bed early, leaving Lily and Jason to sort themselves out. She refused to let herself get cross even when she heard them still moving around at eleven p.m.

It didn't help that sleep came slowly, her mind buzzing with Bart's murder and swirling with Josh and Mags.

She knew Josh was unhappy with the move north and the new job in Manchester probably wasn't good enough for him. And nor did he have a secretary to keep him diverted.

She tossed and turned, fighting the urge to give him a call. That was on him, she was determined, but she did have a horrible feeling in the pit of her stomach about him not coming home that night. She tried not to dwell on it.

Then her mind raced to the Moss gang and that supposed contract they'd put on her. So far nothing had happened. Perhaps they thought killing her was a step too far, even for them. She knew that although nothing could be proved, they were implicated up to their neck in the murder of DCI Costigan (another horrific image that came and went in her brain) and the undercover cop who'd been dredged up from the Thames. That sounded gruesome in the extreme and only grew worse in her thoughts. She took a little solace that Assistant Commissioner Amir had promised to let her know immediately if there were any developments.

Finally she drifted to sleep.

At exactly three a.m., Jason screamed.

Jess woke instantly, shot upright, still asleep really, but her mothering instinct engaged as she scrabbled out of bed and ran towards the noise which was terrifying and did not subside until Jess crashed through his bedroom door and found the poor lad sitting up in bed, sobbing, gasping for breath.

She swooped across and gently took him in her arms, cradling his head into her chest, cooing, 'Darling, darling, what is it? What's going on? I'm here, I'm here now.' She stroked his hair as he sobbed in anguish, unable to draw a steady breath until finally, clinging to her, it started to ebb.

The scream – it had been as awful as any scream Jess had heard before – had also woken Lily who hovered at Jason's bedroom door with a terrified expression on her face. Jess had expected her to be dismissive of this, but she looked concerned and when Jess beckoned her over to sit on the bed, she joined in with the hug like a little girl. Jess had to hold herself together, be strong, until finally Jason was in control of his breathing again and slowly detached himself from the hug and lay back, staring at the ceiling.

'I know it was a dream,' he whispered. 'But it was so real. A faceless man, standing by the bed, leaning over and putting his hand over my face so I couldn't breathe. It felt so real.'

Jess stroked his arm. On her other side, Lily slid her arm around her and squeezed gently, pressing the side of her face into her upper arm.

'It was just a bad dream, that's all,' Jess reassured him.

She could feel him calming down under her touch until his breathing was steady and he was asleep. She and Lily stood up quietly and went on to the small landing where they hugged again and Jess stroked her hair.

'Are you OK?'

Lily nodded. Jess kissed the top of her head and watched her go back into her small bedroom and close the door behind her. Jess waited until she saw the light go out under Lily's door and only then did she exhale and make her way down to the living room.

She checked all the doors and windows were secure – as she had done before coming to bed – and then stood at the foot of the stairs for an extra few moments to listen to the silence. When she was satisfied, she went back up to bed, leaving her door open.

FORTY

Because of her now wide-ranging responsibilities – in that for the moment she was the only regular uniform sergeant covering the whole of the Ribble Valley – Jess had decided to take her uniform and PR home, plus a couple of spare radio batteries, so that as soon as she was up she could listen to anything that was going on, even if she wasn't technically on duty.

And on that third day of her new life in the valley, after dropping Lily and Jason off at school, she was glad she had tuned in because as she drove away from the front of the school, PC Vinnie McKinty's voice came breathlessly over the airwaves, urgent and accompanied by the pounding of running feet, but still saying quite calmy and clearly, 'Assistance, assistance! Currently Lowergate on foot . . . pursuing suspect.'

Jess immediately shouted up, 'I'm Chatburn Road, not far off Waterloo Road, Vinnie. Who are you chasing?'

'Micky Roach . . . wanted on warrant, failing to appear . . .'

Ah, Micky Roach, Jess thought, the subject of the conversation she'd had with Samira the other day, local hard man and drug pusher.

'Describe him,' Jess said.

'Six-two, white trainers, black joggers, red top . . . I'm thirty yards behind him.'

'I'm Waterloo Road now,' Jess said which she knew connected to Peel Street, both of which combined formed the road enclosing the eastern part of Clitheroe like a mini bypass. 'Anyone else about?'

'PCSO Patel turning out from the station,' Samira joined in.

'Anyone else?' Jess demanded.

No response.

'Current location, Vinnie?' she asked.

'Lowergate, still thirty yards behind him,' Vinnie shouted. 'He's gone across the car park, could be going to run up through Swan Courtyard.'

Samira shouted back, 'I'm in the car, up King Street, stopped at the junction with Castle Street, right in the town centre.'

Jess had anchored on, skidded left on to Shawbridge Street, then left on to Lowergate and swerved on to the car park mentioned by Vinnie, only to see the officer disappearing up the steps to Swan Courtyard in pursuit of Roach. The courtyard was a little square just off Castle Street, the main shopping street.

Jess slammed the brakes on, jumped out of her car, leaving it parked at an angle, and sprinted after Vinnie, calculating that by the time she could have driven around to get on to Castle Street, the chase could well be over one way or the other. Or not. Decisions on the hoof were usually only analysed and dissected at leisure later with the purity of hindsight, something Jess knew well.

'Castle Street now,' Vinnie said, 'he's turned right, heading in your direction, Samira.'

Jess upped her pace, taking two steps at a time and instantly feeling the strain on her thighs.

'I see him,' Jess heard Samira say.

'Watch out – he's already thumped me,' Vinnie warned her.

'Will do. Unuph!'

'Shit,' Vinnie said, 'he's rammed her over.'

Samira was sitting on her bum with her back against the stone wall of the old Barclays Bank building on Castle Street with Vinnie crouched down next to her as Jess joined them, wincing with concern for her two officers, both of whom had nosebleeds, both of whom had shown the bravery that most front-line cops show. Samira's car was parked up on the junction with the driver's door wide open, engine ticking over.

'You guys OK?' she asked. Day three and she was already concerned about them.

'I'm fine,' Samira said, annoyed by the fact she hadn't been able to bring down the charging bull of the man on the run. 'Sorry, Sarge.'

Vinnie stood upright and looked down at Samira and tried to stem the flow of blood from his nose with a once pristine handkerchief.

'I'm fine, too,' he said, responding to Jess's inquiring expression, but then wobbled and staggered towards the bank wall to keep himself propped up on his feet. Jess grabbed him gently and eased him down into a sitting position with his head between his knees. 'In the heat of the moment after he'd punched me, I went into autopilot and chased him.'

'And now you're feeling it?' Jess said.

'Oh yeah.' His nose continued to bleed.

Several pedestrians had stopped to gawp at the spectacle, but a man eased his way through the small crowd and asked, 'Can I help, Sarge?'

Jess turned to the voice and despite herself and the situation, she gasped inwardly, recognizing the running-gear-clad figure of Joe Borwick, the firefighter who was the crew manager of the tender up at Dead Man's Stake Farm. He was obviously out for his morning run. Normally Jess would have called it a jog, but by the looks of Borwick's body, this guy definitely ran.

Their eyes met for a moment and Jess saw him react to the sight of her black eye, of which she was suddenly very conscious of herself. However, he squatted down by the two injured officers.

Vinnie now had his head tilted back.

And Borwick was so well equipped that he was wearing a bum bag from which he extracted two man-size tissues and handed one each to Vinnie and Samira.

Jess had been slightly entranced by this apparition but she managed dutifully to tear her eyes away from Borwick's sweaty, running-shirt-clad torso which clung to a definite six-pack, and looked him in the eye, which she found just as disconcerting.

'I think they're OK,' Borwick said, 'but it might be worth them going to the walk-in NHS surgery on Chatburn Road. They're pretty good.'

'I'll make sure of it,' Jess said, 'and, er, thanks for the tissues.'

'You're welcome.'

God! She even liked his gravelly voice.

'In the meantime there's a guy out there now wanted for assaulting two police officers,' Jess said, now more professionally.

'I'm sure you'll find him,' Borwick said.

Vinnie rose tentatively to his feet and helped Samira to hers, but she waved him away and wriggled her fingers towards Borwick so he would be the one to pull her up, which he did and Jess could not help but notice the expression of sheer bliss on the PCSO's face despite her nosebleed, until she was finally upright, steady and glancing at Jess with a secret smile, who in turn was just a tad cross with her, before she grinned.

'How are you both?' Jess asked her officers.

'OK,' they responded in unison.

'Right, let's regroup at the station, arrange to get you to the walk-in and come up with a plan to nab Roach. Are you OK to drive?' she asked Samira, whose car was starting to cause an obstruction.

'Yep.'

'In that case, you take Vinnie to pick up his car, then both of you see me at the station. I'll stroll back and get mine in the meantime.'

Samira and Vinnie got into the police car, the remaining onlookers dispersed, leaving Jess and Borwick.

'How far?' she asked him.

'How far, what?' he asked, then realized. 'Oh, five miles, give or take.'

'Every day?'

'Every other day. I do weights at the fire station.'

'Nice,' she said, trying not to eye him too salaciously.

'Where's your car? Not up Pendle Hill, hopefully?' He grinned.

'Just over the back on Lowergate.'

'I'll walk with you. My flat's over that way.'

'Your flat?' That's handy, she thought.

FORTY-ONE

'I thought Roach'd been locked up,' Samira mused. 'I must've got that wrong.'

'Well, whatever, he's out and about,' Jess said, 'and he needs to know there's no hiding place for him.' She regarded Samira and Vinnie seriously. 'No one gets away with assaulting my officers. Where did you spot him first?' she asked Vinnie.

'Waterloo Road.'

'What's his last known address?'

'NFA as far as I know,' Vinnie said.

Both officers had staunched their nosebleeds but each now, slightly comically, had screwed rolled-up tissues into their nostrils. Neither appeared to have had their nose actually broken which was a good thing.

'Right, let's fill in everyone about this morning and try to pick up some solid intel on his whereabouts. He's only a low-level dealer so it won't be long before he surfaces,' Jess said. 'Pond life has to come up for oxygen.'

'Might be worth giving the town centre pub landlords a heads-up. Most of them will give us a bell on the quiet if he shows up in their pubs,' Samira suggested.

'Unless they're getting a cut of his profits,' Vinnie said.

Jess said, 'Do it anyway, good shout. It'll be good for the dodgy ones to know.'

They were in the sergeants' office, drinking tea, coming down from the excitement of the foot chase and the assaults.

Jess looked at Samira whose countenance was screwed up in puzzlement. 'Something bothering you?' she asked her.

'Nah . . . I'll let you know, Sarge.'

'OK. How are you both feeling now?'

'I'm good,' Vinnie said, carefully removing the blood-soaked tissues from his nose.

'Me too,' Samira said, doing the same.

'You must both check into the walk-in today, please,' Jess said. 'An order, not a request.'

'We will,' they chorused, drank their tea and filed out as Dave Simpson appeared, standing aside to watch them go past. He had a smirk on his face. He'd come on duty at nine a.m., too late to be involved in the shenanigans. Jess clocked Samira's peculiar expression which was locked on to Simpson for a few significant seconds, then she was gone.

He stepped into the office. 'On at nine, Sarge. On time, Sarge,' he said with a hint of mockery – noted by Jess. 'What was all that about?' He cocked his thumb at the disappearing couple.

'Almost caught Micky Roach but he managed to evade us by assaulting them.'

'Ah, bad man.' Simpson was in his shirt sleeves which he rolled down before putting his zip-up top on.

'I've been looking for the actual hard copy of the fail-to-appear warrant that's out for him. Any idea where it is?' Jess pointed to a stack of paperwork in her tray. 'Doesn't seem to be in there.'

Simpson shook his head. 'No idea, Sarge.'

'OK, no worries,' she said. Then: 'Mobile patrol, Dave? Those two will be grabbing a bite to eat, I expect.'

'Sure thing.' He held up the keys for the section Land Rover, which seemed to be his preferred mode of transport, and being the senior PC he had first dibs in the pecking order so no one questioned him.

'Oh, Dave, you didn't tell me you'd visited Pendle View. How come?'

'Nothing to report, Sarge.' He actually gave her a wink, then turned out of the office as Vinnie edged back in.

'Sarge?' Vinnie said. 'Just remind me what powers of entry we have into scrapyards, just so I'm armed and dangerous.'

For a moment, Jess had been put off her stride by Simpson, but she pulled herself together. 'Er, simple enough – we have a power of entry to check the books and the owner must enter every item the business receives which includes contact details for the person bringing in the item and how much was paid.'

'Cheers for that. Thought so.'

'Why?'

'I'm still doing local scrap merchants and car wreckers to see if I can find if the car involved in the fatal hit-and-run I'm dealing with has been traded in or whatever. I went to Primrose Wreckers yesterday and they were arsy with me and their dogs, which I think are those ferocious American pit bulls . . .'

'XL Bullys?'

'Yeah, them . . . well they looked at me as if they could have torn my throat out and I must admit I did a bit of a retreat, but I'm going back today cos I want a proper look around the yard.'

'Want me to come with you?'

'That would be great, thanks.'

'Can you give half an hour? I just want to see what's happening upstairs with CID. I see – and smell – a few extra detectives have arrived.'

Jess followed the aroma of bacon sandwiches up to the CID office and found four detectives she did not know lounging around, drinking coffee and munching the sandwiches.

Dougie Doolan was at his desk, presumably briefing them. On the dry-wipe board behind his desk he had written several names, headed by Bart Morrison and the assumed timeline Jess, he and Samira had worked up the day before.

Jess edged in at the back of the office and listened in. It seemed these detectives would be dedicated to the murder investigation, but looking at them cynically Jess wasn't convinced they would be any more effective than her tiny team of uniformed cops, the big difference being her staff also had another day job and would not be able to commit full time to the murder, which was required for a quicker result.

She was a tad underwhelmed by the distinct lack of enthusiasm on display. They seemed more invested in their refreshments than anything Dougie was telling them and he had a pissed-off look on his face. Jess guessed the visiting DCs had all been skimmed off the big sexy murder in Blackburn and were not impressed by it.

Half-baked at best, she thought, and Bart Morrison deserved much, much more. She almost waded in, broke it all up to send them packing back to the big city, but this wasn't her shout.

A few minutes later they split into two pairs, Dougie handed out some actions for them to follow up, devised by her and Dougie the day before, and they meandered out, not even giving her a second glance.

Finally, just her and Dougie remained in the office.

She closed the door. 'They have no interest in being here, do they?'

He sighed. 'Nope. Out in the sticks investigating the murder of an old guy that a couple of them aren't even convinced is a murder. All a bit sad, really.' He put his jacket on. 'I'm going to the Pendle View for more chats with the residents and staff and, if it's OK, I'd like to keep Samira on the house-to-house in Pendleton. She seems very thorough.'

'I'll send her back up later,' Jess promised. 'Er, any ideas about Micky Roach, by the way? Address, anything? You know what happened this morning, don't you?'

'Yeah, I do, but I don't know where he's crashing at the moment. I'll ask around later.'

'That would be good.'

After this she made her way back to the sergeants' office where Vinnie was waiting for her return to accompany him to Primrose Wreckers. His nose was still dripping blood.

'We'll do the walk-in centre first,' Jess decided for him.

Unsurprisingly there was a queue at the walk-in clinic and even a police uniform didn't get Vinnie to the front, so he and Jess found seats in the waiting room.

'No need for you to stay, Sarge, I'll be fine,' Vinnie assured her.

'I know, but it gives us chance to have a little chat so I can get to know you.'

So they sat and Jess learned a bit about Vinnie's family history and how he'd come to join the police. He had completed his probation of two years and hoped to become a detective eventually but admitted he was still a bit wet behind the ears and had a lot to learn.

'It's a fair point,' Jess conceded, 'but from what I've seen so far – and I know we're only a couple of days in – you seem able enough.'

'How do you mean?'

'Well, this fatal hit-and-run . . . you seem pretty determined to track down the vehicle and driver.'

'I am, though *not* pretty determined, *totally* determined,' he said gravely then squeezed the bridge of his nose with a finger and thumb.

'What are the circumstances, Vinnie?'

'Old guy crossing Edisford Road.' He shrugged. 'Wiped out by a fast-moving car which threw him into the air. He rolled over the car, hit the roof, then hit his head on the kerb as he landed. Massive brain trauma and other severe internal injuries.' Vinnie shrugged again as he recalled the scene vividly. Jess could tell it was affecting him. 'I was there within a couple of minutes, literally nothing I could do for the old fella. Unfortunately I drove to the scene from the direction of Longridge and the car that hit him had travelled in that direction too and made off towards Clitheroe, so I never passed it.' Vinnie held his hands palm to palm, about an inch apart and ran them side to side to indicate passing vehicles. He sighed. 'Git got away.'

'Witnesses?'

'A couple of ladies, but no one else. To be fair, they haven't been much use.'

'And the car?'

'Never seen again, but from some fragments of headlight glass and paint I recovered from the scene, Forensics say it could have been an old blue Peugeot 406. A similar one had been stolen from a second-hand car dealer in Blackburn a few days before, but I haven't had chance to follow that up yet. Thing is there really wasn't any need for the accident to happen. That section of the road has good visibility both ways for both traffic and pedestrians, so an old guy doddering across the road should have been seen from some distance by the driver unless he or she was distracted, on the mobile, maybe, or talking to a passenger . . . or even worse,' he concluded bleakly, 'it was deliberate.'

'In which case you're possibly talking murder or manslaughter.'

'I know. I ran it past Dougie, but CID aren't interested, won't touch it with a barge pole without compelling evidence.'

'Interesting,' Jess said pensively.

'But there is one thing I do know: that old guy isn't going to live to be a ripe old age and that really riles me and I'm not going to give up on it, Sarge.'

'I'm glad to hear it.' Jess took this all in, then another thought struck her. 'What's the story about the woman, the misper, the one you went to Dunsop Bridge about? I haven't had chance to look through the file yet but how come we're so interested in her? Adults go missing all the time. Most show up, some disappear deliberately never to return . . . others, well, we know about the others, don't we?'

'Well, I don't know,' Vinnie admitted. 'Just a gut feeling thing. Maybe it's nothing, but I'm never happy when people just go missing on a walk, that's all. It's possible she's come to grief somewhere in the Trough of Bowland, but we've had mountain rescue out all over the area where she was last seen and they found nothing. I just don't like it.'

'You're very tenacious,' Jess complimented him.

'Thanks, Sarge . . . Dave Simpson says I'm a pain.'

Jess was going to ask about that when a nurse appeared from down the corridor and called Vinnie's name.

'At last,' he said and stood up. But as the blood drained away from his brain, he wobbled, said, 'Whoa there,' then pitched forwards and fainted.

Jess caught him before he hit the floor.

FORTY-TWO

Jess made her way through the A & E department at Blackburn Hospital into the fresh air outside where she took a lungful, then exhaled long and hard.

As soon as Vinnie had slumped to the floor at the walk-in, his nose gushing blood again, and even though he regained consciousness almost immediately, the nurse who had been about to tend him called treble-nine for an ambulance which was there within twenty minutes.

Despite the young officer's protestations – plus the fact he could hardly stand unaided on his shaky legs – Jess did not give him the option: he had to get in the ambulance. She followed in a police car, informing Comms and also wondering about the wisdom of Samira not having yet been checked over. The health and safety of officers under her supervision was something she took very seriously and if she got it wrong she knew someone like Inspector Price would nail her to the wall, good and proper. On that thought, she had given Samira a call via the mobile phone which was integral to the personal radio set and told her to get down to the walk-in, no arguments.

Now outside A & E, she called her again. 'Just checking on you,' she said when the PCSO answered.

'I'm good, Sarge. How's Vinnie?'

'He'll be fine. Slightly concussed and needs a day in bed. His wife's on the way to pick him up when they discharge him.'

'That's good.'

'What are you up to, Samira?'

'House-to-house in Pendleton. So far not much from it but a few people have doorbell cameras fitted, so I'll be asking for footage from them.'

'Keep it up. When I get back we'll figure out how best to get Micky Roach arrested. He won't be at liberty one more minute than necessary.' Even as Jess spoke, she found her voice was starting to quiver with rage and she was surprised at how, in such a short space of time, she had grown to care so much about her officers.

'I'll have that,' Samira said. 'He's done me twice now and I want revenge – in a professional way, obviously. So I'd like to be there when he's arrested and, if possible, be the one who kicks his door down.'

'You and me both,' Jess said. 'You'll be there, I promise.'

Jess ended the call and went back inside A & E where Vinnie was on a bed in a cubicle at the far end of a corridor. A doctor was currently shining a torch into his eyes, gently feeling his skull and testing the bridge of his nose.

The doctor stood back. 'All good,' he declared. 'You can be discharged and we'll give you an information leaflet with symptoms to watch out for . . . it's self-explanatory.'

'Thanks,' Vinnie said.

The doctor left, drawing the curtain behind him. Jess sat on a chair next to Vinnie's bed. 'Take as much time off as you need,' she told him.

'I'll be back tomorrow,' he said determinedly. 'Things to do, people to arrest.'

'I get it, but make sure you're fine,' Jess stressed. 'Otherwise, I'll be for the high jump.'

'Yeah, you'll have to watch your back with Pricey,' Vinnie blurted, then seemed to realize what he'd said. 'Um – loose brain cells talking,' he said quickly.

Jess smiled. Normally she wouldn't have asked, but now that Vinnie had accidentally broached the subject, she said, 'What has Inspector Price got against me?'

'I don't know . . . said too much. Head injury and all that.'

Jess continued to smile sweetly and take advantage of Vinnie's slightly weakened state. 'I get it that I'm the new sergeant from nowhere and noses will be put out of joint. It always happens when new blood steps into established set-ups. Always some resentment.'

'All I can say is this, Sarge – I'm glad you're here and so is Samira, and . . .' He hesitated. 'We're also glad Dave Simpson didn't get the job.'

'He expected to, I believe?'

'He was literally just waiting for the stripes to come in the corrie, if you know what I mean?' He was referring to the internal correspondence. 'He and Pricey thought they had it all sewn up after Luke Baron's suicide.'

'The previous sergeant?'

'Yeah, good, steady bloke,' Vinnie said with a hint of sadness.

'What happened there?'

'Threw himself into the Hodder off Cromwell's Bridge.'

Jess knew the one he meant.

'Supposedly he was depressed.'

'And was he?'

Vinnie shook his head slowly so as not to rattle his brain. 'I don't know . . . however, the upshot was that Dave got temporary stripes and the plan was he'd be made substantive if Pricey had anything to do with it. They're like this, them two.' Vinnie crossed his fingers. 'I think they go a long way back, joined the job together, I think . . . they always seem to be scheming. I wouldn't be surprised if they'd done a jig over Luke's death – and that's one of the reasons I'm glad you're here. Bit of new blood, plus, if you don't mind me saying, bloody good at the job.'

'Kind of you to say,' Jess said modestly.

'But I haven't said this.' Vinnie went on, 'Dave is bad news. He's lazy, a bully and a liar and there's just something about him, so watch him,' he warned Jess. 'He'll trip you up if he can. Off the record, that.'

'Haven't heard a thing,' Jess said.

The curtain opened and a pretty face popped in. 'Darling . . .' It was Vinnie's wife. She stepped in and crossed worriedly to him, hugging him.

Jess stood back.

Vinnie's wife stood back, tears flowing. 'I was so worried.'

'I'm OK, Janine, honestly. Just a punch and a woozy head. I must have a glass nose,' he said with a smile, 'rather than jaw.' He squeezed her hand tenderly and looked at Jess. 'Sarge, this is my wife, Janine; Janine, this is Sergeant Raker, our new sarge.'

'Pleased to meet you, Janine . . . I'll head off now you're here.' Jess looked at Vinnie. 'Need anything, give me or Samira a bell, OK? Anything. Understand?'

FORTY-THREE

I t had been quite a long journey that day for Mags. She would have preferred to go by train and be picked up at the other end but that wasn't protocol and at least having a car meant she could skedaddle whenever she felt like it. Unless of course she ended up with a bullet in the brain which, she thought, was always a possibility when trying to reach a trading agreement with this bunch of thugs who were always on the edge of violence and sanity.

But, she supposed, running a business, the turnover of which ran into billions, she sort of understood it, especially as this business was one hundred per cent criminal.

So she always placated them by acknowledging her place in the scheme of things, keeping her head down and never bringing a gun to the party. She knew how to play the little woman role in order to get her own way, yet play these fuckers at their own game.

Manipulating men, it was called.

However, first things first. There had to be some pleasure thrown into the equation, that being in the form of Tommy Moss, the eldest of the three Moss brothers, son of Billy, and the guy who mostly ran things.

FORTY-FOUR

Samira knocked on as many doors as possible in Pendleton. There weren't many houses anyway and she had a decent success rate, chatting to quite a few occupants, none being much use as witnesses, pleasant though they were. She asked for and was happily given footage from door cams and security cameras on houses, but she wasn't certain how useful any of it would be. She would spend time back at the station perusing the footage.

A few were not home so she pushed letterheaded notes through their doors, asking if they would ring her when they got home.

Then she set off back to the nick.

It was only as she pulled up in the backyard and saw the Land Rover that something clicked in her brain.

In the station she went to the report-writing room which was unoccupied. She sat at the only computer in there and logged in, then entered the custody system which gave her low-level access to the lists of prisoners detained at Blackburn DHQ, plus sparse details of why they had been arrested, but that's where her permissions ended. PCSOs only had minimal clearance to search for information but what she saw was enough. Or to be correct, what she didn't see.

She logged out and, ensuring that no one saw her, went into the sergeants' office where all incoming, pending and outgoing paperwork was kept, plus the personal trays for each officer based in Clitheroe. She quickly shuffled through the in/pending/out paperwork then, rechecking she was alone and not being watched, she looked in one particular officer's tray and, just to be certain that what she was looking for wasn't accidentally in another officer's, all the others. It wasn't. She then checked the sergeants' book which logged all files, warrants, summonses and other paperwork and its current status, but found nothing.

However, the question she then asked herself was: am I right, or am I wrong? And if I think I'm right, should I do anything about it? Also, does it matter, does it prove anything? Or am I just being a silly sod?

FORTY-FIVE

'How do you know you can trust any of those guys not to blab?' Mags asked Tommy Moss as he entered the hotel room and swaggered across to the double bed on which she was posing, already in her silky, skimpy underwear – holding in her tummy – and feeling that movement of anticipation in her lower belly at the prospect of what was to come.

This was always the same with what Billy Moss referred to as 'strategy' meetings, held not at this hotel, which was one of a cheap chain on the outskirts of Banbury just off the M40. The actual business took place in a luxurious one nearer to Oxford. Mags and the Moss gang had been successfully in cahoots for about ten years and twice a year she, and other like-minded crime bosses from around the country, would meet up to discuss this 'strategy'. It was a discussion about logistics, payments, percentages related to their businesses, which was all drug dealing, controlling county lines and how to maintain and improve profits, the bottom line of any enterprise.

Money. Tons of it.

And Mags had been making it for years, during and since school, then college and then when she inherited her father's scrap business which was mostly fed by crime.

And now she controlled, pretty discreetly she thought, a portfolio of businesses ranging from the scrap metal one to running several pubs around the Ribble Valley and the most profitable of all, drug dealing. She took a percentage of every drug transaction in the valley.

Cannabis was hugely popular but she grew a lot of that herself on land adjacent to the two garden centres she also owned. Heroin and cocaine and their derivatives were sourced from other criminals, which is where the Moss gang came in. A healthy relationship was established following some edgy meetings a few years back and continued up to the present day.

But what had really cemented things for Mags – and she kicked herself for her weakness here – was her relationship with Tommy Moss.

Mutual, basic lust.

Eyes across a crowded room and all that shit.

Until after one of the earlier meetings to discuss county lines when both knew they could not hold back any longer and had ended up in the back of Tommy's then car, a spacious Mercedes, making the suspension bounce like it was on a test track as they screwed the life out of each other.

The serious discussion following that, as they lay intertwined on the soft leather seats with Maggie's panties hanging from the head-rest, set out the parameters of their relationship.

Both were married at the time. Mags had since jettisoned that husband, but Tommy was still wed to the same woman who Mags knew to be a dangerous cow. So their mutual lust, they decided back then, would only be satisfied once or twice a year in a hotel separate to the one in which the strategy meeting would take place. They would meet and shag each other's brains out without anyone else being the wiser, especially Tommy's ferocious wife.

'Which guys?' Tommy asked in answer to Mags' question. He had pulled up right in front of her. She had parted her knees. He slowly unbuckled the belt on his chinos and unzipped the fly with a seductive 'zzzz'. Mags reached out and tugged the trousers down around his thighs as he shrugged himself out of his Hilfiger T-shirt.

'The ones who frisked me outside.'

'Because they know I'd kill them if they blabbed,' Tommy said as Mags slowly peeled down his boxer shorts.

FORTY-SIX

Jess motored back from the hospital, trying to marshal her thoughts into some sort of logical order and decide what she needed to do and what could safely be delegated to others. There was always a temptation to do everything yourself and she was frequently guilty falling into the 'if you want something doing, do it yourself' trap, but she knew it was her job, really, to hold back and supervise. The noticeable lack of officers and staff in the valley made that more difficult but she knew she had to give the people she supervised more responsibility.

However, for the moment – until she settled in properly and got to know exactly what was what, who was who – she decided she would do whatever it took to keep things moving forwards.

Top of her agenda was Micky Roach and she wanted to get some sort of operation underway to root him out from under whichever rock he was crashing. Then she wanted to help Vinnie find the car responsible for the fatal hit-and-run on Edisford Road and, of course, assist in the investigation into Bart Morrison's murder in the reservoir. She felt personally invested in the last one, having been there when his body was recovered, attended the post-mortem and got to know something of him as a person since.

That said, she decided to enjoy the journey back from Blackburn. At one point she passed the impressive Whalley Viaduct on her right which she knew from being a child – because her dad had told her every single time they drove past – that it was built in the late 1840s with over seven million locally produced bricks and consisted of forty-nine arches. She had always been impressed by it and it was good to see it looking so well-cared-for. Plus, it gave her a fleeting memory of her father, which made her smile, happy and sad at the same time.

Not long after she was travelling the last couple of miles into Clitheroe where, she had to pinch herself, she was now based. New force, new job, new location. It was quite hard for her to get her head around, having spent all her working life in the Met.

So, so different.

She slowed as she came into the outskirts of Clitheroe, then turned into Primrose Road, driving past a new housing estate, then into a very low-end industrial estate at the end of Woone Lane where Vinnie had told her that the scrapyard he was interested in – Primrose Wreckers – was located. The business was surrounded by a high wall topped by lethal-looking barbed wire. The heavy metal double gate was closed, secured by a substantial padlock. Jess parked parallel to the gate and peered through the mesh into the yard without getting out of the car. There were two 'Beware of the Dogs' signs prominently displayed, each with an outline of a slavering dog that looked like a Pitbull. Another sign read: *Primrose Wreckers – vehicle dismantlers. Cash paid, any condition.* Jess had to get out of the car to read the last line which read: *M H Enterprises* and gave a mobile phone number.

Jess then peered closely through the mesh and through the gaps she could see a large number of vehicles, many scrapped, crushed into cubes and stacked, plus others in a line waiting to be picked up and fed into the jaws of the crusher behind a Portakabin which looked like the office. The whole thing looked exactly like it was – a dirty business.

There was no one around, no sign of activity. Jess half-considered calling the mobile number but decided against it. This was Vinnie's job and if there was any credit to be had, he should get it when he came back to work. Plus Jess did not want to spook the owner of the place. Any search needed to be carried out without warning. She knew Vinnie had already been here, so if there was to be a return visit, Jess wanted it to be an unhappy surprise for the owner.

Then she caught her breath.

Because hurtling silently towards her, appearing suddenly from behind the Portakabin, were two very powerfully muscled, ferocious-looking XL Bully dogs.

Her mouth dropped open and her heart might have stopped, she wasn't sure.

The dogs moved fast.

Jess had to quickly remind herself that she was standing on the safe side of the gate.

The only noise they made was the padding of their feet slapping on the ground until, on reaching the gate, they exploded with rage and terror, hurling themselves at it, making the whole frame crash and shudder on hinges Jess truly believed were about to break and allow the dogs at her.

She jumped back.

The dogs barked, snarled and slavered at her, teeth bared and their strangely shaped ears reminded her of the devil.

She stepped even further back, ready to scramble into her car should the gate actually collapse.

After a few moments of intense fury, the dogs stopped and peered through the mesh at Jess, growling as they paced around each other in a figure of eight.'Good dogs,' Jess said.

She swallowed, then exhaled, so glad she hadn't been able to get into the yard. She had dealt with attacks by such animals down in London, seen the horrific result of one in particular where a little girl's face had been torn off and her shoulders shredded by the 'family' dog.

The girl had died.

Jess had destroyed the dog, wishing she could have done the same to the girl's parents.

Those images still lived with her, occasionally returning in the depth of night when she least expected it.

If there was to be a revisit here she knew she would have to arrange backup from a dog patrol armed with dog catcher poles at the very least. Plus armed officers, too.

FORTY-SEVEN

Dave Simpson was in the report-writing room on the ground floor of Clitheroe police station at the desk with the one computer on it. He had turned away from the desk on the swivel chair and was looking out through the window on to King Street which was fairly busy with shoppers.

Simpson was on his mobile phone, his voice hushed, but from where Samira stood – at the door – she could hear most of what he was saying, although not the other end of the conversation.

Samira had finally decided to speak to him about Micky Roach and the non-appearance warrant she could not find anywhere and assumed was in Simpson's possession.

As she entered, his back was to her. She hadn't intended to be a sneak but decided to be so and, if necessary, bullshit her way out of it if Simpson caught her eavesdropping.

'Redacted how?' she heard him say, and although Samira could not hear the words spoken by the other person, there was something familiar about the tone. 'No way!' Simpson said. 'So your mate in HR can't even access the files on the bitch?' He paused whilst the voice – a man – at the other end spoke. 'And this guy, sorry, woman, has access to the highest level?' Another pause. 'What force has she come from? The Met? And they gave the bint my effin' job? Stinks, Brian, stinks to high heaven . . . summat going on, isn't there? Be nice to know what. Yeah, scuppered our plans for world domination, didn't it? Gonna have to find a way to deal with her, aren't we?'

With a thud in her chest, Samira realized the person at the other end of the phone was Inspector Price and that the subject of their conversation was Sergeant Raker.

Suddenly Simpson sat bolt upright and spun quickly around. 'Got to go, being spied on.' He thumbed the end-call button and looked dangerously at Samira standing helplessly in the doorway. He placed his phone down on the table slowly, deliberately. 'Caught in the act, eh? How long have you been standing there, listening in? Eh?' he demanded nastily.

Samira did not want to be intimidated by him, but she was. She'd encountered him enough times to know he was bad news for everyone, but the vibe she also picked up was that he was even worse towards people like her, meaning a woman, and of colour. Mostly he'd been guilty of eye-rolling, quiet tutting and pulling his face, but she was immediately feeling something different now. Something direct, angry and dangerous. She shook her head. 'Not long . . . only just . . . now.'

'What do you want?' he asked, then smirked. 'You're getting a good ole black eye to go with your brown skin.' He was looking at her injury from the assault.

Samira's throat dried up.

'So what do you want, you lump of lard?'

'I . . . er, came to ask about Micky Roach.'

'What about him?'

'I . . . um . . .' She stumbled on her words, feeling her confidence draining, particularly when Simpson stood up slowly to his full height. He was a big guy, towered over her. Intimidating.

'You said on Monday morning that you'd arrested him on that non-appearance warrant,' Samira said in a meek, quiet voice that embarrassed her.

'Did I?'

'Yes.'

'I don't think so, Sammy.'

'I'm sure you did.'

He shook his head, licked his lips. 'I never said anything of the sort.'

'Yeah, you did, Dave. I heard you on the radio.'

'Misheard, perhaps,' he said, slowly moving from behind the table. 'Misheard. I mean, did anyone else hear me say that?'

'I don't know,' Samira admitted.

'No one, I think you'll find, because you imagined it, darling.' His voice was a low, threatening growl. He walked across and grabbed her face between the finger and thumb of his right hand, her jaw on the curve of flesh between those digits. He slowly squeezed her face so her mouth became twisted, out of shape, and he put his own face just inches away from hers. 'Now then, brown girl, you made a mistake, didn't you?'

He squeezed harder, making her whimper.

'And if you even think of blabbing to anyone, I'll be back for you. You won't see me coming but you will feel real pain.' He jerked her face even closer to his. 'So what I suggest you do is resign because I don't want people like you in this job and if I'd been made sergeant – and I will be made sergeant, make no mistake – I would've made your life a misery, so unbearable you'd have fucked off quick.'

He shoved her ferociously away against the door frame, looking at her as if she was dirt whilst he wiped his hands on his trousers.

'Just remember what I said,' he warned her, then smiled warmly. 'Otherwise, I'll put you out of your misery.'

He barged past her.

Stunned and terrified, Samira sank down the door frame on to her haunches, shaking not just from the assault, which had made her injured face even more painful, but because of something else she had just seen as well.

'Detectives have been here all day,' Elsie Dean said to Jess. The manager of the Pendle View Care Home had, by coincidence, been standing at the front of the large house having a crafty ciggie as Jess pulled up. Elsie Dean had greeted her warmly.

'I hope they haven't been too intrusive or upsetting for the residents,' Jess said.

Elsie Dean chuckled. 'Not a bit. They've loved every minute of it. It's very exciting for them, even though it's obviously a sad time, though to be honest, most didn't really like Bart. But they seem to be having fun and they all think they're in one of those cosy murder mystery novels that are so popular now.'

'There's nothing cosy about murder, Mrs Dean,' Jess said. 'Anyway, could we have a chat?'

'I've been talking to detectives all day, you know? What could I possibly have to say to you?'

'Maybe nothing, but may we anyway?'

'Of course.'

She led Jess into the home and to her office. On the way Jess spotted Dougie Doolan in the large association room, standing in front of an audience of residents. He was making a sign like an old-fashioned film camera.

One resident shouted, 'It's a film!'

Doolan then held his hands out, palms together, then opened them like a book.

Another resident shouted, 'It's a book!'

Doolan then held up four fingers.

'Four words,' a resident shouted.

Jess didn't catch any more as by then she was in Elsie Dean's office.

'That detective has gone down a bomb with our lovely people.' Elsie Dean smiled indulgently.

'Well, to be fair, he's probably not too far from being on your waiting list,' Jess said. 'Which brings me to why I want to chat with you.'

'Ah, I thought I'd emailed it to you.'

'You may have done, but it's been a bit full-on today and I haven't had chance to check, but as I was passing . . .' Jess shrugged.

'I've printed it off anyway.' Elsie Dean picked up a file from her desk and took out a sheet of paper with a list of names, addresses, dates of birth and next of kin on it. The waiting list. Jess skim-read it. Her stomach did a backflip.

'Who has access to this information, Mrs Dean? Other than you?'

'My assistant manager.'

'Do you trust that person?'

'Absolutely – why?'

'Just wondering. Anyone else?'

She shook her head.

'Do you recall telling me that places are very much sought after in the home?'

'I do, and yes they are.'

'Has anyone ever tried to jump the queue, as it were?'

She laughed. 'People are always asking me, trying to bribe me. You know, relatives who want to get their aging mum or dad in.'

'Mm.' Jess read through the list again then said, 'Could you make a list of those people? The ones who have approached you in this way.'

'Er, well to be honest, it doesn't happen that often and when someone's name goes on the list, relatives are told very firmly that it's a queue and if you're at the head of it, you're first in line, if you see what I mean?'

'I do.' Jess's eyes were on the list. She recognized two names and though she didn't want to jump to any conclusions, her eyes dallied over those names for a second or two. 'Can I take this?' Jess asked, referring to the list.

'Of course.'

Dougie Doolan was still leading the charge in the games of charades and his happy audience seemed more than willing to let him.

When Jess walked back to the association room he was indicating the first word of the next subject was a 'The' – which the old folks all shouted in unison. Then he moved on to the second word: three fingers for three syllables, first syllable sounding like – and here he cupped a hand around one of his ears – and then placed his hands palms together and wiggled them towards the crowd.

One did indeed shout, 'Wriggle!'

Another, 'Snakes!'

Another, '*Snakes on a Plane.*'

At this point Dougie saw Jess watching him. He rolled his eyes, then continued with the clues.

'Are we still on the first syllable?' an old man shouted.

Dougie nodded and made an exaggerated popping sound with his mouth, which stumped them.

He did it again and one shouted, 'Goldfish!'

Another sneered at this. 'Have you ever heard of a film called *The Goldfish*?'

'Might have.'

Jess decided to have a punt. '*The Godfather*?'

Dougie pointed decisively at her. 'Yes! How did you work that out?'

'Lucky guess. Sounds like . . . fish . . . Cod . . . God . . . Godfather, maybe?'

'Fair enough.'

'Can I drag you away from all this, please? Y'know, police business?'

Dougie bowed to his people who gave him a perfunctory hand-clap, and he withdrew to join Jess in the entrance foyer, then both stepped outside.

'How's it going?' Jess asked him.

'Nothing much so far.'

'Err, what do you think about this,' Jess began, 'for a serious line of enquiry?' They had walked down the front steps and she leaned against her car.

'Go on.'

She showed him the waiting list. 'A pincer movement: kill a resident, or more, maybe – and then kill someone who's on the waiting list.'

Dougie screwed up his nose. 'To what end?'

'To get your beloved, old, knackered mum or dad into the home quicker than, literally, waiting for dead man's or woman's shoes. A shuffle up.'

'Far-fetched, a bit desperate . . . you were sort of thinking this before, weren't you?'

'Dougie, you and I both know that people get murdered for literally no reason whatsoever, and this is a reason, maybe.'

'True.'

'So, hear me out. Bart Morrison is an old guy, one of the longest standing residents of this place, although that doesn't make him the pick of the crop, but if you were aware he frequently put himself in danger by going on unscheduled walkabouts which made him vulnerable, say . . . I'm just spit-balling here by the way, Doug.'

The detective nodded. 'Be quick about it, I've got party games to get back to,' he joked. 'Bingo next.'

'And if it was known he liked strolling around a piece of open water, it would be relatively easy to push him in and make it look like an accident, if we didn't investigate it properly, that is. Plus witnesses are pretty thin on the ground out there, so it's an ideal location to commit a murder.'

'OK, maybe it could be a reason to murder him.'

'Which is worth following up, as we know already.'

'But all that does is get rid of Bart, who, correct me if I'm wrong, isn't on the waiting list, other than God's.'

'However, what if someone who is on the list, close to the top, is also killed?'

'Then there's a big shuffle-up, one place at the home and one place up the list,' Dougie said. 'But that argument stalls . . .' He left the rest unsaid.

'Stalls because no one on the list has been murdered?' Jess posed the question and looked at him, willing him to make the less than difficult mental leap. He was a detective after all.

She gave him an encouraging 'come on' gesture with her hands.

'Unless, of course . . .' he said falteringly.

'Come on, you're nearly there.' She egged him on.

'Unless someone on the waiting list *has* been murdered!' Dougie exclaimed. Then: 'Is that what you're telling me? This is Clitheroe, not somewhere exactly inundated with murders, so I don't recall any more off the top of my head.'

Jess gave him a 'maybe' shrug.

'Stop teasing me. I need to get to my bingo gang.'

'Does the name Edward Withgill mean anything to you?'

'Should it?'

'How about PC Vinnie McKinty?' Despite the seriousness of it all, Jess was kind of enjoying this low-level mind game with Dougie.

'This is worse than charades,' Dougie whined, but then the thought hit him. 'Vinnie was investigating a hit-and-run accident, a fatal.'

'*Is* investigating,' Jess corrected him.

'Err, Edward Withgill?'

'You remember him!'

It was all coming back. 'Old guy. Edisford Road. Driver not traced.'

'And Vinnie came to you thinking the CID might be interested.'

Jess then noticed how large Dougie's Adam's apple was as it rose and fell with an audible clunk in his throat as he gulped.

'He's on the list, isn't he?'

'Number three.'

'Oh dear.' Dougie's voice was contrite and he looked stunned.

'So it's possible that in recent weeks two people have been murdered whose deaths free up some space in the home and therefore the list like an escalator.'

'Coincidence?' Dougie ventured weakly.

'Fuck off, Dougie,' Jess chortled. 'My arse! All right, it may be, but we still have to talk, nicely, to anyone whose old parents have benefitted from the deaths by moving up the list – which is everyone on the list, by the way.'

'How many is that?'

Jess held up the list. 'Thirty-two.' She handed it to Dougie who skim-read it. She asked, 'Recognize any names?'

'Just the one, really.'

'Which one?'

He placed his fingertip on a name, number five on the list who, when the list was updated to include two deaths, would move to number three. 'I don't actually know the person on the list, but I do know his daughter.'

Jess tilted her head and looked where his finger was placed, and the name.

'Why is that person known to you?' Jess asked.

'Because that person is the biggest drug dealer in the Ribble Valley in terms of supplying. That person runs the biggest OCG in the valley, too, and I assume that the person on the list is that person's father.'

Jess blinked at the information and said, 'We are talking about Margaret Goss stroke Horsefield here, aren't we? Just to confirm?'

'One hundred per cent. Ernie Goss and Maggie's about as untouchable as can be. Smart, violent, the equivalent of your fourth cousin twice removed. You know she exists but for the life of you, you can't work out the family tree. Too many steps to link her to what she does, basically delivering death to the streets of the valley.'

FORTY-EIGHT

Just at that moment Mags was still wafting down to earth from the best orgasm she'd had since . . . well, the last time she and Tommy Moss had screwed and almost broken a bedhead in a hotel. Because that was pretty much how she viewed it: screwing. Not making love. At least that is how she set off viewing it several years ago when they had first done it in his car but now, if she was honest with herself, it was one of the high points emotionally and sexually of her year, highly anticipated, something she yearned for.

And he was so good. He was regularly in her thoughts.

And the relationship had moved on, at least in her mind, from pure sexual attraction – which was still there, obviously – to something deeper. And she hated herself for it. No way did she want to be falling in love with a South London gangster. That would only lead to heartbreak and probably violence, maybe worse.

But as he withdrew from her, himself sated and drained, Mags knew she wanted this big lug of a man all for herself, not just a twice a year sex-fest.

He flopped on to his back and she slithered up next to him, crushing her boobs against his ribcage and sliding her right leg across his thighs.

'That was wonderful,' she cooed.

'You're not wrong, babe.'

It was on the tip of Mags' tongue to begin 'the' conversation about 'them' but she didn't quite dare, which she found unusual, thinking twice about voicing her wants and desires. What she wanted, usually, she went for, including men. Perhaps the difference with Tommy was that he might not submit to her like other men did.

'Need to get moving,' he said reluctantly. 'But I'm feeling so good after that, it'll be hard to keep concentrating with you across from me.'

'I know that feeling.'

Tommy peeled her arm from his chest and sat up as she rolled back.

'Usual suspects coming?' she asked, watching Tommy's firm backside as he walked to the ensuite shower room.

'Yeah, all the usual villains,' he said, 'like some kind of cut-price James Bond film, but none with any class.'

Mags chuckled.

'But my dad's going to be distracted this year,' Tommy said.

'By what?'

'He's put a contract out on the cop who shot and killed Terry, my youngest bro.'

Ironically it shocked but didn't surprise Jess that Maggie Goss, née Horsefield, was a crime boss, maybe the female equivalent of a crime lord. Even way back she had known that Mags' father who owned a couple of scrapyards was a very shady character and she recalled his name, Ernest, appearing occasionally in the local press after some minor court appearances for handling stolen goods. That his daughter – there were no other kids – had followed his footsteps into that way of life didn't surprise Jess one bit.

What did gobsmack her was the level she was operating at, according to Dougie, carrying the mantle of the Ribble Valley Queen of Crime.

Drug dealing, trafficking, and all, if Dougie was to be believed and Jess assumed that he would have his finger on the pulse of valley crime as the longest-standing detective in the area.

The question was would Mags resort to murder just to get her dear old dad into a bloody old peoples' home?

From what Jess knew about her previous character, even though that knowledge was quite ancient now, the answer would have to be a resounding yes.

Mags was selfish, nasty and always relentlessly pursued what she wanted and usually got it through intimidation and violence and from Jess's recent encounter with her, she hadn't changed an awful lot, and her parting shot to Jess about being able to help each other out had a sinister undertone to it. A cop on her payroll would be a useful string to her bow.

But murder? Just to get her dad into a home?

Jess was back in her car now after speaking to Dougie, making her way to the police station, all these things, these possibilities, spinning around her head, and as she pulled the steering wheel down to make a corner, she thought, Who am I kidding? Course Mags would stoop to murder, but bearing in mind she distanced herself from anything that might besmirch her, or drag her down, she would get some other fool to do it for her, wouldn't she? She would not get her own hands dirty.

Also in her mind was Micky Roach, and Jess was hoping to write a quick operational order to go after Roach when she got back, because she felt he should be her immediate priority, so she wasn't really concentrating as hard on the road ahead as she should have until she reached a roundabout which was the conflux of four roads, the main two being Chatburn Road and Waterloo Road, the latter of which she was on.

Traffic was busy and she had to stop at the roundabout behind a motorbike which was waiting for traffic to clear.

Jess still wasn't thinking or concentrating, really, other than on police work.

Perhaps the deaths of two old men connected to the same old people's home was purely coincidental, nothing untoward. Sometimes shit happened.

The biker in front of her seemed hunched over and now Jess clocked that he was constantly glancing in his right-hand rear-view mirror, his head jerking like it was on a broken spring. She understood drivers getting edgy when there was a cop car behind – even she did when off duty – but this guy kept looking and there seemed to be a tension about his shoulders and the nervous, unnecessary revving of the engine now made Jess park her thoughts on Mags and focus on the biker.

She was perhaps three metres behind him when for the first time she actually looked at the number plate. Then blinked a few times after reading it, digesting it and realizing the bike in front was her husband's stolen Honda: the one pinched from the railway car park.

And the guy in front of her was on it, so no wonder his body language was signalling that he wanted to crap himself.

Jess eased forwards.

The guy, a rake-thin lad, looked in the mirror again, but then his left hand came behind him with his middle finger extended, then he revved the bike and surged forwards, pulled a spectacular if unstable wheelie between two unsuspecting cars on the roundabout, and was across the roundabout in seconds with Jess on his tail, weaving her car expertly and precisely through gaps between cars and in pursuit of the stolen bike.

'Echo Charlie Three – in pursuit of a stolen Honda 125 Trials bike, red colour,' she transmitted cooly over her radio, alerting any other patrols in the vicinity, which she knew were few and far between, whilst keeping one eye on the road and street names as she zipped by. She might well have lived in Clitheroe in her younger years but she didn't have a forensic knowledge of the town. 'Waddington Road, heading out towards Waddington itself,' she said.

She dropped a gear. Chase on.

Since her unpleasant encounter with Dave Simpson, Samira found it impossible to get going. It had completely sapped her energy.

She was almost in a trance of terror thinking about it and work suddenly felt an unsafe environment to be in. She had always pegged him as a wrong'un. Something about him: underhand, nasty behind closed doors, nice to your face when not. She had been on the verge of packing the job in – not because he'd been harassing her or anything like that, but because people like him had been, somehow, allowed to thrive and survive in the police. Not that she could ever prove anything against him or had any proof of wrongdoing, just that horrible feeling in the pit of her stomach about him. She had been deliriously happy when Jess Raker got the sergeant's post. The expression on Simpson's face when he heard the news had been priceless; all those months as a temporary sergeant yanked from under him. *Priceless*. And it is what had kept Samira in the job, but now Simpson had shown his true colours again over the Micky Roach warrant, so the big question for Samira was should she speak to Sergeant Raker about it? She had shown trust in her, and Samira was sure she would listen and deal with it in an appropriate way. And that other 'thing' she had seen. Did it mean anything, or was she letting her imagination run riot?

One thing Samira was certain of though was that Jess would not be intimidated by Simpson. She struck Samira as someone who would take on anyone, anything, head-on. And win.

Even so, Samira's contretemps with Simpson had left her mentally bruised. It had sucked all the confidence out of her – which surprised her because she thought of herself as a pretty stoic person who rarely allowed anything to affect her too deeply. Following it she had reluctantly pulled on her uniform and decided to head across to her favourite coffee shop on the corner of King Street and Station Road where she could sit for a while and get her head back together.

As she walked out of the station, Sergeant Raker's urgent call came over the radio – chasing a stolen motorbike – so Samira pivoted in the opposite direction, grabbing a set of car keys and ran into the backyard while transmitting, 'PCSO Patel received, turning out from the station.'

He was off, fast, dangerous, weaving between the cars ahead and oncoming, then at one stage mounting the pavement, causing an old lady to leap out of his path, walking stick and all, probably moving quicker than she had done for half a century.

Jess kept the biker in view on Waddington Road, coolly transmitting progress.

She was keenly aware of the policing conundrum here: pursuing stolen vehicles was a very contentious subject if it went wrong and the offender ended up injured or worse. Usually the police got the blame, although Jess could never quite work out the logic of that narrative, other than the world had changed and, in her opinion, not for the better in many respects.

But as far as she was concerned, this guy had no intention of stopping for her. He was on a stolen bike, he knew she was behind him and she intended to do whatever was necessary to get him into the criminal justice system.

His intention not to stop was made extra clear when he suddenly flung a package about the size of a house brick sideways with his left hand which bounced across the pavement. Jess knew instantly what it was – drugs, bound up in plastic wrap and secured by duct tape. Cocaine.

'He's ditching drugs, Waddington Road,' she said over the radio.

The biker did another wheelie, then ditched another package which flew sideways into someone's front garden. Jess realized they must be stuffed under his jacket like a suicide bomber.

The ones he'd thrown were two quite big packages and there was a lot of money tied up in them.

Two more came out, bouncing across the road, then another over his shoulder, landing right in front of Jess's car. She heard and felt it bounce up under the engine block and under the chassis and despite herself, she laughed out loud when she checked her rear-view mirror and saw the bag had burst spectacularly and behind her was a swirling cloud of white powder.

'Don't breathe in,' she muttered, then relayed this information over the radio . . . at which moment the voice of Inspector Price came over the air and demanded, 'Sergeant Raker, are you pursuit trained to Lancashire standards? If not, you must immediately withdraw from this dangerous situation.'

Jess purposely did not respond.

The biker went under the railway bridge that spanned Waddington Road and once under, he put his left heel down on the road, braked hard, dropped the bike down at a sharp angle and pivoted into Chester Avenue, then came back upright and put his head down almost on to the handlebars and gunned the bike along there.

'Sergeant Raker,' Price said curtly.

'Bike now Chester Avenue, general direction of the back of the railway station,' Jess cut in just as curtly.

Samira skidded out of the police station car park, swerved into King Street. She knew that Chester Avenue had a car park on it used mostly by railway travellers and opposite it was a narrow underpass below the railway line itself from the car park and out on to Station Road and that it was quite possible the biker was heading for this and if he got there first he'd have a great chance of getting away from Sergeant Raker who would have to slow considerably and then, as Samira knew, go against the one-way system in the underpass.

However, Samira also knew that a well-placed car could block it which, Samira thought, was a plan.

Chester Avenue was narrow, cars parked on either side before the car park was reached, and with one last, 'up-yours' flourish, the biker lobbed another parcel of drugs to one side, reared the bike for a spectacular wheelie almost the whole length of the avenue. This even impressed Jess in a begrudging sort of way, although she was also praying for him to misjudge his balance and do an even more spectacular back flip. But he managed to keep control for almost one hundred yards, then just before the underpass he dropped the bike back on to two wheels, swerved, controlled it, then turned sharp left into the underpass, ignoring the no entry signs. He disappeared from Jess's view in the few seconds it took for her to reach the tunnel. She braked hard and was about to go against the no entry sign.

Only to come face-on with the biker speeding back towards her with Samira's cop car right behind him. He had been blocked by Samira but somehow managed to do a full about-face, one-eighty degrees, and change direction completely. Jess stalled the car.

But at that exact moment, the escaping biker was doing an over-the-shoulder check to see where the second police car was, and when he twisted forwards again he was faced by the front radiator grille of Jess's car giving him no room or time to manoeuvre his way out of danger and he was left with no alternative but to slam head-on into the car. The motorbike did a forward flick and hurled him skywards off his seat, arms and legs flailing like a Catherine wheel.

Jess cowered as the biker's head – thankfully in a helmet – smashed into the windscreen, denting the glass before the lad did another flip across the roof of the car. Jess ducked as she reacted to the two bangs he made as he bounced and then rolled off into the road behind the car.

Jess leapt out, dreading what she was about to find: a young biker, neck broken, dead after a police chase. She could almost see the lurid headlines and social media voraciously gobbling it all up and assigning narratives to it.

Her heart almost soared to the heavens though when, as she skittered around the car, she found the lad climbing unsteadily to his feet and with a shake of his head, running away from her.

'Thank God for that,' she breathed and legged it after him.

However, the impact must have had some delayed effect on him as after about twenty yards he began to decelerate.

Jess glanced behind her to see Samira bringing up the rear on foot, having abandoned her car in front of Jess's. Jess unhooked her rigid handcuffs, slowed to a jog, then to a walk and the young lad eased off his helmet, tossed it aside.

He withered to his knees, looking spaced-out and disorientated.

Jess walked up and stood over him, her cuffs swinging on her forefinger.

'You're under arrest. Theft of a motor vehicle for a start,' she informed him, glancing back forlornly at her husband's Honda, now with a buckled front wheel and prongs, probably beyond repair.

'I want a doctor. I need medical attention – now!' the lad demanded. 'You nearly killed me.'

Jess noted his words, cautioned him and said, 'You're also under arrest for possession and supply of controlled drugs.'

'Ha! Nonsense. You won't find any drugs on me.'

As he said that, a plastic packet slithered from under the front hem of his jacket on to the ground. Both cop and prisoner shared a look.

'Hands out,' she ordered him. Beaten, he held out his arms and Jess cuffed him.

Samira joined her. 'Good one, Sarge.'

'Teach him for nicking my hubby's bike.'

FORTY-NINE

M ags made a phone call from the hotel room, demanding information, some of which was, though vague, returned immediately, sending a shimmer of excitement down her spine.

This time it was a greedy urge, not a sexual one, as she wondered if she now possessed information the Moss gang would pay

handsomely for. She might well have some sort of personal relationship with Tommy, but that didn't exclude squeezing money
out of him.

She then got all her things together and left the hotel, walking
across the car park to her car, certain that Tommy and his dad would
be very generous.

She did not see the woman in the car on the far side of the car
park, slumped low in the driver's seat, watching her.

It was all very formal. A nice conference room with a shiny, wooden
oval table in a very posh hotel somewhere near Oxford. Coffee, tea,
a nice finger buffet with the delegates standing around, chatting
affably. They could have been high-level businessmen (and one
woman). But they weren't. They were elite, yes, but what they were,
were twenty of the country's highest level organized crime leaders
here to discuss the next six-to-nine months' business strategies.

All very civilized indeed.

Mags nursed a flute of champagne, observing all this pre-meeting
malarky, not particularly mixing with anyone.

Billy Moss circulated like his lordship and Trevor and Theo were
doing the same. It was easy for Mags to spot that the youngest son,
Theo, had the hots for one of the waitresses who was delivering drinks
and nibbles to the delegates. The animal lust was plain on his face,
unlike Mags' veiled lust for Tommy, who she watched schmoozing
around, chatting lightly, trying not to catch her eye. Mags was keeping
it to herself and was glad she was doing so when the door opened
and Tommy's wife, Leanora, swept in like Cleopatra on heat, all gold
bling, a shimmering, clingy dress and very enhanced boobs that put
Mags' ones to shame, and which moved like deadly weapons. Jeez,
Mags thought, despising the woman to hell and back. *Quelle* bitch.

Mags eyed her as she smooched around, bubbly in hand. She
spoke to one guy from Newcastle, another who had his fingers in
many pies in Leeds, one from Manchester Mags knew well, and
others from Cardiff, Glasgow and the Midlands. Between them they
controlled huge chunks of the drug trade across the UK, plus other
lucrative lines. Mags was quite a small fish in comparison but she
didn't care. Having a stranglehold on the Ribble Valley was like a
crown jewel and incredibly profitable. She had no plans to expand
beyond those boundaries but there were one or two cheeky upstarts
who she intended to put in their place in the near future.

And on top of that she had something very valuable indeed.
Information.

Something she had worked out by adding two and two to turn
that 'information' into fact. And as much as she liked Tommy and
their occasional sexual forays, she intended to use it to full fiscal
advantage.

Currently, though, her attention was riveted by the woman wearing
thick, heavy lipstick reminding Mags of a vampire in a cheap movie,
and who was bearing down on her with a dangerous look on her face.

As decreed by the custody office on arrival at Blackburn nick, Jess
and Samira were instructed to convey their prisoner directly to A
& E for a check-up following the accident.

His name was Lance Drake. He was eighteen, from a broken
home – no dad, a mum who had little time for him who had a series
of boyfriends and 'uncles', many of whom enjoyed smacking Lance
around when he was younger, but since turning sixteen he'd been
more prone to retaliate. He had three younger half-brothers from
different fathers and school was just a place he turned up at occasionally until he reached the age when he didn't have to go at all.

He had fallen into crime as a way of life early on, been in and
out of custody offices many times, been cautioned, been to court,
been sent to youth detention centres and Jess could have written
his life story for him, having come across so many just like him.

Not bright buttons, but not thick either. Let down by parents and
society and with little to look forward to in adulthood other than
an existence of petty crime, joblessness and brushes with the law
which would probably get blamed for all his bad luck.

Jess knew all this.

The police came in at choke points in peoples' lives and had to
react in some way.

But Jess always tried to do something more than just arrest kids
like Lance, whose current lot in life was as a distributor of drugs
for someone further up the food chain. If she could help in some
way, she would.

At A & E – which was horrendously busy – Jess and Samira
settled down for a lengthy wait, sitting either side of Lance on
plastic chairs in a corridor.

With the exception of the packet of drugs that had exploded
underneath Jess's car, they had managed to recover every other

package he'd jettisoned, plus others still tucked under his jacket. Ten in all.

It didn't take a genius to work out that Lance must be working for someone else.

'That was a lot of drugs,' Jess commented. Lance was sitting back in the chair, his cuffed hands in his lap, head against the wall, eyes shut.

'You can't talk to me,' he said. 'I'm not under caution. This isn't a police interview room. I'm saying nowt.'

'I'm not talking to you,' Jess put him straight, smirking at Samira and giving her a subtle wink. 'I'm chatting to my colleague, passing time, making small talk. Don't listen if you don't want to.'

Lance grunted.

'So, yeah, a lot of drugs,' Jess said.

'Huge amount,' Samira agreed, picking up on Jess's intentions.

'I reckon what – a million quid's worth.'

'Maybe more,' Samira guessed.

'Three hundred grand,' Lance interrupted, then shook his head, angry at his inability to keep his gob shut.

'OK, three hundred thousand,' Jess said. 'Not to be sneezed at.'

'Heck of a lot of dosh,' Samira said.

'The kind of amount you associate with a major drug dealer,' Jess said. 'Cream of the crop.'

Lance still had his head tilted back, now with a smug look on his face. The big drug dealer look.

'And every penny of that three hundred grands' worth of drugs now in a police property store, eventually to be incinerated. Plus, didn't we find two grand rolled up in this lad's pocket?' Jess said. 'Nicely locked away in our safe, now. What a result!'

'Boom!' Samira said. 'Cops two, villains nil.'

'Sometimes it's all worth it.'

'Certainly is, Sarge.'

A short silence descended.

Jess looked around at the chaotic scenes in the A & E department and blew out her cheeks. 'So . . . obviously being the big boss of a drug dealing empire, Lance won't be too concerned by the loss, will he, Samira?'

'Take it in his stride,' she answered.

Jess snuck a look at Lance's face. The grin had receded slightly.

'Unless of course . . .' she began.

'Unless . . .?' Samira asked.

'Unless Lance here isn't a major drug dealer, you know, not the snake's head.'

'Ooh, that never occurred to me,' Samira said.

'Unless Lance here is at the bottom of the pile and is actually a nothing, a no mark. Unless Lance here is just a gofer, a delivery boy, using a stolen motorcycle – which in itself doesn't actually shout, "Hey, I'm a big nob". It smacks more of someone who's a rubbing rag. I mean, where's the Ferrari?'

'Exactly. Where is it?' Samira asked.

Lance's head had now tilted forwards, his thin chin angled down.

'Unless Lance here is a worthless shitbag,' Jess said, her voice now taking on a serious tone. 'In which case, he isn't the boss, and the actual boss, whoever that is, will probably view the loss of three hundred grands' worth of drugs and a couple of grand rather differently.'

Lance's shoulders drooped as he hunched over, his body language stating how miserable he was.

'Ooh, that could be nasty,' Samira said. 'And messy.'

'Of all the main man drug dealers I've come across, not one has taken kindly to an idiot losing a shedload of drugs to the cops. And you're right, PCSO Patel, sometimes it's very messy indeed. I've seen some of those idiots unable to walk without agonizing pain for the rest of their lives . . . if they're alive to walk, that is.'

'OK, OK, enough!' Lance cut in.

The mouths of the two lady-cops closed.

'You are a real pair of bitches,' Lance told them.

'Nicest thing anyone's ever said to me,' Jess said. 'So, what are you, Lance? Big dealer or small fry, a nothing guy?'

'Nothing guy,' he whispered.

'Pardon?'

'You heard.'

'A nothing guy who also stole a motorbike – my husband's motorbike, at that. Didn't I tell you?'

'Oh hell, totally screwed then.'

'I would say so,' Jess agreed. 'Unless of course . . .' She purposely left her sentence hanging.

'Unless what? I grass?' Lance guessed. 'Not a chance in hell.'

'I wouldn't put it in those terms exactly. More a back-scratching exercise.'

'Uh?'

'You scratch my back and I'll scratch yours. You've heard of that concept?'

'Uh – yeah.' He swallowed. 'How would that work?'

'Quid pro quo.'

'I literally have no idea what that means,' Lance admitted.

'It means this: I assume you personally know every drug dealer in town?'

'I supply 'em.'

'Good. In that case I want the name and address of one particular dealer and in exchange for that I'll talk to the CID about putting lesser charges to you, ensuring you get bail and stuff like that. But I also want the name of your boss so I can start to move up the chain. Otherwise, Lance, you will be charged with every offence I can think of in relation to the supply of drugs, et cetera and I guarantee you will not see the light of day for the next fifteen years. And if you survive clink, you'll come out a pathetic guy in his thirties who has missed the best years of his life. Do it my way, it's eighteen months tops, out in nine for good behaviour.'

'And I'll be a grass.'

'I promise no one will find out but if you don't come across I also promise that every drugs arrest we make over the next year will have your name behind it.'

He rotated his head slowly and glared at Jess. 'You really are a . . .'

'Don't say it again, Lance. Once is enough. So let's begin. Who is your boss? Where is he now? And what is the best time to catch him surrounded by drugs and money?'

Lance's eyes closed despairingly. He sighed heavily, then turned to look at Samira.

'What?' she said.

'Your face is a mess, love. Someone punch it? And did someone punch another cop's lights out, too?'

Samira touched her bruised face gently. 'Why?'

'Because I won't speak his name out loud, but you can use the cover of arresting him for belting two coppers and also, if you time it right, you'll find him in a counting house where he also crashes for the time being. Money and drugs will be stashed there, ready for distribution and pay-offs. That's who my boss is, girls, and I damn well know that if he ever finds out I told you this, I am a dead man walking. And don't ask me who is above him. He's my boss and that's as far as I know, except whoever is above him won't be happy with my losses. So, this is what I want for my information – bail, pending charges, and then I can leg it.'

A nurse came down the corridor. 'Lance Drake? We can see you now.'

FIFTY

'You're looking lovely tonight, Leanora,' Mags said to Mrs Tommy Moss, gritting her teeth behind the compliment.

'How kind . . . although' – Leanora took a sip of her champagne which made her emit a sort of snake-like hissing noise – 'to be fair, you look a bit bedraggled yourself, Margaret. Through a hedge backwards, kind of thing.' She smiled.

Mags felt her phone vibrate in her clutch bag. 'It's a look I try to cultivate,' she countered Leanora, 'one which reflects the way in which I live – in wild abandon, going for what I want and getting it.' She smiled now.

'Yeeesss, exactly.' Now Leanora did not smile. 'The sort of life principles that could get you into serious trouble, you mean?'

'Yeah – but what a way to go!' Mags lifted her phone out of her bag. 'I need to make a call and then, Leanora, with your permission, I need to speak to Tommy in private . . . about business, obviously.'

'What else?' Leanora said with a dash of frost.

As Mags left the room she could feel the laser-like beams of Leanora's searing eyes, frying holes into her shoulder blades. She sashayed out, swinging everything yet she did feel a tiny bit of dread because she was now certain that Mrs Moss knew that Mr Moss was cheating on her, and Mags doubted that knowledge would lead to anything pleasant.

In the hotel corridor she read the newly landed text: *Sir Lancelot has been skewered, together with lots of goodies XXX*. The triple 'X' ensured she knew who it was from, certainly not a lover.

She quickly typed, *Worried?*

No. Will keep an eye.

She didn't bother to respond to this one, but breathed, 'Idiot,' quietly.

Lancelot, aka Lance Drake, was so far down the chain he was in the plughole, so she wasn't worried about it from that angle. However, the word 'Goodies' gave her pause for thought. She knew what Lance was up to, how much gear he was carrying, so although it was an occupational hazard to get arrested (or skewered), a big loss wasn't something she was prepared to accept.

A big loss would mean trouble for Lance.

Along the corridor the door to the gents' toilets opened and Tommy Moss came out just in time to see Mags put her phone back into her bag.

'You know all phones are banned from the meeting, darling. Even yours.'

She pouted.

He wanted to bite her bottom lip. *Now*. But it was all too dangerous.

'What was that about, anyway?' he asked.

'Trouble at t' mill; nowt that can't be handled,' she said. 'Would you like me to give it to you?'

He looked shocked, then grinned. 'Ahh, the phone, you mean?'

'No.' Her eyes roved over him, head to toe. Then she laughed as the door to the conference room opened. Theo stuck his head out. 'Time to crack on, bro,' he said, eyeing Mags and Tommy with amused suspicion.

'Be there in a mo.' Tommy moved to the door but Mags grabbed his arm and pulled him back.

'We need to speak.'

'Later, babe.'

'Now. I have something you need.' She said it playfully again, then from the expression on his face she said seriously, 'Not that. I'm talking information and in return I'm looking for a good deal.'

'What sort of information?'

'The sort of information that will make your daddy very happy.'

FIFTY-ONE

The problem for Jess was that Lance was entitled to a phone call once he was back in the custody office, a call that could potentially alert people Jess did not want to be alerted, so she had to present a convincing case to the custody sergeant and duty inspector to delay that right to him.

But even if Lance was denied his call, there still wasn't a lot of time to play with. The police had to move quickly and justify their actions ultimately to a court, so there was no time for hanging around. Jess had to get things moving.

In order for Lance to get treated at A & E it was necessary to move him to a cubicle and then remove his handcuffs, which Jess did not want. No handcuffs meant he could run better, so Jess made a quiet plea to a nurse who agreed he could have one hand cuffed to the bed frame.

Then she spoke quietly to Samira in the corridor. 'I need to speak to Dougie Doolan, urgently, and also pre-warn the custody sergeant of my intention to request that Lance doesn't get a phone call when we get him back to the cells. Are you OK to stay with him while I nip outside and make the calls?'

'I am. If he tries anything, I donk him,' Samira said.

'Spot on.'

Jess went back in with Samira and had a quiet word in Lance's earhole just so he understood the situation. He seemed to.

Jess then hustled herself outside, took a breath and made two police-related calls. One to the custody office, the next to Dougie Doolan. After those she tried calling Lily on her mobile phone even though she knew it was against school policy to allow use of phones in class. There was no response so she left a voice message telling her she would be running late and for her and Jason to get a taxi after school. Jess had given the kids numbers of two local taxi firms so, hopefully, they wouldn't struggle to book one. Then she apologized profusely before hanging up and striding back inside the hospital.

Lance's treatment – a head X-ray – seemed to take forever and

Jess was almost jigging from one foot to the other as her anxiety grew.

Finally when it was done and he was given the all clear, Jess and Samira raced their prisoner back down to the cells, only to find themselves in a queue of others being booked in. On one hand this was frustrating but on the other, Jess was glad to see this: it meant that despite the outside pressures and vitriol raging against the police, there were still many officers out there who did the job they loved doing knowing, Jess hoped, that this hatred and lack of support for the organization was just a blip in the ocean.

Her biggest disappointment, though, was that Inspector Price was the duty inspector which made Jess less than confident when it came to making her case regarding Lance's phone call.

As they waited in the prisoner queue, Jess spoke into Lance's ear again. 'I want you to tell the custody sergeant you don't want a phone call, OK? If you want this to work in your favour, just say no. At the same time, I'm going to tell the sergeant that I don't want you to have one, either. Got that?'

'Yuh. I just want feeding,' he said. 'So if you sort me a Super Big Mac meal, it's a done deal.'

'You screw me over, Lance, and go back on your word, I'll stuff a triple cheeseburger down your throat.'

'OK,' he said happily. 'Coke Zero, too, by the way. And hash browns.'

Jess slid a tenner to Samira and sent her on the mercy/bribery mission to the fast-food restaurant which was close to the police station. Jess waited in line with her prisoner.

Dougie Doolan took Jess's phone call at his desk in the CID office at Clitheroe and jumped up a little too excitedly, consequently sending an agonizing twinge down his lower back which creased him up and he was forced to support himself on his desk for a while before the pain ebbed and he propelled himself out of the office where he bumped into Dave Simpson who seemed to be hovering in the corridor.

'Dave,' Dougie said, 'we've got an address for Micky Roach.'

'Oh, oh, brilliant! Are we going for him?'

'No, not just yet. I want to wait until Sergeant Raker and PCSO Patel get back. In the meantime, I'm going to get a warrant signed by one of my friendly neighbourhood magistrates and I'm going to put a rapid entry team together so we do it right . . . hopefully it'll all come together in the next couple of hours. You coming along?'

'Absolutely. That git needs pulling in after what he did to Vinnie and Sam. What's the address?'

Dougie almost blabbed it, but something held him back. Normally he would be fine about spreading such information to the troops, but a gut feeling made him hesitate. 'Sorry, nowt personal, Dave, but this one could be a bit delicate.'

'Delicate?' Simpson said in disgust. 'C'mon, mate, we're in this together, aren't we?'

'Course we are, but just be patient. I want to get the warrant sorted and get a team together and an operational order.' Dougie shrugged. 'Just one of those things. Like I said, nothing personal but I do want you along.'

Simpson's glare could have ignited coal, but then he relented. 'OK, fair do's.'

Dougie watched him go, then remembered what he was going to do. Get that warrant signed.

FIFTY-TWO

M ags did have to admit that Billy Moss did have an aura about him. From, she guessed, inheriting, running and overseeing a criminal enterprise which had existed from the Second World War, right up to the end of the twentieth century and now twenty-odd years into this millennium. Quite a feat and one from which Mags thought she could learn with regards to her business.

The conference room had been cleared of everyone other than the key players for this moment. Billy was in his seat at the head of the table, like an old lion leading the pride, but looking unimpressed at each individual until finally resting his eyes on Mags after he'd scanned his sons, Tommy, Trevor and Theo. There was an uncomfortable pause when a dinky waitress dressed in a tiny black skirt and tights appeared with a tray of drinks and deposited it on the table. Mags watched Theo eyeing the girl's every move, all the way around the table up until the point when the door finally closed behind her. Mags felt sympathy for her. She knew what fate awaited her at Theo's hands and cock. Poor lass. Finally the lad's attention returned to the family gathering – plus one: Maggie Horsefield.

Billy scowled, his heavy jowls wobbling, very annoyed by the waitress interruption.

Mags saw the grin on Theo's face and saw his hand move down to, and adjust, his groin area, his thoughts elsewhere.

The boss looked at Mags. Despite her standing within the criminal world, she felt a shimmer of apprehension and hoped the hand she had to deal was as good as a Royal Flush in poker.

She thought it was.

'This better be good,' Billy said. 'To delay a meeting like this.' His voice was a low growl, threatening with a hint of South London in it.

One thing, though, that Mags excelled at, was fighting her corner in a male-dominated world, both literally and metaphorically. It was OK to feel a bit nervy, but she sure as hell wasn't going to let that influence her. She decided to start by putting Billy on the backfoot. 'It will be,' she assured him. 'But before I start, can I be certain this room is safe? Nothing said here will go further and,' she stressed, 'it's not being bugged by the filth, as I think you southerners call the police?'

Billy looked mortified.

Good, Mags thought.

'I can assure you of those things,' Billy said. He looked at each of his sons, all of whom nodded. 'We've had the place swept for any devices. We're clear.'

'In that case, I'll begin,' Mags said as if addressing a class of children, although the faces of the Moss family were not bearing expressions of expectation. Theo was distracted by his lustful thoughts, Trevor looked bored and Tommy looked as though he wanted to shag her. Most importantly, though, Billy looked challenging and he was the one she spoke to directly. 'Billy, I'm so sorry for your loss and that I haven't been able to say that to you before now. I know Terry was a beloved son—'

'Get on with it,' he said, cutting her short.

'OK. I hear that the police officer who coldly, brutally shot Terry down, this female cop, appears to be difficult to trace. I understand you have someone working on this, but I believe I have information which will expedite this process.'

Billy leaned forwards, interest now stirring a little.

'However, you and I are in business here, first and foremost,' Mags cautioned.

'What do you want?' he asked coldly.

'A much better deal all around. Ten per cent better for the information I have – for the next twelve months, that's all, not forever.' Mags, if nothing else, was a realist.

Billy's head almost came off as he threw it back and laughed at that outrageous demand which Mags knew would not be accepted, at least not straight away.

'Not a chance,' Billy confirmed after his eruption. 'Two per cent. Six months.'

'Five per cent. One year.'

'Two and a half. Three months.'

'Four per cent. One year. Final offer.' Even that would line her pockets to the tune of an extra twelve thousand a month. Serious money.

'OK.' Billy relented begrudgingly. 'But only if what you tell me will lead me straight to this cop.' That was the small print.

'And I need a reassurance that whatever action you choose to take will never, ever rebound on me. No link, no trail.'

'There won't be. There won't even be a link back to me,' Billy said. 'We're a year down the line from Terry's unjustified killing and I've made no attempt at retribution against the cops, so why would I start now? Terry is dead and buried and the law said it was justifiable homicide. Who am I to argue?'

'In that case,' Mags said, taking an intake of breath, 'the cop you are seeking is called Sergeant Jessica Raker. I've got some inside information on her. She's now on my patch and from my sources it seems her appearance and background have been kept secret; no one knows anything about her past. Except me. We were both brought up in Clitheroe and our daughters go to the same school now, so I know that she was living in London and working for the Met until she suddenly moved back up here. She took the job with no notice, a job another cop was in line for. I even know exactly where she lives. And the thing is, Billy, if you take her out you'd also be doing me a favour. She's too damn keen and could be a thorn in my side. I want people on the inside I can control.'

Billy nodded, looked at Tommy. 'You get together with her' – he jerked his head at Mags – 'see what she has, then you set The Saint

to do the dirty work. No comebacks on us. Clean. Tidy. No
witnesses.'

'Understood.' Tommy nodded.

'Now – can we please get today back on track?' Billy said.

As if on cue, the door opened and the delegates who had been
kept out of the room sauntered in and took their places around the
table. The waitress Theo had lusting eyes for also came in and
cleared away the empty glasses on the same tray on which they had
been delivered. She left with a nice sway of her bum for Theo.

Five minutes later, she was gone completely.

Mags needed an urgent pee break. She made her excuses and dashed
to the ladies. Whilst perched on the loo she had her phone out,
checking for messages or missed calls. A text landed from 'XXX'.

It read, 'BIG trouble.'

She frowned and dialled the number whilst her knickers were
still around her ankles.

'What?' she asked.

She listened, then said, 'Sort it and there's a big bonus in it and
I mean big. But I also mean sort it.'

FIFTY-THREE

D ougie Doolan had done magnificently, Jess thought. Within
the space of a couple of hours he managed to get the
promised search warrant signed, even though, at a pinch,
they could have used the failing to appear warrant which still existed,
even though they couldn't find a physical copy of it.

The new warrant was a good one, though, covering a search for
drugs, drugs paraphernalia, money, account books and anything else
that might be related to drug supply and distribution. It was pretty
much a catch-all which meant the place where Micky was supposed
to be could be torn apart legitimately. The failing to appear warrant
didn't give such powers.

Dougie had also roughly drafted an operational order, much of
it a tick-box exercise, but very necessary when everything the police
did was open to challenge somewhere down the line. Jess had a lot

of experience with operational orders, appreciated what Dougie had achieved, and sitting at his desk with him looking over her shoulder, she went through it until she was fully satisfied, then printed it off and signed it. One thing she didn't like was the thought of going blind into a premises, but Dougie assured her, from his own experience, that there would be nothing at the flat which would cause the entry team a problem. The team would just have to exercise the usual care in checking for any nasty surprises that Micky might have laid in wait for them.

Jess was also impressed that Dougie had managed to gather a nice number of officers for the entry and search. Half a Support Unit team – six beefy cops who specialized in forced entry – plus an Armed Response vehicle with a pair of tooled-up cops just to hang back in case. There was nothing to suggest that Micky would be in possession of a firearm, but you never knew. The ARV was mentioned in the Operational Order and their presence had been sanctioned by the divisional commander. Four uniformed officers from Blackburn had also been brought in to make up numbers, supporting the local ones which included Dave Simpson, two PCs who were on the afternoon shift, Samira and another PCSO – plus Jess and Dougie.

The Support Unit would force a fast entry, then step aside to allow the local cops in, led by Jess with Samira at her shoulder.

That was the plan, anyway.

Jess sat back in Dougie's desk chair and exhaled. He suddenly held his back and winced with an 'Umph' noise.

'You OK, Dougie?'

'Yeah, yeah, Sarge. Age, y'know. Everything hurts from dawn to dusk and beyond.'

'I know it well,' she confessed. 'Anyway, this all looks great,' she said of the Operational Order. 'No reason for it not to be straightforward. If anyone else is there with Micky, they get locked up too. Could be a good bust, this.'

'It might open floodgates,' Dougie said.

'Or at least give the local drug trade a kick in the nuts.' Jess pressed the 'print' button again and a dozen orders began clattering out of the printer.

The last time she had been involved in any sort of briefing had been a year earlier at New Cross police station in South London on that fateful day – and she couldn't but think of it as anything but *the* fateful day – when her professional and personal lives came crashing down around her ears. 'Hm,' she said inwardly.

Dougie hobbled across to the printer and started stapling the orders together.

'Is everyone ready?' Jess asked him.

'Yep. Inspector Price has rocked up too.' He looked at her, stapler in hand, knowing through the CID grapevine – probably the most efficient rumour factory in any force – that she and Price had not gelled in any way. 'Thought you'd want to know.'

'Cheers. Reckon he'll be arsy with me?'

Dougie considered this, then shook his head.

'Good.' Actually Jess had been surprised at Blackburn nick where she and Samira had been dealing with Lance Drake and Price had appeared and been fairly amicable and supportive about the request to delay Lance's phone call. He had questioned her intently and professionally about it, as he should have done, but he'd been happy to authorize the delay, yet there had been something about his demeanour that slightly unsettled Jess, something just not right. As it happened, he hadn't held anything up. 'I need to make a quick call before the briefing, if that's OK?'

'Kids?'

'Yep, kids.' Jess stood up and went into the corridor. She had texted Lily and Jason a few times without any response. Not unusual for the pouty, Little Miss Up-Her-Own-Chuffer Lily (and Jess asked the lord for forgiveness on that summation of her daughter who she loved to the moon and beyond) but Jason was usually fairly responsive, so that worried Jess slightly.

This time she rang Lily, got no reply.

Then Jason. No reply either.

Both calls went to voicemail and she left a terse message on each. 'Call me now!'

To her astonishment Jason came back with a text: 'Both OK.' And that was it.

'*Breathe*,' she instructed herself like a yoga teacher.

'You OK?' Dougie asked from the CID office.

She pulled herself together, brushed down mentally, got a grip, turned to the detective. 'You betcha I am.'

FIFTY-FOUR

T he shop above which Micky Roach was supposed to be living at was one of the kind Jess referred to as 'Tat'. According to Dougie it had changed ownership and use many times over the past few years and to the best of his knowledge it was self-contained on the ground floor with no access to the flat above, so in terms of an escape route for Roach he would be unable to use that means; he could, however, use the window on the first floor that overlooked Castle Street.

With that possibility in mind – and Jess had seen wanted people leap from even greater heights to avoid capture – two officers were detailed to make their way discreetly to the shop front and linger under the window just in case.

The briefing went well as far as Jess was concerned. She was not remotely cowed or intimidated by the fact that every officer on the operation was a man – except for herself and Samira. Jess was right in the vortex of her own environment, loved doing stuff like this. Loved it.

She went through the details as she knew them and could tell each officer was listening to her. She went through the tactics, which were straightforward: the covering of the front possible escape route, the entry by the Support Unit and the fact they had to take care because Roach was known to be violent towards police. She stressed that officer safety came first, that body cams should be activated and to remain one hundred per cent professional.

She concluded, 'Any questions?'

There were none.

Jess raised her eyes towards Inspector Price who lounged indolently at the back with one of those 'come on, impress me, girl' looks that were still a feature of police life. She gave him a pointed look and her expression asked, 'Well, mate?'

She almost smiled when he lowered his eyes.

'OK, folks, let's go. Remember – cams on, safety and professionalism.'

With a few laughs and some muttered remarks, they all stood up and made their way to the vehicles out back whilst the two officers on below-window duty set off on foot towards their destination. Once they were in position, the operation would begin.

It went brilliantly.

Jess was behind the Support Unit as they quietly climbed the steep wooden steps leading up to the door of Roach's flat and arranged themselves on either side of the door. Two officers equipped with manual battering rams or, more informally, 'big red keys', took a step back and on a descending finger count by their sergeant, swung them backwards in unison and then smashed the door open easily. The two officers stood aside and four raced into the flat shouting warnings, fully prepared to tackle whatever might be encountered.

Jess waited for the 'all clear' shout. She didn't want to get in the way and was puzzled when everything went quiet. It seemed extremely odd until the moment the SU sergeant stuck his head back round the door and beckoned to her. 'You'd best come in.'

She entered the flat and saw Micky Roach's body on the floor, limbs twisted grotesquely, with blood pooled under his head, neck and shoulders from a deep wound right around his throat which she knew must have been caused by a wire garrotte.

'He's dead,' the sergeant confirmed to her.

Jess nodded and said to him, 'Clear the room, please. This is now a crime scene.'

She waited as the Support Unit team withdrew, then she radioed through to Dougie Doolan who had been waiting at his desk with his PR propped up on his CID desk diary.

'Doug, you need to get here now. You know those sexy murders that only happen somewhere else? Now there's one in Clitheroe for you. Yeah . . . Micky Roach . . . strangled to death by the looks of it.'

Jess glanced around the scene, knowing she too had to withdraw and seal it but as her eyes took in everything, she saw something glinting on a battered armchair by the front window, tucked down between the seat cushion and arm rest.

She moved delicately over to it, pulling on a pair of disposable gloves. She ensured her bodycam was recording and what she did next was recorded with her commentary as she reached down for the thing and pulled it out and found it to be a key fob with two car keys attached to it. She held it up to see it better and read the words on the tab written in felt-tip pen and said, 'No shit,' before remembering that everything she did and said was being recorded.

It was another two hours before Jess could get away. She took initial charge of the scene until the first pair of CSIs arrived, closely followed by Dougie Doolan and the on-call DCI who demanded she give him everything she knew about Roach, which was of course precious little because she had never met the guy and had been in post less than a week – although by now, to her, it felt much, much longer.

By the time she had completed the practicalities of protecting a murder scene, something she'd done on numerous occasions on the streets of London, it was just gone nine p.m.

Yet, although home was calling, she still wanted to have a quiet word with Dougie and Samira, and back at the station she managed to usher them out into the privacy of the yard for a chat.

'I know I shouldn't have, Dougie, and grass on me if you want, but I took this sneaky photo.' She produced her phone and showed Dougie a picture of the key fob she'd found at Roach's flat. 'I wouldn't have done it if I'd thought it was crucial to the actual crime scene.'

Dougie looked, not quite understanding its importance until he enlarged the image using his finger and thumb on the screen. 'The hit-and-run!' he gasped.

'Yep. The old guy on Edisford Road, the job Vinnie is looking into,' Jess said.

'This is insane!' Dougie said, shocked.

The photo showed two Peugeot ignition keys on a fob that read: *Salah's Garage, Whitebirk, Blackburn* and gave a telephone number plus the words: *Peugeot 406, Dk blue, 2001* and a registration number.

Dougie passed the phone to Samira.

'Vinnie told me a similar car had been reported stolen from a forecourt in Blackburn,' Jess said. 'Which begs the question: why is Micky Roach in possession of the keys and the fob which was probably hanging from the car dealer's hooks inside an office, maybe inside a locked cupboard or safe, perhaps?'

'Maybe Roach didn't steal the car at all,' Samira suggested.

'Maybe he was given it,' Jess added.

'Yep, but whatever,' Dougie said, 'Micky Roach looks like he has the keys for a vehicle responsible for killing that old guy.'

'But now he, too, is dead,' Samira said sombrely.

'An old guy who was on the waiting list for Pendle View,' Jess said.

'We need to go back to the dealer for a start,' Dougie said, 'and ask some questions.'

'And we could do with recovering the car – or what's left of it,' Jess said.

'How do we do that?' Samira asked.

'Vinnie was checking car breakers. It may have ended up at Primrose Wreckers, so we need to get that checked ASAP,' Jess said.

'Which is owned by Maggie Horsefield,' Dougie said.

'Really?' Jess said. 'And whose father is on the waiting list for Pendle View, and who has now been bumped up two places with that hit-and-run and Bart Morrison's murder.'

Dougie nodded, taking this all in. Then, brilliantly, he said, 'Coincidence?'

'My arse!' Jess snorted derisively. 'I've crapped better coincidences!' she blurted. Then she said, 'Pardon my lingo and excuse the fact that what I just said doesn't really make sense.'

'You're forgiven, Sarge,' Samira said. 'I'm always crapping coincidences.'

They all laughed. It was a welcome release from the build-up of tension gripping them.

'I think we all need to get home, get our heads down and have an early morning meet-up for a little strategy about this,' Jess suggested, 'and link in with whatever's happening re Micky Roach. I think it might be as well to be armed with a warrant when we go to the breaker's yard, and also pay a visit to the car dealer in Whitebirk who has some tricky questions to answer.'

'I'll sort the warrant for the breaker,' Dougie promised.

'OK, folks, let's call it a day. I'm off to see what exactly my children are up to.'

FIFTY-FIVE

The crime strategy meeting went well once the private matter had been addressed. New county lines were ironed out, new ideas tossed around, more percentages worked out, although the deal that Mags had come to with Billy was never discussed. That was solely between her and the Moss gang, no one else needed to know a thing.

There was a big Chinese banquet at the end of the day, when too many crackers, spring rolls and Cantonese curries were eaten, and Chinese beer drunk.

Mags was very much the honey pot to which the other men were attracted, and all assumed that a few choice words and winning smiles would be enough to entice her away into a bed chamber.

Mags did not drink alcohol that evening. She knew she had to keep her wits about her because she didn't trust any of them not to try and force themselves on her. That's how they were: expectant of their powers. That didn't stop her flirting dirtily, playing along with them but making it clear that was as far as it went.

All the while, though, her eyes kept flitting to Tommy – and his to her – even though his wife clung desperately to him like a sad limpet.

'Pathetic,' Mags muttered under her breath as she watched Tommy peel Leanora from around his neck, not for the first time. His eyes caught hers just at the moment Mags was detaching herself from a young buck down from the North East who she did not know well but who was becoming a little too unpleasant and insistent in his advances, talking about having an older woman like her and speculating whether she'd had 'tightening' surgery down below to complement her obvious boob job. He bragged that he would be able to burst any stitching.

Mags forced him away roughly and stalked out of the banqueting suite to the ladies' loo down the corridor. Exhaling, cross, she settled herself down in a cubicle for a wee and to check her phone on which there was just one text from an unknown number which read:

Done XXX. She smiled and deleted it. There was nothing else on the phone and as she sat there with her lacy panties around her ankles she wondered what mess she would have to sort when she got home tomorrow. Just as long as the job had been done, all would be good and she would be well out of the equation.

She heard the door of the ladies open and close, then footsteps, soft ones. She hoped she wasn't going to be accosted by Mrs Tommy Moss again. She was about to pull up her knickers when the cubicle door crashed open, knocking her back on to the loo. Standing there menacingly, leaning on the door frame, was the man she had just escaped from.

He had an expression on his face she recognized all too well.

Drunken lust. Entitlement.

And body language she also recognized.

Shoulders hunched forwards. Threat. Bad intentions.

'Mrs Moss told me you need fettling,' he growled, slurring his words. 'And I agree. I mean, how long is it since you've had anything worthwhile up there, old lady?'

You'd be surprised, she thought as she slid her hand surreptitiously into her clutch bag whilst her eyes and his were locked. Her fingers circled around the handle of the stiletto she always carried in there for defensive purposes.

'You need to back off while the going's good,' Mags warned him in a flat, unemotional voice. 'I don't do rape.'

'That's where you and me differ, babe.' He grinned and as a statement of intent he reached down and slowly unzipped his chinos.

Mags sighed. 'Just don't. One way or another this will not end well.' She kicked her knickers off from around her ankles and began to rise slowly from the toilet seat. She supported her clutch bag with her left hand, her right still inside it, gripping the knife. It was her intention to simply show it to him and hope he got the hint, but he moved as fast as a blur at her, covering the one-stride gap in a microsecond, his right hand shooting out, fingers grabbing her neck and forcing her backwards into the corner of the cubicle, crashing her skull against the wall.

A moment later the man emitted a grunt of surprise. His fingers relaxed and let go of her neck and he stepped back a pace, looking down his body with wide eyes at the fast-spreading blood stain on his tight shirt, just below his ribs where the stiletto had penetrated and been withdrawn.

He became limp and wilted to his knees, gripping the toilet for support, his eyes wide open in terror and realization.

Mags did a delicate sidestep over him, picking up her knickers, then backed out of the cubicle and watched the young man's nerve-twitching body as the life flowed out of him and the beat of his heart stopped and his blood poured down him, puddling around his knees, running under the cubicle divider into the adjoining one.

Then she looked at the knife in her hand . . . which was suddenly plucked from her grasp and, in a haze, she found herself being bundled out of the toilets. She resisted at first and then not as she heard Tommy's voice cajoling her along, saw his face close to hers as she craned around, then felt his strong arm around her, supporting her, keeping her moving through a fire escape, into the car park, and finally she was lifted into the back of a car with Tommy saying, 'I'll fix this, I'll fix this,' into her ear.

FIFTY-SIX

Jess called Lily and Jason as she drove out of Clitheroe towards Chatburn but got no reply. Even though she knew they could take care of themselves, as a mum she couldn't help but be worried, verging on frantic. Suppose something had happened? Suppose Lily had been lured away by Mags's daughter and was currently smoking crack in some hellhole?

Put those damned thoughts out of your mind, Jess chastised herself.

However . . . they lingered.

She drove along a road that was becoming very familiar to her now: out of Clitheroe, through Chatburn, on to the A59, then through Sawley and up to Bolton-by-Bowland where she managed to find a parking spot fairly near to the cottage as the usual space out front was taken up by a Ford Focus she didn't recognize. By now, Jess knew every regular vehicle in the village and this Ford wasn't one of them. As she drove past the cottage, she saw the lights were on, intimating that the kids were home.

Warily she walked back, then up the short path to the front door. Glancing through the window she could see the TV was on but because the curtains had been partly drawn, couldn't see what else was going on unless she put her nose right up to the glass.

She stepped through the vestibule, then into the living room.

Yes, the TV was on: a noisy Tom Cruise film playing.

Lily and Jason were sprawled on the settee whilst helping themselves to slices of two huge pizzas in boxes on the coffee table which had obviously been delivered, plus a huge bottle of cola, already half-drunk.

And in the middle of the two kids sat Josh who was first to notice Jess's presence. He jumped to his feet, beaming. 'Jess! Babe!'

Lily and Jason looked around, saw her, then their attention flipped back to the TV screen.

Josh stepped over the kids' legs and, arms open, went to Jess, who growled, 'What the hell's going on?' under her breath.

Instantly deflated, Josh said, 'Whaddya mean?'

'C'mere.' Jess crooked her finger, beckoning him to follow her outside, her expression leaving him no choice in the matter. Shoulders drooping, he followed.

On the TV, Tom Cruise was carrying out a dangerous manoeuvre in a high-powered jet fighter that screamed across the screen.

Jess spun to face Josh outside. 'Like I said, what's going on?'

Josh half-shrugged, trying to find the words. 'I hired a car in Manchester, managed to sneak off early and thought I'd surprise the kids and pick them up from school.'

'Without telling me?'

'I told them not to. It would be a surprise for you, too.'

Jess took a steadying breath, hoping to control what came out next. 'I've been run ragged at work today and at the same time I've been texting and calling them like mad, Josh, and all the while you've been here with them, treating them to pizzas and coke and a film! Any other pressies for them?'

'I bought Lily a necklace and Jason a football.'

'Marvellous. You really take the biscuit.'

'I bought you some Chanel.'

Jess stopped. Her jaw was rotating, nostrils dilating with anger. Then she said, 'Don't think they'll be fooled by you, Josh. They'll see right through you. They'll take what you give them cos they're kids but a surprise pick-up from school and not allowing them to call me will not impress them. And why the hell did you even think of Chanel? If you knew me, you'd know I don't even use the stuff.'

Jess barged past him into the house, pulling off her jacket and tossing it under the stairs, plonking herself down between Lily and Jason and grabbing a big slice of New York Special pizza because she was ravenous.

'This looks a good film,' she said, seeing Tom Cruise now flying upside down in his jet.

'It's brill, Mum,' Jason agreed. He hunched up to her, hip to hip. On the floor she saw a football, still in its packaging. On her other side, Lily snuggled in tightly too and held out her wrist on which the new bracelet was displayed. It looked nice and expensive.

'I like it,' Jess said. She had never once said anything disrespectful or nasty about Josh to the children and never would. 'You had a good day at school?'

Jason, with a mouthful of pizza and his attention on the film, just nodded.

'It was OK,' Lily said.

Obviously with a not well-thought-out agenda, Jess asked her, 'And how's your new chum, Caitlin?'

'OK,' Lily said, inspecting her new jewellery with pleasure.

'Did she get picked up from school by her mum?'

'Nah. She's away on business. She got a taxi. Why?'

'Nothing, nothing,' Jess said airily and took a bite of the pizza which tasted amazing. She glanced over to Josh who was standing by the door looking like he didn't want to be there. 'There's a bottle of white wine in the fridge. Get me a glass, will you?' Jess asked him with a smile as she chewed a chunk of peperoni.

FIFTY-SEVEN

Detective Superintendent Jack Marsh, seconded to the National Crime Agency, knew he was taking a huge gamble putting anyone undercover ever again to gather information and intelligence on the Moss Brothers crime family. They were extremely violent, nasty people as had been shown by their treatment of the undercover cop who had been found brutally murdered on the banks of the Thames. It had been impossible to prove anything against the Moss gang but another undercover officer had been quickly extracted because of it.

Marsh also believed the gang were responsible for the murder of DCI Costigan in central London, but again that was purely conjecture.

The Moss gang was, as one of Marsh's colleagues colourfully described it, 'Tighter than a duck's arse.'

He had to agree.

But the gang was number one on Marsh's to-do list and he wasn't about to let go of them as long as he remained in law enforcement. He wanted to bring them down, but wasn't sure how this would ever be achieved.

He had a pair of intelligence analysts dedicated solely to collecting every speck of information that could possibly be linked to Billy Moss and his three remaining bastards of sons, and report anything back to him. Not least because he still believed that the threat from the Moss's in relation to Jessica Raker still existed, even a year down the line. He knew they had long memories, played the long game.

He hated them.

When his analysts picked up a thread of intel from various forces across the country that there was to be some kind of meeting of criminal heads somewhere in the South Midlands which might include the Mosses, Marsh was very interested. Despite Marsh authorizing his 'two geeks' (as he lovingly called the analysts) as much overtime as they wanted, intelligence was sparse. That is until they came across these snippets from a few gangs known to have dealings with the Moss gang, who were heading to a luxury hotel somewhere near Oxford.

Marsh knew he was taking a leap, but quite often good detective work involved stepping across the void.

A hurried, clandestine trip to the hotel and a word in the manager's ear revealed a mini-convention of sorts was due to take place imminently. The booking had been made by one of the Moss gang's legitimate subsidiary companies for ten luxury suites, though no names were mentioned in the booking.

Following several hastily convened meetings between the NCA, the Met and Thames Valley Police (which covered Oxford), it was decided to take a chance and put someone in. The method was simple enough. Because hotels often employed temporary staff, it was just a question of who, how and when.

Using his extensive police contacts, Marsh made some very urgent enquiries and came up with an answer – who he was now looking at, slightly open-mouthed and, despite the age difference, a little breathlessly, although he didn't let it show.

DC Angie Thomas was twenty-four years old and, although Marsh didn't want to go there, was the girl of his dreams in terms of her looks.

Except he knew she had been approached very early on in her career after being identified as a possible undercover cop who, firstly, couldn't possibly be a cop and secondly would be useless undercover.

Neither of which was true, as Marsh knew full well.

The very pretty, shapely, demure young lady had been the biggest thief-taker of them all during her first two years of service in uniform in the rough house that was Cardiff city centre. She held her own. Overpowered more big men than most other male cops and had an eye for a crim. She was always underestimated by people who didn't know her, much to their subsequent humiliation.

Her qualities as an undercover cop after training were very evident and she proved ideal to be parachuted into short-term situations such as the Oxford meeting because mostly, things like that involved men who might well have been as hard as nails and wary career crims, but rarely suspected pretty girls of being undercover cops who were usually considered airhead females.

Then, job done, she was gone with the wind, leaving her target none the wiser.

'I didn't think I'd be hearing from you so soon,' Marsh told her. They were at a fast-food restaurant on a motorway service area near Birmingham. It was close to midnight.

'I thought it best, boss.'

'So, go on,' he encouraged her.

'Well, firstly there was a big meeting of criminals and I've managed to identify most of them, though strangely,' she smirked, 'I could not find a written agenda.'

Marsh half-smiled too at the thought of a conference of crims with a written circulated agenda. Although he did know of some very high-level crime bosses who had been ruined by accurate record keeping.

Thomas continued, 'The main meeting was about to get underway when it was suddenly delayed by Tommy Moss who I just caught whispering to Billy – and then suddenly there was just Billy, Tommy, the other two sons and a woman who I was unable to ID having a meeting of their own.'

'A woman?' Marsh asked, his eyes narrowing.

'Yeah, mid-to-late thirties, bit of a boob job, heavily made-up, a looker once-over,' Thomas described her.

'No ideas?'

She shook her head. 'Northern accent, though.'

Marsh wondered if this was significant.

'Anyway, it all seemed very urgent. So I took a bit of a punt and went in and served them drinks, just the Moss gang and this woman around the table. They went schtum when I was there.'

'So you didn't hear anything?'

'I didn't – but I hope to hell this did.'

She reached down beside her into a rucksack on the floor from which she pulled out a round drinks tray. She placed it top down on the table between them, slid her thumb across the centre of the base of the tray and opened a wafer-thin slot, less than two milli-metres deep in which sat a tiny SD card.

With her long nails, Thomas picked the card out of the recess and held it in the palm of her hand. 'This whole tray is locked and loaded,' she explained. 'There are a couple of tiny mics hidden in the rim and this little beauty is designed to record any conversations within a five-metre radius. I left it in the middle of the conference table after I'd given out drinks and collected it after the confidential chat. So, hopefully . . .' She shrugged. 'Sometimes it's brill, some-times not, but I figured it was worth a try to find out what was going on. Let's see.'

'I don't have the equipment to listen to it,' Marsh said. 'Not here, anyway.'

Thomas reached back into the rucksack and pulled out a media player about the size of an iPod.

There was a slot in one end into which she inserted the card, pressed a few buttons and then plugged in a set of earphones which she gave to Marsh.

He fitted them. She pressed play and he concentrated hard. The recording wasn't brilliant, the clarity came and went, some words and phrases were indistinct, hard to understand and would need further analysis.

But some things did stand out.

The name Jessica Raker.

And, more terrifyingly as far as Marsh was concerned, the mention of another name.

'Jeez!' Marsh said as he yanked out the earphones. He knew he had gone pale. And he felt nauseous.

Thomas looked at him. 'What?'

'The Saint.'

FIFTY-EIGHT

Because Micky Roach's death was a meaty affair, a full-scale murder investigation was launched by FMIT, headed by a very self-important detective superintendent. A murder squad then moved into the cramped CID office, pushing all the desks to the side of the room, including Dougie Doolan's despite the look of annoyance on his face. Suddenly the police station was an ants' nest.

Jess wasn't surprised to get sidelined once she'd briefed the detective super about Roach, information which included the Peugeot key ring and the suggestion it would be worthwhile to get some experienced detectives to interview Lance Drake who was still in custody at Blackburn. Any promises Jess had made to him were now no longer applicable following Roach's murder and it seemed obvious that Lance's knowledge would be worth mining even though Jess was sure the lad was nothing more than a low-level grifter and little else. He did jobs for cash, asked no questions, lived hand-to-mouth like so many others at that level in the drugs trade. Many, Jess knew, would be better off as shelf-stackers in supermarkets although most didn't have the self-discipline to be reliable.

The superintendent promised he would 'action' Jess's information which meant that once a functioning Major Incident Room (MIR) was established, jobs would be allocated to detectives. Jess knew that forensic and CSI teams were working the scene of the murder and that the Support Unit – who also specialized in crime scene searching – were already deployed and house-to-house enquiries were due to commence around the town centre.

Jess was laid-back about all this. She wasn't a detective, she was a pro-active response and community sergeant and so far, in her first week in that job, she hadn't been able to draw breath, get her feet under the table and start doing the job properly. She'd had notice that her presence was required at a parish council meeting out in Longridge next week and, incredibly, that thought really excited and terrified her in equal parts.

Vinnie was back at work, looking battered still but fine and was buzzing about the car key find at Micky Roach's flat and raring to go and visit the car dealer in Blackburn and Primrose Wreckers, though Jess told him he had to hang fire for the moment whilst the murder squad sorted out their investigative strategy.

He looked crestfallen and Jess said she would try to get the superintendent to allocate an action for him to follow up. That seemed to appease him a little.

'When the big boys move in, Vinnie, us minnows end up in the muddy water.' She bulled him up. 'You have the makings of a good detective, so, my advice, for what it's worth, is watch and learn while all this is happening here.'

'Understood. And anyway, if you don't mind, I'd like to go and have another look at that misper in Dunsop Bridge.'

'Go for it,' Jess said. 'Oh, I need to do a return-to-work interview with you today, sometime.'

'I'm fine, honest.'

'I know that, you know that, but HR need to be assured of it – health, safety and welfare and all that. We'll do it later.'

'World's gone mad – and I say that as a twenty-three-year-old!'

'You're not wrong,' Jess said, looking at her desk and the pile of equipment still to be straightened and put away that had been scattered there since Monday morning.

That would be her first job so that the office at least looked professional. She was doing this when Samira came in looking bright and fresh.

'Morning, Sergeant Raker,' she said, bubbly.

'Hi, Samira. You OK?'

'Not bad, thanks.'

'Good to hear,' Jess said, although she got the feeling that all wasn't as it should be.

'I see the lunatics have taken over the asylum.' Samira jerked her eyes upwards to indicate the noisy assembly of detectives drafted in. There was a lot of foot-clomping going on, plus the usual aroma of bacon, sausages and coffee.

'Do bacon sandwiches offend you?' Jess asked seriously.

'Nah, not in the least. I don't eat it, obviously, but I say each to their own.'

'OK. I'm assuming you know we've been sidelined at the moment but it won't do any harm if you still pay attention to Pendleton and keep knocking on doors as regards Bart Morrison. Keep a visible presence. It must be disquieting to have someone murdered on the doorstep. Drive up, stroll round this morning and afternoon, yeah?'

'I'll do that, Sarge, and oh . . .' Samira started to say something and her demeanour changed from bright to serious. But before she could begin, there was a rap on the office door behind her.

It was Dave Simpson. He'd managed to snaffle one of the bacon sandwiches from upstairs and was folding it messily into his mouth. 'Sorry, Sarge,' he apologized, talking through his chewing.

Jess saw a look of absolute disapproval verging on hatred on Samira's face and didn't like what she was witnessing.

'I'll tell you later, Sarge,' Samira said and retreated from the office. Simpson stood aside, grinning and eating with his mouth open, something anyone would find offensive.

'Shut your mouth when you eat!' Jess snapped at him.

'Sorry, Sarge,' he replied, wiping his mouth with the back of his hand, leaving a smear of ketchup on it.

Jess shoved her police jumper into her locker and said, 'Inappropriate, Dave.'

'What?' he whined innocently. His mouth drooped open again to reveal a mashed-up combination of bread, bacon and saliva.

Jess turned to him slowly. 'If you tease Samira again about her religion, I'll nail your career to the carpet, Dave. Promise. One and only warning.'

The two of them held each other's gaze for a very icy few seconds before Simpson swallowed, spun and left without a further word. A shiver ran through Jess, knowing further trouble was going to come between him and her. As she hung a spare uniform shirt in the locker she wondered how she was going to sort him out but knew it wasn't an option.

Out in the corridor Simpson scoffed the last corner of his free sandwich, and stood to one side as Dougie Doolan walked past with an affable nod.

Simpson strolled away, checking one of the two extra mobile phones he always carried with him. He was expecting a very urgent call, a request, he didn't know who from and didn't know exactly what it would be or what he would be expected to do, but he did know it would be a big payday and would involve Sergeant Jess Raker.

FIFTY-NINE

Tommy Moss sat on the edge of the twin bed in the hotel room and watched Mags worriedly as she dressed in the tight jeans and T-shirt he had bought for her.

'I'm fine. Honestly,' she said, irritated at his fussing. She slid her feet into a pair of flat shoes he'd also bought. 'I know it's not often I have to knife someone for trying to rape me in a toilet cubicle, but hey! Shit happens and you've gotta deal with it.' She slid her hands into the denim jacket, also bought by Tommy, and looked critically at herself in the full-length mirror inlaid into the wardrobe door. Not her usual guise, but she quite liked what she saw, though there was a slight regret in not instructing Tommy to get her some high-heeled cowboy boots to finish off the look.

'What was it all about, again?' Tommy asked, screwing up his face.

'A drunken guy with a hard on who thought he could get away with it. Y'know, the big "I am",' Mags explained for the nth time but again wasn't sure why she didn't tell Tommy the exact words the guy had blurted out about Leanora Moss telling him that she, Mags, needed fettling. It felt wiser to keep that arrow in the quiver. It might come in useful at some stage because Mags was one hundred per cent certain she and Leanora had unfinished business which wouldn't be pretty.

That said, she was glad that Tommy had appeared in the toilets when he had, to pluck her out of a very horrible situation.

It had all been a bit of a blur.

Tommy had quickly arranged for her to be driven to a nearby hotel – not the one where they'd had their lovers' tryst – where he bundled her into a very iffy room, helped her strip and got her into the shower with instructions to take a very long time over washing herself from head to toe, then to wrap herself in a dry bath towel.

He'd scooped up her clothing and disappeared with it.

He was away for over five hours before returning with the brand-new set of clothes by which time Mags was in bed, half-cut after draining the mini bar of its spirits.

Now it was the morning after.

'So what did you do last night?' Mags asked him. 'Pray tell.'

'Shut down the meeting, cleared the lot of them out, no explana-tions given, shifted the body – which has now been fed through a stone-crusher – and got our clearing guys in to sort the scene, which is now pristine.'

'And my attacker? Isn't he going to be missed? Aren't questions going to be asked?'

'Unlikely, but if we have to quash anything, then we will,' Tommy said with confidence.

'Promise?' Mags pouted. She stood in front of him and lifted his chin in the palm of her hand, looked deep into his eyes.

'Yes,' he said, the word catching in his throat as he slid his hands around her arse and eased her towards him. Then his fingers moved to the front and began to lower the zip on her jeans – but she caught them tight.

'No,' she said firmly despite herself. There was so much tension inside her she thought she was going to burst and having a big sexual blowout with Tommy would have been a great release. 'I need to get home. Things to sort.'

'Yeah, I get it, but . . .' he moaned.

'Things which include your family business, I might remind you.'

'Yeah, yeah.' He dropped his hands on to his thighs.

'And that guy? Definitely road fill?'

'Already under.'

'Good. Now take me to my car. I want to pick my daughter up from school this afternoon.'

'Then we'll talk?' Tommy asked hopefully.

Mags said, 'No, we won't. Normal business resumed between you and me, Tommy. Your life, my life. Occasionally meeting for business and fucking, nothing else. That's how it has to be.'

'You're right,' he demurred reluctantly.

'So be a good boy, go back to Leanora and give her one from

me, eh?' Mags raised his chin again, winked salaciously and made a double-clicking noise with her tongue.

Tommy drove her to her car and not long after Mags was on the M6 heading north, wondering what sort of shitshow awaited her back home. One thing she was certain of was that she was far enough removed from it all for it not to be a direct problem for her. Low-level pushers were always unreliable. The other thought swirling around was that although she insisted she and Tommy were back to what they had been – no stupid emotional entanglements – she had not even started with Leanora.

SIXTY

That day for Jess did prove to be much less frenetic than the previous ones and did allow her to get her feet under the table and do what she called 'sergeanty things'.

Not being part of the Micky Roach investigation did not bother her at all, though she did feel for Dougie Doolan who seemed to have been shouldered aside, so much so that he eventually appeared at her office door, holding his painful back, and asked if he could relocate there for the time being. As there was a spare desk and computer terminal in one corner, Jess waved him in and watched him walk creakily to the spare chair, wincing with each painful step.

Over in the Blackburn custody office, Lance Drake was going nowhere for the time being as detectives were very interested in everything he knew about Roach, his drug dealing and all the connections from it. Drake knew very little but the fact he had a huge amount of drugs and money on him when arrested made him a character of interest.

Which moved Jess's thoughts on to his mode of transport: Josh's stolen motorbike.

She went into the backyard of the nick where the bike had been stored inside a secure cage in one corner of the yard. Jess peered through the metal mesh at the twisted bike: a definite write-off.

Josh would need another or a cheap runaround car.

That morning he'd set off early to Manchester in his hire car, leaving Jess to run Lily and Jason to school. He didn't know what his day would bring other than it would be busy. Jess had waved him off just after six a.m., not sorry to see him go. She hated to admit it, but he stressed her out and there was a growing part of her that thought the move north with him was perhaps not the best of ideas. As she mulled that over whilst looking at the broken motorbike, her personal mobile phone rang. It was her mother.

There were no pleasantries, just straight into the meat: 'Jessica, dear, just to let you know I've sold the house and I'll also be moving back up north so I can be there for you, darling,' she announced.

'Sorry? You've sold up?' That was news to Jess.

'Contracts signed and exchanged. Done, dusted, storage arranged for the furniture and I intend to buy somewhere around Clitheroe. Views?'

'Yes, yes, get somewhere with views.'

'No, silly girl. Your views. What do you think?'

Jess was shocked, overwhelmed and pleased at the same time. Her mother had been acting more covertly than an undercover cop and Jess hadn't known anything about her intentions. 'Erm . . . jeepers!' She was starting to get emotional.

'I know Josh still works all hours God sends. As do you. The kids need picking up and dropping off and all that . . . I mean it won't be overnight, but I plan to be up there in six weeks, probably rent somewhere first, maybe in Bolton-by-Bowland? What do you think?'

'I think you're amazing and a lifesaver.'

Jess couldn't wait to let Lily and Jason know about their grandma coming to live nearby in a few weeks' time. They doted on her and she on them and Jess could only see benefits and not just from a selfish perspective. Her mum, somehow, although very much a person of a different generation, had always given the children a more rounded view of everything, plus a grounded outlook on the world.

Jess was bursting with happiness later that afternoon as she parked the Citroen opposite the school and waited for Lily and Jase to come out.

Then she saw Mags pull up in her Range Rover a little further down the road, obviously to pick up Caitlin, which got her thinking again.

Could Mags really be the biggest drug dealer and organized criminal in the Ribble Valley?

On reflection, Jess wouldn't be surprised.

She had the credentials and personality to fit the bill.

But could she really have ordered the killing of two old men just to move her father up a waiting list for the best old peoples' home in the area? That seemed so bloody unlikely and even as Jess mulled this over, she struggled to convince herself.

Yet . . . that nagging doubt.

Jess's cop instinct then took over; that predisposition which revelled in making suspects feel uneasy, plus – maybe – getting one over on a vicious bully from her teenage years. She got out of the Citroen and, unzipping her windjammer which was over her police shirt just to show she was a cop – a psychological thing – she walked along the line of waiting cars and stopped by Mags' Range Rover.

Mags was in the driver's seat slunk down with her head tilted back against the rest, eyes closed, not having noticed Jess's approach.

Jess looked at her critically for a few moments.

Mags seemed to be asleep. Her mouth drooped open and she looked well whacked out. Recalling she had been on some business trip or other, Jess wondered if it had been like some of the jollies she'd been on – some work, a lot of play – and she had only just got back and was completely knackered.

Jess didn't even consider letting her rest.

She tapped loudly on the window with her nails and was pleased the interruption made Mags almost jerk out of her skin, spluttering and wiping dribble from her chin. She seemed slightly disorientated for a moment until her brain got into gear and she glared at Jess before lowering the window a few inches.

'You just back?' Jess asked.

Still slightly not with it, Mags said, 'Back?'

'You been away on business. I'm guessing from your looks that it was one hell of a thing.'

'That supposed to mean?' Mags snarled.

Jess bent slightly to look through the gap. There was no trace of make-up on Mags' face, her hair looked half-brushed and big bags hung under her eyes. Certainly nothing like the dolled-up alley cat Jess had encountered the other day.

'Nowt,' Jess said. 'Anyhow, I was just wondering how your dad, Ernie, is?'

Mags' tired-looking eyes half-closed with suspicion. 'Why are you asking me that?'

'Just curious.'

'But why?'

Jess decided to have a go at prodding the long grass to see if a tiger came out. 'I presume you've heard about the death of the old guy who was a resident at Pendle View Care Home? Fella called Bart Morrison? Murdered, as it happens.'

Mags shook her head. 'Can't say I have. Why?'

'Oh, OK. What about the old man killed in a hit-and-run on Edisford Bridge a couple of weeks back?'

'Again, no; again, why?'

'He was on the waiting list for Pendle View.'

'What of it?'

Jess sensed Mags getting irritated. 'Just putting it out there.'

Mags seemed, or pretended to seem, at a loss. 'Why are you telling me this?'

'Heads-up, I suppose. In due course everyone on the waiting list for the home and their relatives will be getting a visit from the police. And I've seen your dad's name is on the list. Just a line of enquiry, you understand?'

'No, I don't understand. What is there to understand?' Mags really was getting shirty now.

'Hm.' Jess's mouth twisted. She was quite enjoying this. 'That everyone on that list, until they've been eliminated, is a murder suspect.'

Mags guffawed. 'Really?'

'Like I said. A line of enquiry. With Mr Morrison's death as a resident and the old guy who was killed by a stolen car, suddenly everybody gets bumped up the list. We know competition is fierce to get into Pendle View and that everyone wants their best for their aging parents, even you, Mags.'

'So I had two old men murdered? Utter cock, Jessica, and you know it. You want to watch who you discuss this with because I feel slander in the offing.'

'Thing is, I know you so well, Mags.' Jess smiled sweetly. 'All I'm doing is giving you, as an old mate, a heads-up. Detectives will be coming round to chat to you sooner or later. Oh, look!'

The school bell rang signalling the end of the day and almost immediately children surged out of every door like a tsunami, including Jason who was straight away doing keepie-uppies with his new football and behind him Jess spotted Lily and Caitlin amongst a crowd of other girls. Those two seemed to be at the centre of things.

Jess turned back to Mags. 'The kids are here, and by the way' – her voice lowered to the key of menace – 'keep Caitlin away from Lily. I don't want my daughter to be influenced by someone like you.'

'Someone like me?'

'Yes, someone like you.' With that Jess moved away from Mags's car but clearly heard two obscene swear words directed at her. She kept on walking with a smirk on her face.

Blue touch paper lit, she thought. Tick!

SIXTY-ONE

'Just get in the damned car!' Mags snapped at Caitlin who was still messing around with a couple of other girls, not including Lily who had gone off with Jess and Jason.

'What's eating you, grumpy git?' Caitlin said.

Mags was on the phone, staring menacingly at Jess who drove slowly past in the Picasso.

Jess gave her a wave whilst wondering who she was on the phone to.

'Steve?' Mags said as the call was answered.

'Boss?'

'That car Roach dropped off?'

'The Peugeot?'

'Yeah. Has it been crushed yet?'

'No.'

'In that case, do it now. Lock the gates, let the dogs out on the prowl and make effin' sure that the car is no bigger than a cardboard box in ten minutes and then ship it out immediately. We have a lorry load ready to go, haven't we?'

'Yes, but not a full one yet.'

'Don't care. Crush it and get it out of there and don't willingly let any cops in until it's off the premises and after you've finished, shut the yard down for the week. I'll pay you, no probs.'

'If you say. What's happenin'?'

'Damage limitation.'

'OK, understood,' Steve said. He was the yard manager at Primrose Wreckers and had crushed many a stolen vehicle for Mags after cannibalizing them first for spare parts.

Mags slid the phone back into its holder on the dashboard and rooted in the glove compartment for another, an unused one but already set up and charged.

Caitlin said, 'Nice to see you, too,'

'Sorry, love – I have missed you.' She smiled at her daughter who she just about tolerated. 'Business,' she said, switching on the burner phone, then making a call to the only contact listed in the menu.

'Me,' she said. 'Have you sorted out what you're going to do yet? How it's going to play out? . . . Good, make sure it works because by lunch time tomorrow I want to hear one thing, and one thing only – that she's . . .' She glanced at Caitlin who had already inserted earphones and was fully fixated on her own phone. 'I want to hear that the bitch is dead.'

SIXTY-TWO

The brilliant news that their grandmother was going to come and live nearby in a few weeks' time cheered up Lily and Jason no end and both spent a long time on the phone to her, deliriously happy. The fact that Josh had at pretty much the same time messaged Jess to tell her he would not be able to get home that evening – more big client business – didn't dampen their spirits and after tea both sat in the living room and were happy to watch the Tom Cruise film again, which Jess also thoroughly enjoyed. They seemed happier than they had been for a while which in turn made Jess feel a bit more confident about things.

She ran them to school the morning after and promised to pick them up when they'd finished their after-school activities. Jason was playing rugby and Lily was doing some sort of art class.

Jess arrived at work at eight thirty-five a.m. and sat down at her desk to check the overnight incident logs. As she was doing this the detectives working Micky Roach's murder were filtering in for a nine thirty a.m. briefing which Jess decided she would also attend and try to get a chat with the lead detective.

Everything seemed quiet and orderly.

Dave Simpson and Vinnie McKinty had come on duty at six a.m., covering the mobile beats. Samira had come on at eight a.m. and two other PCs were due to come on at nine a.m.

Jess found a sticky note on her desk from Samira saying she had already gone to Pendleton to pick up some doorway footage from a householder who had been uncontactable but had emailed her that morning to say she could come at any time for the USB on which it had been downloaded.

Jess also took some time to familiarize herself with the misper Vinnie had been dealing with, the woman who had disappeared in circumstances that the young constable wasn't comfortable with.

After this she stood up and looked at the large-scale Ordnance Survey map of the Ribble Valley tacked to the office wall. Once more she appreciated how immense the area was. In population terms it was small but in terms of square miles was vast.

'Big area,' a voice came from behind her: Dave Simpson. She glanced over her shoulder at him. He was leaning against the door frame, smiling pleasantly, and emanating a completely different aura to the one Jess had so far experienced from him all week. Friendly, charming, almost.

'Certainly is,' she agreed.

She returned to her desk and plonked herself down, slightly wary of Simpson and this change in him. 'Much going on this morning?'

'Nah, quiet. Visited a couple of shops that had their windows broken overnight, not much else to be honest.'

'Good.'

'Er, Sarge,' he said hesitantly, meekly almost.

Still wary, Jess said, 'Yeah?'

'Look, erm' – he gestured towards the map – 'I know there's a murder enquiry going on' – he pointed to the ceiling above him through which came the incessant thudding of CID footwear – 'but they seem to have it under control and I don't suppose we'll get a look in . . . I was just wondering, y'know, I realize we got off on the wrong foot.' He held the palms of his hands over his heart. 'My bad, so I wondered if we could have a clear-the-air chat? Was wondering if you fancied a drive out in the Land Rover – the only way to travel around here – and I'll show you the sights?' He pointed to the map again. 'And we can chat at the same time?'

Jess smiled, half expecting him to add, pretty please. But she had to admit he was transformed from the usual scowling, bad-tempered piece of work into something more amenable.

But yet there was just something that failed to completely convince her of his about-face. She wasn't sure what. Maybe it was just his effort at making an effort.

'OK,' she said.

'Excellent.'

She grabbed her jacket and equipment and followed him out, passing Dougie Doolan in the corridor who was just arriving for work.

'Off out, Dougie. Back in an hour or so, maybe, then we can have a chat about Bart Morrison, perhaps?'

'OK. Can I still use your office?'

'Knock yourself out.'

'Cheers, and you be careful out there,' he said, voicing a line from an old TV cop show.

'I will.'

Samira arrived back at the police station five minutes after they had driven away, clutching the USB she'd picked up from the householder in Pendleton she hadn't been able to contact previously.

She popped her head around the sergeants' door and saw Dougie easing himself down at the spare desk with a big mug of coffee.

They said good morning and Samira went along to the report-writing room, sat at the computer, then plugged in the USB. Normally it wouldn't be possible to open up an external drive on up-to-date computers because of the risk of viruses spreading on to the main-frame, but this was one of the remaining older computers still in use and Samira hoped like mad there was nothing nasty on the USB, otherwise both her job as a PCSO and any aspirations to become a PC would vanish.

The stick opened its contacts immediately, each day of the door-bell recording being a separate, dated file. She clicked on the day in question, the one on which Bart Morrison had died, then went to fetch herself a cup of tea and began the tedious task of reviewing footage.

She had done the same for eight other houses so far and got no results of significance.

As ever. She prayed that this would be the one with that crucial bit of evidence that would crack the case wide open. She was that sort of person: an optimist.

There were beautiful places in London without a doubt. Iconic buildings, awesome parks, inspiring sights and sounds and as a place to live, if you were lucky enough to be able to afford it, it was virtually untouchable.

But on this amazing morning in the Ribble Valley as the sun rose across the hills, and Simpson drove Jess out of Clitheroe and within moments the car had cleared the pretty village of Waddington and was heading north, climbing up Bradford Fell, she was stunned by the scenery, the amazing colours, a vast, seemingly endless sky and once more it dawned on her how fortunate she was to be here, even by default, even if her arrival had triggered some very negative vibes from others. Such as Dave Simpson.

'Look,' he said suddenly, unprompted, 'I know nothing about why you came here, what the circumstances were . . .'

Jess opened her mouth to butt in; he held up a finger.

'And it's nowt to do with me. You got the job, the hierarchy must be sure that you're the right person for it and I have to accept that, even if it all seems a bit murky, shall I say?'

'I applied, went through a process, end of,' Jess said shortly.

'I know and I get it. I overreacted.' Simpson dropped a gear to give the Land Rover some umph on a steep gradient. 'So, sorry.'

'Apology accepted.'

'I'll get another chance, probably sooner than you think.'

'What does that mean?'

'Well . . .' He shrugged. 'I bet you move on pretty quickly. Person of your calibre . . .'

Jess's face screwed up quizzically.

'I mean, you're clearly destined for greater things. I'm just hoping that when that moment comes, I'll fill your boots. So, let's just bury the hatchet, eh?' He smirked.

'Uh, OK, yeah,' Jess said shifting uncomfortably at his choice of words. She looked out of the side window, trying to appreciate the vista again. 'Anyway, Dave, all I ask is that we forge a decent working relationship because I'll need to rely on your local knowledge and experience. We have the makings of a decent team.'

'We do.' He nodded sagely.

Samira sipped her tea. She tilted back the aging, creaking office chair, swung her heels up on to the edge of the desk and watched the doorbell footage. It was all very clear and sharp, as all the footage from the houses had been. The house this was from was a terraced house with a small front garden with a low stone wall right on the main street. The camera was fixed in the framework of the front door and set to record continually, twenty-four-seven, catching anyone who approached the door, plus giving a decent view of the road also.

No one came to the door, but several vehicles passed on the road. The camera recorded a side view of the ones driving past. It was not at an angle to pick up registration numbers, but it was possible to tell what make the cars were. She stopped the footage each time a car passed and screen-shotted it just in case it became of interest. The screen showed the time of each download.

Next, though, was an image that made her sit up abruptly and almost spill her tea: Bart Morrison trundling slowly past along the footpath.

Samira gasped and rewatched it several times, noticing the exact time Bart went past, using his cane for support and with his flat cap on his head. So far this was the only door cam that had filmed him.

Samira went cold, despite her hot tea.

Were these the last images of Bart before his death?

She felt a tear forming in her eye as once more she watched the old man shuffle past not knowing that this would be his last day on planet earth.

'Damn,' she whispered as Bart went off screen. She knew that his next turn right would put him on the road to Audley Reservoir and his watery grave.

She pulled her emotions together, sat back and let the footage run on.

Rising up Hallgate Hill and crossing the River Hodder, they reached the pretty village of Newton which was really nothing more than a tight junction, right to Slaidburn, left to Dunsop Bridge. Simpson took the left turn.

'Seems very sad about the previous sergeant, though,' Jess commented.

'Mad as a box of frogs,' Simpson said harshly. 'Jumped off Cromwell's Bridge into the Hodder.'

He was referring to the old packhorse bridge built around 1561 near to Stonyhurst College named after Oliver Cromwell who led his New Model Army across it in 1648 to fight the Royalists at the Battle of Preston.

Jess knew it well enough from her youth. It was a tourist attraction and no longer in use, but was possible to walk across it.

'So I hear . . . the jumping bit, anyway,' she said, now annoyed again by Simpson's harsh attitude. His halo was slipping. 'Was no help offered to him for any mental problems? Counselling, or whatever?'

'Don't know.' Simpson shrugged uncaringly, then smirked. 'When you got to go, you gotta go.' He chortled.

Stunned by this, Jess could hardly believe what she was hearing. 'Not nice,' she said stonily, looking forwards through the windscreen, her annoyance simmering into anger.

'Everyone knew he was doolally.'

'And then he committed suicide! He got that far? That desperate? And no one saw it coming, or did anything to help the guy?'

'Well, to be honest, there's a lot of things people don't see coming.'

They reached the next village, Dunsop Bridge, coming at it from the east. Simpson pulled into a layby across the road from an ice cream parlour named, cutely, Puddleducks.

'Buy you an ice cream?' Simpson pointed to the quaint village shop, got out and crossed the road before Jess could accept or refuse. She exhaled, glad of the respite from him because he was making her feel sick to her stomach.

'Bastard,' she whispered. In her gut she now knew a decent working relationship with this guy would never happen.

She got out and leaned on the vehicle, watching him at the short queue for ice cream, checking his watch and then on his mobile phone before ordering the cornets and coming back with them.

He handed her one which she took and licked, then said, 'You do know you and I are not going to get on, don't you?'

'Never thought any different, Jess, but like I said, we'll probably find out that things will move on quicker than you think.'

'You seem sure of that.'
'Oh, I am.'

SIXTY-THREE

Samira jerked forwards, almost tipping her tea on to the computer keyboard.

She was a young lady who rarely swore.

But now she said, 'Shit!'

She rewound the footage.

She watched Bart Morrison walking past again, then watched that a few times more, before allowing the picture to move on.

'Woaw! I'm not wrong.'

She re-ran the clip, back and forth, rewind, play. No definitely, not wrong.

She jumped to her feet and dashed out of the room, along the corridor into the sergeants' office.

'Dougie! Dougie! Oh no!'

She knew Dougie was working temporarily in that office whilst ousted from his own office to make room for the influx of detectives investigating Roach's murder. When Samira spun into the office, he wasn't there. She assumed he'd gone out but then she spotted his shoes sticking out from behind the desk and with horror, realized he had collapsed. Heart attack or something major like that.

'Dougie, oh no!' She crossed quickly to where he was laid out full length on the carpet, eyes shut, and she wondered if the CPR training she'd had would come back to her.

Jess was surprised when Simpson turned right after passing through Dunsop Bridge to travel on the road to the Trough of Bowland. She'd expected him to head back towards Clitheroe. So she asked the question.

'There's something I want to show you,' he said mysteriously. 'One of those quirky things, I suppose.'

'Maybe we should be getting back,' Jess said. 'We've swanned around long enough. I have things to do. As lovely as it's been,' she concluded with a white lie.

'No, no, no,' he said. 'Honestly, five minutes tops.'

Jess sighed irritably but sat back not liking that Simpson was calling the shots, even on a sightseeing trip. It made her uncomfortable.

'What the heck!' Dougie said groggily from his position on the floor of the office as his eyes flickered open and looked at Samira kneeing over him, fingers interlocked, about to place the heel of her hand on the middle of his chest, with the beat of the Bee Gees 'Stayin' Alive' already thumping in her brain to time compressions.

'Dougie! Blimey, I thought you were dead, had a cardiac arrest or something,' Samira gasped and sat back on her heels.

'Oh, sorry dear. It's my back, really killing me and sometimes if I lie down flat on the floor it helps to ease the pain. I must've dozed off. Can you help me up?'

Samira hoisted him carefully into a sitting position, then all the way up to his feet where he stretched his spine and did a little circular rotation of his hips.

He smiled. 'That has actually helped,' he said. 'Thanks for the lift – and waking me up. Now, what can I do for you?'

'Doug – how easy is it to check a cop's DNA?'

'Well, every serving officer's DNA is on file, but it's not just that straightforward, not something done as a matter of course. Why ask?'

'Come with me, will you?' She beckoned him.

Other than from a gut feeling, Jess could not really say why she felt very uncomfortable – a feeling of trepidation which plunged to even greater depths when Simpson turned off the Trough of Bowland road and headed east along the track which she recalled vividly from her first day as a sergeant in the Ribble Valley: the one she and Samira had driven up to the serious incident at Dead Man's Stake Farm where the wildly drunken farmer Bill Ramsden was holding a firefighter hostage, a shotgun pointed at the unfortunate guy's head.

Seeing the track now, Jess was astonished they'd made it in a small police car which struggled to mount speed bumps in town. She was also amazed that a fire engine had made it too, to the tyre fire. The Land Rover, though, found the going easy.

Needs must, she thought, and for a moment allowed herself, once more, to take in the fabulous scenery which was wild, empty, stark and stunning. To be honest, she was lost for words.

'You can go for days up here and not see another living soul,' Simpson said.

'No doubt,' Jess replied, bringing herself back to reality and not liking what he had just said, which sounded ominous. 'But why are we going to Bill Ramsden's place?' She knew Ramsden was still on remand, that his farmhouse had been secured and there was no reason for the police to revisit it now.

'Ever wondered why it's called Dead Man's Stake?' Simpson asked, avoiding the question.

'Not particularly. I just know there's a waterfall close by to the farm and there's a stone stake in the ground where someone may have died in the dim distant past.'

'So you do know,' Simpson said, then stopped the Land Rover in front of a structure by the track. 'I wanted to show you this,' he said as he cut the engine, slid out of the driver's seat, stretched and breathed in the air. 'God, that's so good,' he said as he filled his lungs with fresh, cool air.

'Show me what?' Jess asked.

'This.' He pointed to the stone building he'd parked close to. Jess recalled passing it on the way up to and back from Ramsden's place, but never thought anything of it other than it was the only structure on the bone-jarring journey. Simpson gestured for her to join him outside the car. Reluctantly she got out and walked around to him. 'It's called Langden Castle.' He shrugged. 'Dunno why?'

'It's a derelict barn with a tin roof.'

Which it was, but with an ornate mitred door and windows, all boarded up. On closer inspection it was quite a nice building.

'I want you to see this, too,' Simpson said. He jerked his head for her to follow him around to the back door of the Land Rover, which he opened. 'This,' he said, pointing.

Samira plonked Dougie down in front of the computer in the report room and talked him through the door cam footage.

'This is Bart Morrison walking past a house in Pendleton.' She pressed play and they watched the old guy making his way up the road. 'Probably the last image of him alive,' Samira said sadly.

Then she slow-forwarded the footage, stopped and rewound it slightly, letting Dougie watch, making no comment herself.

Twice.

'Er, what about it?' he asked, not seeing what she had done.

'It's the police Land Rover going past the house, three minutes after Bart.'

Dougie was clearly perplexed. He made an 'And?' gesture with his hands.

Samira dragged another chair alongside him and sat on it. 'With Dave Simpson at the wheel.'

'Go on . . . officially intrigued,' Dougie said.

'I'd heard him on the radio saying he'd arrested Micky Roach on a warrant and that he was going to take him to Blackburn and yet, here he is in Pendleton not long after. He didn't go to Blackburn so he didn't execute that warrant, though I haven't been able to find it, yet I'm sure I distinctly heard him say so on the radio, but when I asked him about it, he denied it. Yet I did hear it,' she said firmly, 'but there was no one else to hear or remember it. Vinnie was on his way to an inquest and HQ Comms won't even have acknowledged it.'

'And? I say again.'

'And I saw him rolling down his sleeves the day after.' Samira paused. 'I saw four scratches on his right forearm as though someone had gouged him with their fingernails.'

Dougie blinked. 'Bart Morrison had flesh and blood under his fingernails.'

'Hence my DNA enquiry.'

'You think Dave Simpson killed Bart? Bit far-fetched, wouldn't you say?'

'I know he told me a lie about the warrant when I asked him, but I don't know why. I now know he was a few minutes behind Bart in Pendleton. I saw scratches on his arm which fits with what we learned from Bart's post-mortem, and he threatened me not to say anything about the warrant.'

'He what?'

'I'll never be able to prove it. It was just him and me.'

Dougie watched Samira's face crease with emotion. 'But why kill Bart?'

'Maybe for the reason that Sergeant Raker thinks?'

'To clear a space on the waiting list for Pendle View?' Dougie said, still not convinced.

'Can we just do a DNA comparison with what was found under Bart's fingernails? Can you arrange that?'

'Yes,' Dougie said. 'But I wonder if it's worth calling him in for a chat?'

'Where is he?'

'He went out with Sergeant Raker.'

He was about to say more when the phone started ringing in the sergeants' office. 'I'd better get that,' he said, picked up the phone in the report room and intercepted the call.

Jess followed Simpson to the back of the Land Rover. He opened the back door and the inner prisoner cage door. On the floor, inside the cage, was a large holdall alongside a smaller one.

'Ta-dah!' he said dramatically.

'What am I looking at, Dave?'

He leaned in and dragged both holdalls to the edge of the door, unzipped and pulled them open. 'This lot,' he said, reaching into the large one and lifting out a brick-sized parcel, wrapped in plastic and gaffer tape. 'One kilo of heroin,' he said proudly. He dropped it back into the bag, reached into the smaller one and picked out a tight roll of bank notes. 'Two grand in each of these . . . forty of them in here.'

Jess's mouth and throat suddenly went dry as she tried to process this.

Instinctively her right hand moved to the canister of PAVA spray in the holder affixed to her belt. She took a step away from Simpson.

'What's going on, Dave?'

He tossed the money back into the holdall. 'I just wanted to share this with you because, if I'm honest, I've brought you here under false pretences.'

Jess tried to draw the PAVA spray.

But Simpson moved with incredible speed. With one hard, accurate punch, he slammed his right fist, haymaker style, into the left side of Jess's head. That single punch put her down.

'DC Doolan, Clitheroe CID, answering the patrol sergeant's phone, can I help?' Dougie said, although his mind was really focused on what Samira had revealed to him and whether any of it hung together in any way, shape or form.

'This is Chief Constable Newby. I need to speak to Sergeant Raker, please. A matter of urgency,' said the voice on the line.

The voice sliced through Dougie's thoughts. He recognized

Gail Newby immediately, having spoken to her on a few occasions in the last eighteen months and heard her give talks and interviews.

Comically – and as a result of old-fashioned institutional conditioning – Dougie shot to his feet and came to attention.

'M-ma'am,' he stuttered, 'I'm afraid Sergeant Raker isn't here. She's out on patrol.'

'Can you locate her and get her to phone me – urgently?'

'Would you just hold on a moment, please?' Dougie covered the telephone mouthpiece and hissed to Samira, 'It's the chief constable, wants to speak to Jess urgently. Can you call her up?'

Samira nodded. 'Yeah, yeah, yeah.' She also leapt to her feet.

'Ma'am, we're just about to call her,' Dougie informed the chief.

'Thanks, Dougie, I'll hang on.'

Dougie's mouth popped open at being called by his first name by Newby.

'Clitheroe to Sergeant Raker, receiving?' Samira said into her radio. 'Sergeant Raker?'

There was no reply.

'Uuh!' Jess's head lolled forwards, then her eyes opened and she tried to focus on the floor. A searing pain jolted like a million volts arcing across her brain. She uttered another gasp and then her head jerked upright as she realized her hands and ankles were bound together with cable ties and she was sitting on a dining room chair in a room she did not immediately recognize.

'Ah, there you are.'

Dave Simpson dragged a chair in front of her and sat down. He smiled, put his fingertips underneath her chin to hold up her head which had started to droop forward again.

Take it, Jess, she ordered herself. Hold yourself. Whatever comes, hold yourself.

She remembered the drugs, the money and Simpson's punch. She'd seen it coming from her left, tried to dodge it, tried to make it a glancing blow at least, but she wasn't fast enough. Then she recalled nothing until waking up just now.

'What's going on, Dave?' she slurred.

He gripped her face between his finger and thumb so her head could not move. He tilted her face one way, then the other, as though assessing the value of an antique vase in a shop.

'That was one hell of a black eye old Ramsden gave you,' he said. 'It'll go well with the concussion.'

Sense was dribbling back now. She could feel it returning drip by painful drip.

Don't let him know, she ordered herself. 'Whaaas goin' on, Dave?' she slurred again, hoping she was fooling him and kept up the pretence of insensibility by dribbling and slurping back saliva.

He thumbed it away with disdain.

'Y'won't . . .' she began.

'Won't what? Get away with it? Duh! You don't even know what I'm going to get away with yet.' He used a thumb to peel up one of her eyelids and winked at her. 'Basically everything.' He removed his hand and let her face fall. Then, as though she was making a huge effort, she looked up slowly, allowing her head to wobble, and in doing so she realized exactly where she was, recognizing the living room of Bill Ramsden's farmhouse in which she had effectively begun her career in the Ribble Valley and in which, it seemed, she would end it. Plus she was now sitting there in just her uniform shirt, trousers and shoes.

'I need to know I can trust you, Dougie.'

The detective was still on his feet, still at attention, phone to his ear and the chief constable on the other end of the line.

'Of course you can, ma'am,' he promised. 'One hundred per cent.'

'Who is in there with you? I heard a female voice.'

'PCSO Patel, ma'am.'

There was a pause. Then: 'Is she trustworthy?'

Dougie glanced at Samira who gave him a helpless shrug, not knowing what was being said by the chief. 'Yes, ma'am, one hundred per cent.'

'Anyone else there?'

'No, ma'am.'

'Dougie, stop calling me ma'am, it's grating me. And stand easy, please,' she said as if she could see him. 'Now close the office door and put the phone on speaker so you can both hear me.'

'Yes, ma— Yes, will do.' Dougie relaxed a tad, covered the mouthpiece and said, 'Shut the door,' to Samira.

As she did this, Dougie set the phone on speaker.

'Door closed, speaker on,' he announced to the chief.

'Dougie, it is imperative you contact Sergeant Raker somehow and fast. She needs to return to the police station as quickly as possible.'

'Yes, ma'am, I mean, boss.'

'So you know – I've just been on the line to an assistant commissioner in the Metropolitan Police who has received information that Sergeant Raker's life is in imminent danger and it is vital we get her into some sort of protective custody. To put it bluntly, a hitman has been contracted to kill her and is aware of her location.'

'Jesus!' Dougie gasped.

'So it's down to you, Dougie. Contact her, bring her in now, please. I have a team from our witness protection unit currently en route to Clitheroe to deal with the situation but there is something else you need to be aware of, Dougie.'

'Yes, boss. That is?'

'It is believed that this hitman, this contract killer, may be being assisted by someone inside our organization, a corrupt police officer possibly.'

'You are a deranged nutjob,' Jess managed to say, trying to keep her focus on Dave Simpson's face despite her head throbbing in pain from his punch. It was a comment that, Jess could see from his expression, hit a nerve, enraged him.

Good, she thought. An enraged villain is a villain who makes mistakes. Keep him enraged, she thought. This whole thing had gone way past pacification anyway.

She tried subtly to test the tension of the cable tie on her wrists. Tight.

Simpson snorted derisively and checked his watch. 'I reckon we have about five minutes more in each other's company.'

Jess tested the cable tie again but any movement just seemed to tighten them more. One thing she realized, though, was that her ankles, though fastened together, were not bound to the chair legs which meant she could stand up.

'Where do I begin?' he asked.

'You sound like a fucking bad Shakespearian actor.'

'Well, one thing is certain, Sarge – this is a tragedy and one which began when you appeared on the scene with no baggage, no known police career, no background, which all *stunk*!' He yelled the last word right into her face, then stood upright which was when she noticed a roll of gaffer tape in his hand which she hadn't seen him pick up. He started to unpeel it. 'But now I do know where you're from, I know your whole backstory, which is why we come to be here. And it's not pleasant, is it?'

'I don't know what you mean.'

He pulled out a length of tape from the roll then held it in place with one hand and quickly began to wind the tape tightly around Jess's chest and arms, walking around the chair as he did, binding her to it, round and round from her sternum to her waist. Then he bent down and fastened her ankles to a chair leg.

He checked his handiwork.

'Now then, I feel I need to unload, as one does these days. They say it's good for the soul but for me it's a gloating thing and – big plus – what I tell you won't go any further because you've well and truly reached the end.'

Jess squirmed against the tape and said, 'Yep, definitely deranged.'

He spoke on as though he hadn't heard her. 'First off, you took my job. From under me . . . after all I'd done to line it up.' Whilst he spoke, he circled around her like a lion. 'Thought I'd well sorted it by pushing Luke Baron off that bridge. Thing is, he was on to me, so he had to go. His depression helped and there's me trying to talk him down and – wheee – he jumps! Splash. Well, he was pushed actually, but I came out of it the hero, the last person he spoke to. So sad. I even gave the eulogy at his funeral. Ironic, eh? Anyhow, that got me the three stripes temporarily which would have been permanent if *you* hadn't arrived. Just think, there's so much a sergeant can cover up, isn't there?'

'Such as?'

'How shall I put it?'

'As it is. No need to mince words.'

'OK. Bottom line: running the drugs trade in town, or should I say supervising it?'

'A bent cop.' Jess shook her sore head whilst at the same time flexing all her upper body muscles against the tape wrapped around her. 'You don't know how much I despise you.'

'I can guess. But, y'know? Water off a duck's back.'

'I assume that means you and Inspector Price?'

'Him? He knows nowt. Just an old mate. Bit of a thicko really. Would've liked to see me with the sergeant's stripes, though.'

'You work for someone else, then?'

'Spot on.'

'Who?'

'Even in this scenario, I won't say.'

'Maggie Horsefield?' Jess guessed. 'Is that how you know my backstory? You and Maggie figured it out?'

He shrugged, said nothing, but in his face Jess saw she was right.

'Dave, you need to let me go. We can sort this before it gets beyond silly.'

'Arf, arf,' he said in a mock laugh. 'So how exactly will we sort the fact I killed Micky Roach?'

'What?' A tremor of cold fear ran through her. She was in the presence of, and at the mercy of, a murderer.

'He was a wild twat, knew too much, could have blabbed under pressure to name names, rather like that idiot Lance Drake did. I wouldn't have wanted that and nor would the people I work for. Plus there was no way we could have allowed the police to seize all those drugs. We took too big a hit when Lance was arrested.'

'Who's "we"? You and Maggie Horsefield?' Jess tried again, but this time Simpson's reaction was blank, so she asked, 'How come Roach had the keys to the stolen car that killed the old guy on Edisford Road?'

'Mm, you see, he would have had to answer that question, too, wouldn't he? And I for one would not have liked his answer.'

'Which is another answer related to Horsefield,' Jess ventured. 'Trying to jump the waiting list for her dear old dad to get him into Pendle View.'

'I'd heard you were working on that hypothesis, Sarge. Very clever-ish.'

'True, innit? Just like Bart Morrison.'

Simpson smiled indulgently. 'Ahh, Bart – he bobbed up and down a few times before he went under, I can tell you. Feisty old guy, that one.'

'Did you kill him too? You won't get away with any of this,' Jess warned him, but it felt a feeble, pathetic thing to say.

He stood directly in front of her. 'Wanna place a bet on that? I'll be the hero of this little scenario, too.' He spun a finger around. 'Like I was with Luke Baron.'

'Run me through that because I just can't see it somehow.'

'OK, let's spitball here. For some reason you wanted to come and check out this house which you knew to be unoccupied . . . bit of old-fashioned police work, which I totally respect . . . looking after life and property and all that and lo and behold, we discover the place being burgled. A terrible fight ensues and, unfortunately, you don't come out of it at all well. Whereas I survive with some minor injuries – not sure what just yet – probably caused by chasing the fleeing, armed burglar over to the waterfall at Dead Man's Stake where I stumble, twist my ankle, say, and the guy's gone – across the moors. I limp back here but there's nothing I can do for you. Sadly. Obviously the finer detail needs working on but it'll all drop into place.'

'Like I said: deranged. And anyway, who is this mysterious burglar?' Jess asked. Her voice trembled.

'I don't know the full story, but I've been tasked to deliver you to a guy. Seems you made some very bad enemies from your time in the Met and now it's payback.' He made the shape of a gun with his right hand and pretended to shoot Jess in the head.

'No response from either,' Samira said to Dougie. She had been trying repeatedly to contact Jess and Simpson on the radio and via their mobile phones, and had also asked force Comms to do the same. Nothing was coming back. 'Not liking this,' she said.

'Me neither,' Dougie agreed.

Jess heard a text message land on a mobile phone in Simpson's pocket. He took it out and Jess saw it was a basic, black Nokia model, not the smart phone she had seen him with and she knew immediately it was a disposable burner that would be destroyed afterwards.

He read the message, then grinned at Jess. 'Not long now.'

Then her phone started to ring on the table. Simpson checked it but did not answer it, allowed it to ring, then checked the screen.

'Ah, a message for you,' he said.

He selected voice mail and turned up the volume. Samira's voice came on. 'Sergeant Raker, PCSO Patel here. Please call me back as a matter of urgency. Thank you.'

Simpson laughed. 'They seem to be missing you for some reason.'

He split his burner phone, removed the battery and the SIM from its slot and cracked it in two, putting the pieces into his pocket. Jess watched him carefully.

He put Jess's phone in his pocket then his own personal mobile phone rang but he didn't answer it. 'Sometimes, when you're in jeopardy, it's impossible to answer your phone. I'll give 'em a breathless, devastated call when it's all over.'

A shadow passed the front window.

Simpson said, 'Here we go.'

SIXTY-FOUR

Samira looked accusingly at her phone as the call to Simpson went straight to voicemail and she told him to contact her urgently, as she had just done to Jess's phone when it wasn't answered.

She looked at Dougie. 'What's going on?'

The detective shook his head as worried and mystified as her.

Samira looked up at the ceiling for inspiration and to get her thoughts into order when suddenly something clicked with her as she flipped the events of the day of Bart's murder quickly through her mind.

There was something.

'Dougie, excuse my language, but fuck!'

'Excused,' Dougie said.

Then she said, 'Got it. Won't help much, but got it. Come with me.'

Simpson said, 'Wait there,' to Jess. Then chuckled and added, 'As if – you're tied to that chair with industrial strength gaffer tape. Not gonna go far, are you?'

He went to the front door, stepped out into the farmyard, and closed it behind him.

Jess gave it one moment before bracing herself and starting to squirm desperately against the ties and the tape, realizing she had very little time because whatever was planned for her would be executed – *she would be executed* – as soon as that front door reopened. She had to break free somehow and one thing was absolutely certain: there was no chance of her ever giving up while she had breath in her body – ever!

She rocked the chair back and forth whilst still tensing and expanding her muscles in the hope of loosening the tape, but it stayed well stuck. Then she started kicking and bucking like mad to try and kangaroo the chair across the concrete floor, twisting her torso as the feet of the chair legs jumped an inch and then another inch across the room as she writhed and fought against her bindings, straining her biceps and trying to raise her forearms against the tape whilst at the same time moving her bound wrists against each other as if she was rubbing her hands together, just trying to lessen the grip of the tape.

'*Christ* – come on, girl,' she said through gritted teeth, and looked at the open inner door leading into the kitchen at the back of the farmhouse – the way in which she had sneaked into the house and surprised Bill Ramsden with 50,000 volts from a taser. About a million years ago.

Because now she had a sort of plan in her mind based on what she remembered seeing whilst making her way through Ramsden's kitchen, in the hope that nothing in there had changed since his arrest. No reason why anything should have. Everything should be exactly as she remembered.

She tried to speed up her rock-and-rolling journey across the floor: twisting, turning, wriggling against the tape and the plastic ties on her wrists and ankles, loosening it all a fraction, but also realizing that time was running out. It would only be moments before Simpson came back in with whoever had turned up.

'Shit! C'mon,' she urged herself.

Then she pushed herself too far, too hard. The chair started to tilt sideways and then, inexorably, in what seemed slow motion, it tipped and crashed over and because she was strapped to it, there was nothing she could do to prevent gravity doing its thing. Now she was trapped on her side.

'This might not help anything, I know,' Samira admitted, leading Dougie along the ground floor corridor to the locker room into which she turned and went to stand in front of Dave Simpson's locker.

'What are you thinking?' Dougie asked dubiously behind her.

'Breaking and entering.'

'Is that Dave's locker?'

She nodded. 'It is.'

'You can't just do that,' Dougie warned her. 'You don't just break into other people's lockers. At the very least they have to be present.'

'Just watch me,' she responded, then turned seriously to the detective. 'If I'm wrong, I'll say sorry, pack my bags and resign.'

Dougie capitulated and said, 'Just tell me why and then I'll back you up. We just need a reason.'

She closed her eyes, thinking back. 'When me and Sergeant Raker were in her office after coming back from booking Bill Ramsden into custody at Blackburn on Monday, Dave came in and said he was responding to a report of a body in Audley Reservoir, which was fine. But just moments before that I'm sure I heard a locker door slam shut, which must have been his because there was no one else about. Yeah?'

'OK.' Dougie accepted that.

'He came in tightening his trouser belt and wearing a brand-new shirt.'

This time Dougie screwed up his nose. 'How do you know that – the shirt thing?'

'Because of the creases in it from the packaging. Y'know, across the chest and the very creased sleeves. It had obviously just been taken out. Plus I'd seen him earlier in a shirt that had been ironed. And he had a different pair of shoes on from earlier. I think he came back after he killed Bart and did a quick clothing swap.'

'Meh,' Dougie said.

'Whatev.' Samira shrugged. 'I'm going to look in his locker. If I'm wrong, then like I said, I'll pack up and go home.'

'Tell you what, I'll do it,' Dougie said. 'No point losing a whole career. At least I've had one. Of sorts.' He looked at the locker door which was secured by a small simple padlock looped through a hasp. 'One minute,' he said and scuttled off, returning shortly with a claw hammer. He jammed the claw head underneath the hasp and, with not too much force, using the head as a fulcrum, snapped it open.

He opened the locker door slowly, standing aside to let Samira see.

She uttered a sad, 'Tch!' and reached in to lift out a pair of police trousers discarded on the bottom of the locker on top of a pair of black shoes. She lifted the trousers up. The legs unfurled to reveal that the bottom hems were speckled with mud. Underneath the trousers was a pair of shoes on top of a shirt. Muddy shoes.

'Imagination running riot,' Samira admitted. 'He murdered Bart – for whatever reason – then came back here and did a quick change before turning out to the report of Bart's death, knowing it would probably be noticed if his clothing was already speckled with mud from the path around the reservoir.'

Dougie listened to her as he bent down and picked up the shoes which were caked in mud which resembled the colour of the mud from around the reservoir. He looked at the soles, remembering that Bart had imprints from a shoe on his neck. He then picked up the shirt and saw blood specks on the right-hand sleeve.

He didn't say anything.

Samira hung the trousers over the locker door and reached on to the shelf at the top of the locker and pulled out a sheet of paper and read what was on it. Her heart literally sagged in her chest.

'It's the arrest warrant for Micky Roach.'

Dougie heaved a big sigh.

Samira said, 'I really do think he killed Bart.'

'I'm getting there too,' Dougie admitted.

***

The crash sideways, although not intentional, helped Jess because the chair to which she was tied was old, rickety and not well constructed, with legs like thin spindles and loose joints, so when it hit the concrete floor, assisted by Jess's struggling, it came apart at the joints and the seat separated from the back. With difficulty, because the back of the chair was still wound to Jess's body, she managed to get to her knees and then up on to her feet, even though her ankles were still bound by the ties.

Her head was still woozy, but by concentrating she managed to hop towards the kitchen door and was relieved to see nothing had altered in the room and what she remembered from last time she was there, was still there: a small workbench in the corner with a vice and still in that vice was a steel-shafted hand axe with a rubber grip that Bill Ramsden must have been sharpening.

Jess continued hopping across to it.

The axe head was secure in the vice with the blade facing upwards.

Jess held her wrists over the axe and brought the cable tie quickly but carefully down on to the fine, sharp blade which instantly severed the plastic and freed her hands.

She quickly loosened the vice, took the axe out and holding the head, bent over and sliced through the cable tie around her ankles.

Then she began to tear off the gaffer tape which was still holding parts of the broken chair to her body. She did this as she went to the back door and by the time she reached it, other than for some pieces of tape still stuck to her, she was completely free.

She tried the handle of the door, found it locked.

She swore again. It hadn't been much of a plan, but she had decided that she was going to run for her life out of the back door.

A terrible dread washed through her as she rattled the solid door whilst casting her eyes around for a key hung up or discarded somewhere.

She could not spot one. Which meant she was trapped in the house and could not scramble across the old sink to the kitchen window because that was boarded up from the outside.

Axe in hand, she turned and made her way back into the living room and over to the front window. Keeping low, she raised her head so she could see into the farmyard where Simpson was talking animatedly to another man, smaller in stature, with a rucksack over his shoulders as if he was on a country ramble. Simpson was gesticulating, pointing towards the farmhouse and at himself. He looked annoyed and frustrated by the smaller man who seemed to just stand there and take what Simpson was verbally throwing at him.

But then it seemed the man had had enough.

Jess watched in horror as the man's right hand came up from his side. There was a pistol in his grip. There was nothing said, no foreplay, he simply shot Dave Simpson in the face and the cop dropped where he stood.

'Oh my God!' Jess said as the man moved slightly to one side of Simpson's body and shot him in the head twice more.

Then he shrugged the rucksack up on to his shoulders for comfort, retightened the straps and walked towards the farmhouse holding the gun at his side.

He looked cool, unperturbed. A plain, neutral-looking man with no outstanding features.

And Jess thought, is this what death looks like? A man with a rucksack? She sank down out of sight, but then something surged through her whole being because her only option left was to fight. There was nowhere to run and the prospect of giving in was something she did not even consider, not while she had an axe in her hand and breath in her lungs.

Keeping her back against the wall by the door, even though her legs were shaking weakly, she slid up from her crouching position until she was upright with the door itself on her left, knowing it would open inwards on hinges on the opposite side of the frame and the man would be fully exposed. Those few micro-moments would be all the advantage she would have. She had to move quickly, without hesitation. To do otherwise would not lead to a happy ending because she knew this man was a professional killer.

She brought the axe up in front of her sternum.

The latch on the door lifted. The door started to open, creaking on its old, rusted hinges.

Jess held her breath, even though her heart was whamming wildly inside her chest.

The man shoved the door wide open and stood on the threshold, at which point Jess screamed like a medieval warrior, hopefully loud enough to cause the man to freeze, then pirouetted faster than a ballet dancer but with less finesse, and swung the axe downwards in an arc, fully aware that the gun in his hand was already rising and her body was open and vulnerable.

He saw the axe coming towards his forehead, managed to jerk his head slightly sideways meaning the finely honed blade did not embed itself in his skull – as Jess had intended – but scraped down the right side of his face and without any effort simply sliced off a sliver of flesh no thicker than a minute steak, like a kebab shop owner cutting off chunks of meat from the kebab, and took off the man's ear with one perfect downward cut.

The flesh and ear fell away on to the floor making a sickening slapping sound as it landed, and blood instantly flowed out of the large wound on the side of his head.

He twisted away, screaming in agony, a scream which doubled in volume when he saw his bloody ear and sliced skin on the ground.

Very aware he was still holding the gun, Jess flipped the axe around in her grip and with all her might smashed the hard, square butt of the tool across his face. It connected with a loud, satisfying clunk of hard metal against his jawbone. He crashed to his knees, but Jess knew she hadn't hit him anywhere near hard enough because he looked up at her and through the agony he must have been experiencing, he turned his grimace into a twisted smile and brought up the gun.

But Jess was on a roll now. She nimbly sidestepped and once more, using her hips as a fulcrum for power, struck him across the head with the butt of the axe, this time hard and very accurately.

For a moment he looked at her accusingly, then his eyes rolled to the back of their sockets and he toppled over.

Jess kicked his gun away and stood over him, breathing heavily.

SIXTY-FIVE

One month later

Sunrise was at seven ten a.m. that day and in order to ensure they were well on time, Jess arranged to meet Samira at Clitheroe nick at six a.m., armed with a flask each, and they set off in Jess's Citroen, taking the road out of town towards Waddington, onwards to Newton, through Slaidburn, up to Stephen Moor where Jess turned left on to a mostly single track road, going upwards on to the fells, driving past Stocks Reservoir on the left, continuing the journey upwards through the Forest of Bowland, mainly in second gear until the road flattened out slightly, where they rattled over a cattle grid and Jess pulled on to a small parking area.

'Here we are,' she announced.

'And here is?' Samira asked. This whole thing had been one mysterious journey, literally at the crack of dawn.

'Bowland Knotts. Top of the world,' Jess said, getting out of the car, beckoning Samira to do the same, and pulling her knee-length, down-filled Puffer jacket tightly around her and clutching her flask, she led Samira up a slight incline to a bench, on which they sat.

This was the highest point of the trip, an elevation of 420 metres above sea level, from which, on this gritstone crag, were stunning views in all directions across the moors to Settle in the east and the Lancashire coast to the west.

'Wow!' Samira said admiring the view as she settled on the bench and gave Jess a smile. 'So, what are we doing here?'

'Bear with,' she said, and after checking the time – six forty-five a.m. – she unscrewed her flask and poured steaming hot coffee into the cup. Samira did likewise, but with tea.

Then Jess sat back and looked east, just starting to see the glimmer of sunrays on the horizon.

She knew it was going to be a magnificent one today even if it was very chilly now. The coffee warmed her body and soul.

'So, how are you doing, Sarge?' Samira asked. 'We don't seem to have had much time for chats. All been a bit busy.' She now knew, mostly, the background concerning Jess.

'We're off duty – call me Jess, please.'

'OK, same question, Jess.' She pulled her duffel coat tight around her.

'More than OK,' she said truthfully. 'On most fronts, that is.'

Which was true, although sorting out the mess hadn't been a ball of fun.

'The thing is we'll probably never quite know everything,' Jess mused philosophically. 'The guy who turned up to kill me? Known as The Saint? Still not positively identified even though he's been in custody since and will probably never see the light of day again. Was he contracted by the Moss gang? He sure as hell isn't going to say a thing, otherwise he'll end up dead in the prison showers.' She shrugged. 'Probably he was hired by them, but they're not saying, are they? But at least the Met and the NCA now have a dedicated task force to bring them down, and they've also had a hard word in the gang's lugholes, so I'm pretty sure that if they did hire that guy, they won't try again. They're not stupid, so I'm not too worried on that front.'

'And Dave Simpson?'

'Mm, Dave Simpson . . . oh, by the way, Dougie was so impressed by you putting all those bits of snippets together about him murdering Bart. Me too. You should reapply to become a cop, you know? I'd happily support your application.'

'That's good of you. I might.'

'As for Dave?' There was a strained expression on Jess's face. 'In too deep, maybe. Greed? Arrogance? Again, not sure we'll ever know the full facts. The financial unit is scrutinizing his bank accounts and there's a lot of money in them which they're trying to source, and also a lot going out on the horses and other forms of gambling. He ran the dealing in the town centre pubs and Roach worked for him and he was concerned about Micky blabbing if he got arrested.' Jess shivered as she said, 'Which is why he garrotted him as soon as he knew we were going after him.'

'I still don't get the non-appearance warrant thing, though,' Samira admitted.

'I know what you mean. Maybe he arrested Micky so he could deal with him and keep him away from other officers, but then perhaps saw Bart out walking, chucked Micky out of the van and went for Bart. Speculation,' Jess admitted.

'Working for Maggie Horsefield?'

'I think so.'

'Who gave the Moss gang information about you . . .' Samira said. 'Pardon the expression, but she fingered you!'

'Well, we don't know for sure, do we? In typical NCA fashion, the sneaky recording they got from the Moss gang's meeting seems to have mysteriously gone walkabout,' Jess said bitterly. 'It's likely it was Mags but, again, we don't know for certain.' She sipped her coffee which had that strange metallic taste of coffee made in a flask which Jess quite liked. 'She seems to have come out of this all untouched, but her DNA is all over everything if you ask me: Bart's death, the old guy in the hit-and-run, Micky Roach's murder, all those drugs we seized from Lance Drake, who is also not speaking now, clammed up like a . . . clam.'

'She must terrify people.'

'But also there are enough firewalls between her and the dirty deeds on the streets to make it almost impossible for us to nail her. But one thing is for certain, Samira, I'm going to make it one of my life goals to take her down. I'm going to finger her back.'

They sat in silence for a while, sipping their drinks, watching the sky brightening.

'At least Dave admitted killing Luke Baron to you.'

Jess nodded. 'The investigation into his death will have to be reopened.' Jess checked the time on her Fitbit.

'Are you expecting someone?' Samira asked.

'I am.'

Once more they sat and watched the sun rise, slowly, surely and spectacularly.

'How's your family?' Samira asked.

'Kids are great, well settled now, I think, thanks for asking.'

She didn't mention Josh and Samira didn't enquire, which was a plus because Jess would not have been able to answer that without getting emotional.

In the distance came the sound of a car approaching from the south. Jess stood up, shaded her eyes, and looked.

'He's here!'

Samira watched quizzically as the car came over the cattle grid and pulled in alongside Jess's Citroen. A man got out.

'What's Dougie doing here?' Samira asked. 'What am I doing here, come to that?'

Dougie Doolan gave a quick wave, then reached into the back seat of his car and carefully lifted out a package covered by a small throw, then made his way up to the two women and placed the package on the bench between them.

'Thought I might find you here,' he said jokingly.

'No problems?' Jess asked him.

'None at all.'

'Great.' Jess looked at Samira, then at Dougie. 'Might be a bit unusual, this,' she began, 'but I hope you won't mind.'

Samira's eyes narrowed, trying to work out what the hell was happening and what was under the throw, a package or vase or something. Her unasked question was answered when Dougie whipped off the throw to reveal what looked like a container for a large bottle of whisky.

'It's called a scatter tube,' Jess said. 'And it's eco-friendly.'

'A scatter tube?' Samira said.

'It's basically an urn for ashes, as in the cremated ashes of a person.'

'Right,' Samira said cautiously.

'Remember when we were looking through Bart's stuff in his room – which was called Bowland Knotts – and we found his will which seemed to indicate he had no family to leave his estate to?' Jess said. Samira nodded. 'In the file there was a letter written by Bart saying what he wanted to happen to his ashes. And when I read it, it kind of took me aback.' Jess swallowed. 'Because he wanted his ashes scattered here, at Bowland Knotts.' She paused. 'Thing is, this is where my dad's ashes are scattered.'

Samira placed a hand over her heart.

'So I thought that if no members of Bart's family were traced – and they haven't been so far – it would be a nice gesture to scatter his ashes here for him and he can get to know my dad. I think they'll make a good pair because my dad was pretty crotchety, as I believe Bart was too.'

'Oh, that's beautiful,' Samira said.

'I know we only came into Bart's life after he'd died, if you will, and we did the best we could for him after that point. Seemed only fitting we could do this too. He was cremated last week, the ashes have been kept at Pendle View, so I ran it past Elsie Dean who was all for it, because she didn't know what to do with them. She said yes and Dougie, bless you' – she smiled at the detective – 'went to pick them up this morning and I hope you, Samira, will forgive me for dragging you out here.'

'Nothing to forgive.'

'Great.'

Jess picked up the scatter tube and checked her Fitbit which showed 7.08 a.m. Looking east, the sun suddenly rose quickly, showering the landscape and the sky with every bright colour imaginable, reminding Jess of being a kid and looking through the kaleidoscope her dad had bought her for her fifth birthday.

Then there was a rush of a breeze around her legs. She twisted the lid off the scatter tube and began to sprinkle Bart's ashes through the perforated inner lid of the tube, allowing the wind to whisk them away across the moor.

'Hope you guys will get on,' Jess muttered.

The trio stood for a few moments of reflection, then Jess put the lid back on the empty tube and looked at the others.

'Work to do,' she said. 'Villains to catch, a beautiful valley to keep safe – what do you say?'

'I say yes,' Samira agreed.

'Me too,' Dougie said.

They walked back to the cars as the sun rose magnificently in the sky.